"O'KANE DELIVERS A SATISFYING WHODUNIT, WITH SO MANY SUSPECTS AND MOTIVES THAT THE KILLER'S IDENTITY WILL STARTLE YOU."

—*San Francisco Chronicle*

"WHENEVER THE GOING GETS ROUGH, MOLLY FALLS BACK ON HER OWN SENSE OF HUMOR AND HER AFFECTION FOR HER CHILDREN."

—*Denver Post*

"WITH ENDEARING CHARACTERS, TOUCHING FAMILY AND FRIEND RELATIONSHIPS, AND A FEISTY HEROINE, *DEATH AND FAXES* IS SURE TO PLEASE."

—Diane Mott Davidson, author of *Killer Pancake*

"A SPARKLING DEBUT...YOU WILL TREASURE THE CLEVER PLOT, GREAT KIDS, AND A CHARMING CLASS COMPOSITE THAT TUMBLES RIGHT OUT OF A HIGH SCHOOL YEARBOOK."

—*MLB News*

Death
and
Faxes

Leslie O'Kane

W🌐RLDWIDE.

TORONTO • NEW YORK • LONDON
AMSTERDAM • PARIS • SYDNEY • HAMBURG
STOCKHOLM • ATHENS • TOKYO • MILAN
MADRID • WARSAW • BUDAPEST • AUCKLAND

DEATH AND FAXES

A Worldwide Mystery/September 1997

First published by St. Martin's Press, Incorporated.

ISBN 0-373-26248-5

Printed in U.S.A.

To my husband, Mike O'Kane, an even better husband than my alter ego's fictional one, and to my wonderful children, Carol and Andy, who never cease to provide me with material

ONE

Woe Does My Garden Grow

THEY WERE DEAD. All of my mother's perennials. Gone. So were the annuals I'd planted just last week. They had been nibbled to dirt level by the rabbits, leaving only the plastic identifiers as miniature tombstones.

Frustrated, I scanned the neighborhood's manicured lawns and picturesque flower beds as I continued down the driveway to the mailbox. How long would it take my neighbors to catch on if I were to "plant" silk flowers?

I grabbed a handful of mail and sorted through it as I wandered back toward the house. Amid the advertisements and bills was a crisp parchment envelope addressed to Miss Molly Peterson. I hadn't called myself a Miss nor a Peterson for more than ten years. Though I didn't recognize the bold, looping handwriting in black ink, I did recognize its implement: a fountain pen.

Oh my God. It's her. I've only been in town for three weeks. Who told her I was back?

I ripped open the envelope and read:

Dear Molly,
 You have no doubt grown wiser during the many years that have transpired since you graduated from Carlton Central. Perhaps, if you have been lucky, you have gained enough wisdom to balance your wit.
 If so, you have learned that one can only conquer

*one's demons face to face, not by outrunning them.
I hope, my dear, that you no longer consider me a
demon. In any case, rest assured that I am not as
fleet of foot as I once was.*

*Please contact me as soon as possible. It is of the
utmost importance. We have much to discuss, and I
have precious little time.*

*Yours truly,
Mrs. Kravett
(Phoebe)*

*Oh, Mrs. Kravett, you were never my demon. Even
seventeen years ago, I realized that much. You just held
up the mirror.*

But what did Mrs. Kravett mean by "precious little
time?" Was she ill? I glanced at the postmark. It had
been mailed three days ago, last Friday.

"Where should I put this, Mommy?" Nathan asked,
jarring me from my thoughts. He was carrying an aluminum pie plate filled to the brim with sand.

"Are you going to make mud pies with that?" I asked
hopefully. I'd been watching for signs that my five-year-
old was outgrowing his neatnik stage. If he'd learn to
appreciate mud play, maybe he'd be less of a fussbudget
around the house.

"I have to hurry. I'm going to drop it!"

"Just put it down, then."

I winced as he set the pan on the tallest remaining
petunia stem.

"It's for bird footprints," he explained. "Like those
people in Hollywood who make footprints in sidewalks."

"Oh, I see. What a fun idea. Are you going to put
some bird food on it?"

"It's not a bird *feeder*," Nathan said firmly. "It's for bird *footprints*."

"I realize that, but birds are more likely to walk across a plate of dirt if it has bread crumbs on it." Unless the rabbits get to the crumbs first, I thought sourly and headed toward the house.

On the front porch, Karen, my seven-year-old daughter, was jumping rope, her teeth clenched in concentration. She stopped her whirling rope and grinned at me.

"You're getting really good at skipping rope."

She nodded. "Now watch how long I can do it backwards." She took a deep breath, purposefully set her angelic features, and mistimed her first jump. She giggled, rolled her eyes, and said, "Wait, Mom. I can do better than that."

She started jumping again and I watched, though my thoughts were with Mrs. Kravett. *Precious little time.*

At about the thirtieth jump, the rope caught on Karen's feet. She panted but smiled broadly.

"That's really good. I've got to make a phone call. Be right back."

I glanced again at the letter and its envelope. No phone number. No return address. This was so like Mrs. Kravett. More than once she'd answered a student's question with, "You expect *me* to do *your* research? Do I have *Encyclopedia Britannica* written on my forehead?"

I chuckled at the memory. Her number was listed in the phone book. I dialed. To my disappointment, there was no answer. I wanted to see her. I wanted to express my gratitude for the difference she'd made in my life. And I had a heartfelt apology to express as well. One that was long overdue.

Back outside, my children raced up and down the driveway, in defiance of the sticky heat. They had adapted to upstate New York's humidity better than I had.

"Look, Mommy!" Nathan suddenly cried, pointing. A cottontail was crossing the Wilkinses' yard toward ours.

Waving my arms, I charged toward it. The rabbit nonchalantly hopped away.

"You just chased away the Easter Bunny!" Nathan cried.

"There's no such thing as—"

"Karen," I interrupted, sending her a warning look. I returned my attention to my son. "That wasn't the Easter Bunny. He comes in April; this is September. More important, the Easter Bunny wouldn't *dream* of eating Grandma's gardens. Especially not while we're in charge of them. Which reminds me, I've got to go get some gardening tools from the shed."

Muttering a satiric rendition of "Here Comes Peter Cottontail," I rounded my parents' white two-story colonial, then swung open the shed door. The air was so hot, thick, and stagnant, I imagined myself inhaling gnats. I grabbed the hoe as a possible bunny bludgeon and a fertilizer made from dried blood. My mother had advised that it doubled as a rodent repellent. When I returned to the front garden, Nathan was crumbling a chocolate chip cookie into his sand contraption so that "the birds can have dessert!"

I started weeding, my children having immediately claimed the hoe for themselves. At least for once I could recognize which plants were weeds. They were the only uneaten ones.

Karen and Nathan made horrid scraping noises as they hoed the blacktop and, equally gratingly, bickered about whose turn it was now.

The neighbor's garage opened. An instant later, little

Rachel Wilkins bolted outside and ran across the yard. Her blond curls bounced and she sported a wide missing-front-teeth smile. "Hi, Karen."

"Rachel," her mother, Lauren, called after her, "we don't have time to visit now." Lauren leaned out of the garage to see that, indeed, Rachel was ignoring her. The two girls were already jumping rope in tandem. Lauren shook her head good-naturedly and approached.

More than once, I'd heard Lauren Wilkins described as big-boned and round-faced. She was also beautiful and moved with an elegant grace, as if her steps were choreographed to ballroom music. She'd been my best friend from first grade through senior high. Living near her again after all this time was like finding a long-lost lucky charm.

"Rachel and I are on our way to the store," Lauren said to me. "Need anything?"

"If you see any 'Bunny Be Gone,' I could use a gallon or so."

Lauren chuckled. "Gee, Moll. It's only been three weeks. Will your plants survive a whole year till Jim gets back?"

"I doubt it." My stomach clenched a little at the mention of my husband's absence. Jim, an electrical engineer, had agreed to a temporary assignment in Albany, New York, but upon our arrival here, his employer changed it to the Philippines. "The lawn will probably go next, soon as the grass blades catch on that Molly Black-Thumb Masters is their new caretaker."

Lauren glanced with interest at the sand-filled pie plate, already crawling with ants attracted to the cookie crumbs.

"Welcome to my garden. First rabbits, now ants. Pests are the only things that flourish in my presence."

"Oh, I wouldn't say that. Your children are certainly flourishing."

"Thanks. And bless you." Lauren had a rare gift for saying just the right thing. Then again, if Lauren's knack were commonplace, the greeting card industry would be cut in half and I'd be out of a career. "Why don't you let Rachel stay and play with Karen while you get your errands done?"

"I wish I could, but I need Rachel to help choose school supplies. With school beginning tomorrow, it's now or never."

Nathan dropped the hoe and gaped at us. Fearful at the prospect of starting kindergarten, he clung to the hope that tomorrow would never arrive if no one talked about it.

I gave him a reassuring smile and said to Lauren, "Guess what? I just got a letter from Mrs. Kravett. She wants me to get together with her. I'm looking forward to seeing her again. I'll finally get to truly apologize to her."

"That's wonderful." She met my eyes and smiled. "Be sure and tell her hello for me."

"She wrote in her letter that she had 'precious little time.'"

Lauren winced. "Oh, no. I saw her two months ago. She seemed healthy then, but I think she's on heart medication." She sighed and ran her fingers through her shoulder-length brown hair. "Funny, isn't it, how your opinions about authority figures change once you get older? Remember how our class voted her Most Likely to Be Killed by a Student?"

I nodded. The category had been my invention.

After a minute of cajoling that rapidly changed into parental threats, Lauren and her daughter left. I waved as they drove away from the house Lauren had recently inherited, fortunately for me. Her proximity made the mixup with my husband's year-long temporary assignment more bearable.

Karen shouted. Nathan, upon realizing the hoe was no longer prized by his sister, was now playing dodge-Karen's-jump-rope-while-she-yells-cut-it-out.

"I'm going to be downstairs in my office for a little while."

Lauren's news about Mrs. Kravett's possibly having a heart condition worried me. I pressed the redial button on my phone. Still no answer.

I put it out of my mind and went to work. Three weeks earlier, along with moving halfway across the country, I had started my own company that specialized in personalized faxable greetings. Customers for Friendly Fax so far had been referrals from friends and from my former place of employment, an alternative greeting cards company in Boulder. I'd recently run my first ads in greeting card trade magazines and a few metropolitan newspapers.

Within a few minutes, I'd sketched a concept for a new greeting card. It was a cartoon drawing of Moses standing in a flower bed surrounded by dozens of floppy-eared rabbits as he commanded, "LET MY GARDEN GROW!" The card was somewhat lacking in what was known in the industry as sendability, but it made *me* feel better.

With tremendous thundering of little feet, the children raced downstairs to the office doorway. I braced myself, for they rarely interrupted my work without good reason.

"Mom?" Karen panted. Nathan stood beside her, their expressions mirror images of deep concern. "Which of us do you like better?"

I held out my arms, and they rushed into a hug. "I

love both of you the same amount and more than anything in the world.'' That was true and was voiced without forethought, but now I paused to consider what had
made their question so pressing. "So does your daddy.
You know how much he wishes he were here with us,
don't you?''

"But which of us is your favorite?" Karen insisted.

"You're my favorite daughter, and Nathan is my favorite son. I love you both. Just like you two love both
me and Daddy.''

"Unh, *unh-h-h,*" Nathan loudly corrected. "I like
Daddy *more* than you.''

"Thanks, Nathan,'' Karen said, giggling. "Now Mom
definitely likes me better than you.''

I started to chuckle at my daughter's unexpected com-
ment, but instantly sobered as Nathan sank to the floor
and began to cry. I lifted him onto my lap and kissed his
damp, salty cheek, as a sudden dowsing of self-doubt
spilled over me. Could I handle being a single parent?
Maybe I'd be so bitter by the time Jim returned, I'd greet
him with, "Welcome back, but the kids and I are outta
here.''

With the thirteen-hour time difference, it was dread-
fully early Tuesday morning in the city of Manila but
Jim was an early riser. "I think this is a good time to
call Daddy.'' I dialed his hotel and when Jim was on the
line said, "There's a little man here who needs to talk to
you.'' I handed the phone to Nathan, who spoke in one-
word responses.

Karen soon claimed the phone from her brother and
chattered happily about plans with Rachel and starting
school in the morning. She ended with, "Okay. I'll put
her on,'' then tossed me the phone and announced she

was going back outside to await Rachel's return. Nathan followed Karen up the stairs.

Jim said sweetly, "Hi, honey. How are things in Albany?"

"Okay, except that we miss you. And Nathan says he loves you more than me. Everyone always talks about building children's self-esteem. If I were a trained therapist, I'd start a course for *mothers* called Rebuilding Your Own Self-Esteem."

Jim's chuckle in response sounded rather sad.

"So anyway," I said. "How are things in Albania?"

"Okay, I guess. I miss you, too."

We chatted for a while, then hung up. The reference to Albania was a private joke. Upon first hearing that Jim's assignment had been changed to overseas, I'd asked whether his boss had said the job was in Albany when he meant Albania.

I felt more depressed now than before the call. I reminded myself about the sound reasons behind my being husbandless and once again living at 2020 Little John Lane. Jim and I had shuddered at the thought of trying to feed "highly seasoned dishes" to children who firmly believed the four food groups were macaroni and cheese, Rice Krispies, peanut butter, and pepperoni pizza.

Not to mention the likelihood of subjecting them to typhoons.

Karen could adjust to such a radical change, but Nathan couldn't. He became so stressed out last year when we bought a new dining room table, he'd tried to run away. As it was, we had taken many weeks to carefully prepare him for the move to Carlton, the Albany suburb where my parents' house was located.

Our own house was rented out, so a return to Boulder meant battling CU students for the few choice rental properties. Plus, there would have been the matter of explaining the change of heart to my parents, who'd generously offered us their northern home while they stayed year-round in their Florida condo. Not one of my imaginary conversations with them had evolved such that I sounded the capable thirty-five-year-old I fancied myself, and not the flaky teenager I sometimes saw reflected in my parents' eyes.

Determined not to second-guess my decision to stay in Carlton, I stretched and rose. Too often people missed beautiful scenery all around them when they daydreamed about the path not taken.

I decided to join the children outside. Partway to the stairs, I heard my machine receive an incoming fax. I returned to the office and waited, hoping for an order of dozens of cards.

I snatched the fax out of the tray and read:

This is all your fault. You think no one knows you're guilty. But I do. You made that dear lady's life pure HELL. Now she's gone. If you want to stay alive yourself, get out. NOW. Leave us alone. Or you'll be sorry. DEAD SORRY!

My heart pounded. I had a paralyzing fear that the "dear lady" was Mrs. Kravett. There was no tag line giving the phone number or the name of the sender.

I called her house again. I let it ring and ring. No answer.

Sensing a small person's eyes, I turned and lowered the handset into its cradle. My son was standing behind me, staring at the seat of my shorts.

"Mom? Why is your butt attached to your legs?"

"So that you can sit," I answered numbly and dropped into the chair.

TWO

Buns of Day-Old Jell-O

I USHERED NATHAN outside with me. I wanted to keep both children in sight till I could make sense of this threat. The fax was crazy; it implied I'd deliberately tormented somebody. *Me,* torture someone? I felt bad enough just forcing the kids to eat their vegetables.

I sat on the bottom step of the front porch while Nathan and Karen made sidewalk chalk drawings. Maybe the "dear lady" was my mother. I'd spoken to her earlier today. The temperature in Florida was ninety-five, with humidity roughly the equivalent of pea soup. Not exactly hell, but close enough. Maybe she had complained to some crazy neighbor with a fax machine.

I reread the note, then folded it and stuffed it into the pocket of my shorts. No, this dear lady had to have died recently.

Could Mrs. Kravett have died this weekend, after mailing me her letter? But if so, no one in their right mind could think *I* had anything to do with it. I hadn't *seen* the woman in seventeen years. Then again, the key phrase might be *in their right mind,* and there was no denying that the poem I'd written about her, published in the school paper, had brought her a lot of grief.

Many people were aware of the unintended ramifications my poem had caused her. Though it hadn't made her life "pure hell," she did lose out on a teacher-of-the-year award she'd been nominated for, and possibly a promotion to principal, while they investigated the "charges" I'd made in the poem.

I made a silent prayer for Mrs. Kravett.

Lauren's gold Volvo neared and pulled into her garage. "Stay right here, you two. I want to talk to Lauren for a moment."

Karen raced ahead of me into the Wilkinses' garage. Fifty percent of my children had heeded my instructions to stay put. That was at least better than Captain Bligh's crew.

"Hi, Moll." Lauren opened the trunk and glanced at our daughters, who were noisily chattering by Rachel's bike in the corner of the garage. She ignored the grocery bags in the trunk, touched my arm, and said quietly, "Mrs. Kravett died yesterday. Apparently she had a massive heart attack. I'm so sorry."

I felt as if I'd been smacked in the face with a two-by-four. *Dear God. Mrs. Kravett is dead. Some mentally imbalanced person with a fax machine wants revenge!*

Lauren gave me a moment to collect myself, then said, "The funeral's sometime midweek. Maybe we can get someone to watch all three kids. I can ask Carolee," she said, referring to the sweet, single-but-still-looking nurse who lived across the street.

"She must have been in her seventies or eighties, right?"

"Sixty-six," Lauren said, studying my face. "She'd just retired this past June. I know this is a terrible shock. You just got a letter from her...and everything."

I did some mental arithmetic. Mrs. Kravett had been only forty-nine when she was our teacher. She'd seemed ancient then. Now, sixty-six seemed way too young to die.

Karen announced that she and Rachel were going to Karen's room to play. They raced off before we could respond.

"It's not just that." I pulled the folded-up paper from my pocket, realizing now that Lauren's husband, Steve, was the ideal person to show the threat to. He was a computer-security consultant. His BMW was not in the garage. "Does Steve get home from work soon?"

"Hard to say." Lauren's face tensed slightly. "He spends so much time working, he acts as though our house is a walk-in closet."

"Someone sent me this fax."

As Lauren read the message, her expression grew somber.

"Whoever sent it knew enough about fax machines to suppress their phone number and name," I said. "The sender must have known about my troubles with Mrs. Kravett. A former classmate of mine or a colleague of hers, maybe." I sighed. "I haven't even unpacked yet. The closets are so jammed I'm surprised anyone can find my skeletons, let alone rattle them."

Lauren met my eyes. She still looked grim, showing no reaction to my closet joke.

"Do you suppose this could just be today's version of an obscene phone call?" I asked hopefully.

"I don't know, Moll. I'll check it out with Steve, though. Can I keep this and show it to him?"

"Sure." I peered outside to check on Nathan. He was still on our driveway. "I read somewhere children twelve or older are least likely to be permanently traumatized by a parent's death. That means I have to keep myself alive for seven more years."

Lauren smiled, though her eyes showed her concern.

She told me not to worry and that she'd send her husband over as soon as he arrived. Then she rushed to put her groceries away before they slow-cooked in the muggy heat.

"Mommy?" Nathan called to me as I neared, pausing from his chalk drawing. "Can you put your toys away? They're in my way."

"Toys?" I spotted the hoe and the bag of dried-blood fertilizer. I gritted my teeth as I moved them onto the lawn. *Isn't it enough that he nags at me to clean the house? Now he's worried about the outside?*

Determined to solve at least one problem, I set to work on the garden with a vengeance. I mixed the fertilizer with the hoe and carefully patted some around the remains of the flowers. I forced my thoughts away from the fax and Mrs. Kravett as best I could, but couldn't force away a sense of imminent danger that chilled me despite the late afternoon heat. In the meantime, Nathan announced that he was going inside to wash the chalk dust from his hands and change his clothes.

Minutes later, a human-shaped shadow appeared across my garden bed. I gasped and turned. A woman holding a bowl stood behind me. *Uh, oh. Alms for the spousely deserted.* Apparently, just as the gardens had become fodder for half the rodent population in Carlton, so my life, and especially my absent husband, had become fodder for the Carlton gossips.

"Um, Molly?" she cautiously queried.

I brushed the dirt from my knees and stood, gradually recognizing the small, silhouetted form. Denise Meekers, once nicknamed Meeky Mouse—by me, I was sorry to admit.

"Denise? Hi! How are you?"

She was still tiny. Even at five-six, I towered over her. Her face hadn't changed, the same dimpled cheeks, button nose, clear blue eyes. Because of the large bowl in her arms, I resisted an impulse to hug her.

She shrugged, maintaining her impish grin. "Same as always. Still here. And how are…" She let her voice fade away as she lowered her gaze to the green ceramic bowl. She thrust it into my arms. "I'm so sorry about your husband. I've been there, believe me." She added apologetically, "It's just Jell-O salad. I was in a bit of a rush when I heard."

Judging from her demeanor, she must have "heard" that my husband had left me and the kids penniless and that I was being supported by my parents. I peered through the pink plastic wrap. There was enough Jell-O in there to feed an elementary school. And there was some sort of flowered centerpiece bobbing on top. Nice touch.

My instincts warned that Denise was here needing to receive at least as much sympathy as she purportedly wanted to lend. I must have missed a page; last I'd heard she was still married, for sixteen years or so.

"My husband, Jim, is just in the Philippines for a year. His first vacation is in November. Why don't we go inside and—"

"I can't. My daughter's got a piano lesson. You can bring the bowl back to me at the PTA meeting tomorrow night. You *are* going, aren't you?"

"PTA meeting? So soon? School doesn't even start until tomorrow."

"Well, you know how Stephanie is."

"You don't mean Stephanie Geist, do you?"

"She goes by Saunders now. She's the PTA president. Surely you heard."

I nodded and felt myself pale a little, remembering now that Lauren had indeed forewarned me. "Good ol' Stephanie. Ever the cheerleader."

"So you're coming? Stephanie will be thrilled to see you."

"I'm sure she will," I responded, trying to keep the sarcasm in my voice to a minimum. "I'll try to make it."

"Seven o'clock. At the elementary school cafeteria."

The screen door slammed and the three children emerged. Nathan and Karen ran toward us, calling good-bye over their shoulders to Rachel, who went home. Karen was holding a clipboard and a pencil.

"Oh, you have such cute twins!" Denise said.

"I'm two years older than he is," Karen cried.

My children were both thin and fair-skinned, with fine, sandy-colored hair—a stubborn recessive gene since my husband and I both had thick, dark brown hair. Nathan had the curls Karen coveted and he detested. He also had a band of tiny brown freckles across his nose and chubby cheeks. Otherwise, they did look like twins.

I introduced them to Denise, who greeted them with so much forced enthusiasm she reminded me of Binky the Clown. Then Denise said under her breath, "I ran into Lauren at the store. She said she'd tell you about Mrs. Kravett."

"She did."

Denise's lower lip trembled. Her sorrowful expression reminded me that Denise had been Mrs. Kravett's star pupil.

"Had you stayed in touch with Mrs. Kravett since graduation?"

She nodded, her eyes downcast. "She used to have several of her former students over for a barbecue each summer. I'm sure you'd have been invited, despite your differences, but you took off for Colorado the first chance you got."

There was a hint of resentment in her voice, which surprised me. I didn't know quite how to respond.

"Well," Denise said, turning, "I'd better run."

I thanked her again for the vat of Jell-O and watched her walk toward a black Chevy Suburban parked a few houses down. What appeared to be teenage-sized bare feet were sticking out the rear window. I felt guilty for not having kept in touch with Denise, or with any of my childhood friends except Lauren. That hadn't been deliberate. Maybe Denise needed me to tell her so.

"Mom," Karen said, pencil poised on her clipboard, "have you lost anybody?"

"What do you mean?" I shifted the bowl to my hip.

"Nathan and I are making a list of lost people. Then when we find them, we write where they were and cross their names off the list. Rachel lost her cat, Missy, yesterday and found her in Carolee's tree."

I peered at the sheet of paper on the clipboard. The first column read: *Who are you missing?* The second column read: *Did you find them?* Below the headings were: *Misy. Fond in tree. Daddy. In Filupeens.*

Suddenly I had a painful lump in my throat. I missed my husband. I missed my friends in Colorado. Someone was faxing me hateful accusations. I'd lost a chance to see my former teacher and clear the air. Now she was dead.

Karen was watching me expectantly, her dark eyes focused right on mine. I forced a smile. "I lost my appetite recently."

"That's not a whole person." Karen took a seat on the stone edging of the garden. "I know. You lost somebody named Mrs. Kravett."

I sighed. I wished my children were even half as attentive when I spoke to them as they were to my private conversations. "That's right. She was a teacher of mine."

Nathan pointed at Karen. "Write down, 'Mommy lost her teacher Mrs. Cavity.'"

Karen wrote, *Mrs. Kravit.* Then she said, "And she was found dead, right?"

"That's right." I didn't want to discuss Mrs. Kravett or think about her death until I had a chance to be alone. "Maybe there are some cartoons on television."

Karen wrote, *Fond ded,* then followed Nathan into the house.

The children told me they were too full for Jell-O. So much for that advertising slogan. The flowered centerpiece bobbed as I struggled to cram the bowl into my refrigerator, giving me an idea for a card. Work had long been my catharsis, something I was especially in need of now.

While my children watched *Tiny Toons,* I grabbed my sketch pad from under the couch and made a drawing of a plump woman working out at the gym. The woman was saying, "My aerobics instructor claims this exercise gives you 'Buns of Steel.' Personally, I'd settle for buns of day-old Jell-O."

Afterward, I appraised my newest creation. It could get me sued by Kraft Foods, the producer of the *Buns of Steel* workout tape, and NOW. Three special-interest groups offended by one card. A personal record. I went into my office, having decided to scan it into my computer now and consider its marketing potential later.

There was a letter in my tray. I picked it up and read:

This is your last warning, Molly. It's YOUR fault she's dead! You'll pay for it! LEAVE NOW OR YOU'RE GOING TO DROWN IN YOUR OWN BLOOD!

THREE

As Talented as the Former First Dog

THE FAX MACHINE began to whir again. Moments later, my hands were shaking as I pulled the fax from the tray. I breathed a sigh of relief as I read:

> Just wanted to let you know we still haven't agreed whether we want you to set our Christmas letter to the tune of ''The Twelve Days of Christmas'' or ''Away in a Manger.'' Mr. Styler still wants ''Wesley had gallbladder surgery'' in the place of ''Five golden rings,'' but I think that's overkill, don't you? We'll keep you posted.
>
> Mrs. Wesley Styler of Manhattan

In early September, this was a matter they found considerably more pressing than I did, though I agreed with Mrs. Wesley Styler of Manhattan about her husband's gallbladder.

I calculated the time in Manila. It was a few minutes after 6:00 a.m. there. Jim was probably already en route to his office. I decided against calling. There was no point in worrying him when there was nothing he could do anyway. I looked again at the death threat. With two of these, I could no longer dismiss it as some random prank, and the second one identified me by name.

How could anyone possibly blame *me* for her death? Maybe because I didn't look up Mrs. Kravett as soon as I arrived in town. No, that made no sense. But someone who knew about my poem and was overwrought with grief at her death might feel justified in venting at me.

Any relatives of hers shouldn't have known I was back in town, let alone know the number for my fax machine. That wasn't true of former classmates. Stephanie Geist and Denise Meekers were still here. Plus Jack Vance, the class hunk, now school principal, of all things. Could one of them have sent the faxes?

Jack had never noticed me in school. I doubted he cared one way or another about my return. Though Stephanie and I had never been friends, she had no reason to hate me, nor was I aware of her having bonded with Mrs. Kravett.

Denise, on the other hand, was certainly mourning Mrs. Kravett. Hopefully Denise had forgotten who tagged her Meeky Mouse. I had an excuse for that, though admittedly lame. My full maiden name is Molly Octavia Peterson, Molly being my mother's choice and Octavia my mathematician father's. Neither of them stopped to consider what it would do to a kid to have MOP monogrammed on her clothing. It introduces you to the name game early, and I always was the sort who figured the best defense was a good offense.

Now that my last name is Masters, I do my best to smile when someone learns my middle initial and points out that it spells MOM, as if I'd never realized that.

It occurred to me that I could check the handwriting on the letter to make sure Mrs. Kravett had really written it. I grabbed the letter and dashed upstairs to my daughter's room, which used to be my room. On tiptoe, I rifled through stacks of memorabilia and mothballed blankets. This closet wasn't as jam-packed as the one in my sister's old room, which now housed all the unwanted presents my parents had received over the years. During Christmas gatherings, we'd watch Mother open gifts and joke about who made the closet this year. Aunt Louise has the record. Fourteen consecutive Christmas closets.

My dusty old yearbook was still on the shelf. I sat on the bed, the squeak of the box springs striking a familiar chord, and looked up Denise Meekers's picture. Her inscription read: "To my dear friend Molly, I'll never forget all the fun we've had. I know we'll be friends for life. Love always, Denise." Again I felt a pang of guilt at my aloofness.

The glossy paper still bore that lingering smell unique to photo albums, yet I glanced at the pictures with a sense of detachment I once wouldn't have believed possible. With the exception of Stephanie Geist and Jack Vance, we were all somewhat less than gorgeous. At the time, it felt as if I were the only truly ugly kid there.

Between back pages, I located the note I'd saved from Mrs. Kravett.

She'd stood in front of her English class and said, "I know who wrote that poem about me in the student newspaper. Though you chose to humiliate me in public, I will allow you to apologize to me in private. The poet can report to me after class. Otherwise, you risk receiving an F as a final grade."

There had been no furtive eye contact between us, nor was any necessary. Even as I'd tried to kid myself that she didn't *really* know it was my poem, I was well aware that my burning cheeks had betrayed me. I didn't stay after class. I was too ashamed. I merely left a sheet of paper on her desk, with the words *I'm sorry*.

Now I compared Mrs. Kravett's letter with the handwriting below my apology to her. It was the same.

In English class the day after I'd anonymously left her the note, I'd found it inside my desk. Below my words she had written with a fountain pen, "Not good enough. If I ask more from you than I do from most of my students, it is because you have more to offer. You need to discover that about yourself someday."

During class, I'd sat at my desk with tears streaming down my face. She called on me and asked me to interpret a passage from the book we were studying. I no longer remember which passage, which book, or my answer. But I do recall her response. "Good, Molly." Then she called on another student, as if nothing out of the ordinary had occurred. And I recall my final grade. A plus.

I replaced the note in my yearbook. In the master bedroom across the hall, I stashed the book in the nightstand and called the police. To my surprise, the sergeant said he'd come out and take a look at the messages.

Nathan had built a duck family with Legos and now lined them up, midwaddle, across the family room. Karen was hypnotized by the TV. I stood in front of it and said, "I'm going next door to get something. I'll be right back."

"To Rachel's house?" Karen asked. "Can I come?"

Nathan objected to being "left all lonely," so the three of us made the short but humid trek past the consumed garden and the lawn in need of another mow. If only rabbits would graze on grass. The Wilkinses' property, in contrast, was meticulous. They used a lawn service.

The same one I'd told my parents they wouldn't need now that *I* was in their house.

No one answered the doorbell. My children looked at me as if this were my fault. When we were halfway home, Lauren's car rounded the bend. We followed her into the garage. I felt self-conscious about intercepting her in her garage twice in the same day. As she got out of the car, I joked, "You've got to start shutting your garage faster. Otherwise, all sorts of neighborhood riff-raff might wander in."

She laughed and lifted a grocery bag from its perch beside her daughter.

"Didn't you just get back from the store?"

"I forgot the milk. Rachel said I forgot a couple of boxes of double-chocolate chewy something-or-others as well."

"Let me give you a hand." I grabbed the bag from her and widened my eyes to signal that we needed to talk sans children. We made a quick kitchen-garage round trip that included my update and her returning the first fax to me. She also graciously offered to keep Karen and Nathan at her house until the officer had gone.

As I returned home, the sergeant's last name rang a bell. More like a gong, in this case.

At the first sound of a car pulling into the driveway, I raced to the front window in time to see the officer climb the front steps. He was indeed Tommy Newton, the runt of my graduating class. Didn't anyone in this town ever *leave?* Was I the only one who got out?

I opened the door. He still had his thick red hair, which poked out from beneath the brim of his cap. In fact, he looked every inch the boy I went through my school years attempting to ignore. He was merely larger, like an image on a balloon inflated by another breath or two.

Plus, back then Tommy had a face that attracted dirt. All my recollections of him were with his having a runny nose, but his sinus condition had apparently cleared.

He nodded somberly at me. In flat tones, he said, "Hello. I'm Sergeant Newton." He pointed at my house number. "And this is twenty-twenty."

"Very amusing, Tom."

He whipped off his mirrored shades and grinned. "Hello, Molly. Long time. Heard 'bout your husband. You want I should try 'n' track him down?"

What was it with this folksy John Wayne drawl? The man had never stepped a hundred yards outside of upstate New York. "No. I just thought I should report the threats I'm receiving on my fax."

"Uh-huh."

We went inside and sat at the cherry-wood dining table. I resisted the impulse to offer him something to drink, because young Tommy had been such a klutz and I was still paranoid about Mom's furniture. He pulled his cap off and dropped it onto his lap. His cap had left a comical band-shaped impression in his red hair. I handed him the faxed threats.

"Should I show you my computer setup? I've got an office downstairs."

"Just the fax, ma'am."

I grimaced, and Tommy held up his hand, laughing. "Been waiting for a straight-line like that for years."

"Yes, well. You're welcome."

As Tommy studied the two faxes, I stared at him in disbelief. What if I needed help from the police to protect my family? He was a sergeant. That meant he had people *under* him.

Tommy dragged the back of his hand across his lips, then asked, "So you got both of these this afternoon?"

"The exact times are printed on them. My machine is set up to print the time and date automatically on the top margin."

He said, "Uh-huh" and nodded. "So you got one at ten after four, and the other an hour later. Got any idea who sent 'em?"

"Not really. But I got this letter from Mrs. Kravett in today's mail." I handed it to him, along with the envelope, and while he read it, continued, "I'm worried that the references to 'dear lady' and 'she's dead' mean Mrs. Kravett, and the sender thinks I'm responsible."

He finished the letter, set it down, and reread the faxes. "Why do you s'pose someone might think that?"

"Remember the nasty, anonymous poem about her that was published in the school newspaper? I wrote it."

His face remained blank.

"A lot of people figured that out. Including Mrs. Kravett. But anyone who thinks *that* had anything to do with her death almost twenty years later would have to be crazy."

Again he merely said, "Uh-huh" and nodded.

"There was all that furor when the poem first came out over whether or not she used corporal punishment. Surely that must have died down quickly, though, right?"

Tommy shrugged.

His lack of response was getting to me. *Did* he remember that blasted poem after all these years? Was his silence geared at tempting me to say more? He might be a good policeman after all. "Tom, I—"

"Call me Tommy."

"Tommy, I'll understand if you can't answer this, but is there any chance Mrs. Kravett's death wasn't simply a heart attack?"

"What do you mean?"

"Could she have been murdered?"

"No, no. Was a heart attack, all right. Had a weak heart. Shoulda quit teaching long ago." He stared at the first fax as he spoke. "This line here says, 'You think no one knows you're guilty.' You got anything to feel guilty about? 'Sides the poem, I mean."

"I'm a mother. I feel guilty by definition."

"Pardon?" He studied my eyes.

"Do you have kids, Tommy?"

"Got two teenage boys."

"Don't you worry that something you're doing either too much or too little of is going to warp them for life?"

"Can't say as I ever worried about that."

"Well, ask your wife. I'm sure she'll know what I mean."

He lowered his gaze. "Can't do that. My wife died last year."

"I'm sorry to hear that." How awful! She must have been only about my age. Her children were left without their mother. At least his sons were older than twelve.

"Lemme take these for evidence." He picked up my letter from Mrs. Kravett, too.

"Could I have... Please be sure to return the letter to me."

He nodded, stood up, and slipped his cap back onto the groove in his hair. "Call the station next time another of these here threats arrive. Be sure 'n' ask for me."

"Do you have any advice for ways I can *keep* from getting more of them?"

He shrugged and said, "You could turn off your fax machine. Course, I don't suppose you'd get any faxes that way."

"Can you trace my line? See where these are coming from?"

He shook his head and chuckled. "On our budget? For two nasty messages? We're not exactly talkin' a matter of national security here. You s'pose they're from your ex?"

"I don't have an ex. My husband and I are still happily married. He just happens to be overseas."

"Uh-huh."

That "uh-huh" of his was as annoying as a hangnail. "He's in Manila on business. He...makes envelopes."

"Uh-huh. Well. Great seeing you again, Moll. Let me know if I can be of any assistance again."

Again. As if he'd actually done something. None the less, it was nice of...Sergeant Newton to come all the way out to my home, and I thanked him sincerely as he left.

I fetched my children who, so far, were unaware of my current troubles, though that wouldn't last. Five minutes at home proved sufficient time for them to get into a fight. I told them if they wanted to pick on someone, to throw rocks at the rabbits in our gardens. That horrified them into temporary silence, and I set out to drown my sorrows in a sea of lime Jell-O.

Thomas Wolfe was wrong. You *can* go home again, provided you don't *want* to. All of this trauma was giving me the same feeling of claustrophobia I lived with during my teen years.

The doorbell rang. It was Steve Wilkins, plus Lauren and Rachel. Steve was a large person. With his pale complexion and white-blond hair, he looked a bit like a polar bear. Though I'd liked him from the moment we'd met, he was stingy with his laughter and often wore a furrowed brow. At the moment, he looked frazzled. Lauren smiled at me as she stood beside him, but their body English hinted at some marital discord.

As soon as the children had run off to play, Steve said, "Lauren already filled me in about your unwanted correspondence. Do you have any idea what this could be about?"

I shook my head. "I hope it's just some sort of joke someone from our class is pulling."

"Lauren and I haven't gotten any threats," he said matter-of-factly. "I'm also doing a consulting job for a company owned by the husbands of two of your classmates. They didn't report anything of the sort. I'm going to go down and tinker with your software, if you don't mind."

"No, go ahead. Thanks."

He was already down the stairs by the time I'd finished speaking. I glanced at Lauren, who was staring into space. We sat down, but she declined my offer of iced tea or lime Jell-O. I asked, "Whose husbands is he referring to?"

"Stephanie's and Denise's."

"Denise stopped by a while ago. Is she divorced?"

"No, but I've lost track of how many times she's called to ask me if her husband's having an affair. She thought since he and Steve were working together I'd know. As if Steve would tell me something like that, even if he was privy to it."

Perhaps I'd just found a motive, albeit bizarre, for a classmate to send me hate mail.

There was a weighty pause. Lauren was chewing on her lower lip, a nervous habit whenever she was upset. She was probably just frustrated with the long hours Steve put into his work, but this wasn't the time for me to inquire.

"Are you going to the PTA meeting tomorrow night?"

She smiled faintly. "No, I avoid those things like the

plague. But I'll watch the kids while you go. Be sure and say hi to Jack Vance for me.''

"I can't get over the thought of Jack Vance as a principal. Bet that keeps attendance among mothers pretty high at meetings.''

"What do you mean by...'' Lauren stopped, then chuckled. ''You haven't seen him in a while. Well, I won't spoil it for you.''

"Uh-oh. He's not drop-dead handsome anymore?''

She gave me a sly grin. ''He's not exactly bad-looking. He's just not *the Vance.* Too bad, too. He's single again.''

Lauren hopped to her feet as Steve trudged up the stairs. "We can install Caller ID on your fax line,'' he said. ''That will let you know the phone number of the fax sender. Let me look into it, and I'll get back to you in a few days.''

"Great. Thanks.''

He still hadn't cracked a smile. Lauren and he seemed to be avoiding any eye contact. I had a sinking feeling in my stomach I used to get as a child whenever my parents argued.

"Listen, Molly,'' Lauren said, ''you've had a big shock. How about if we watch the kids for a couple of hours?''

"Thank you. That's really nice. I'll send them over after dinner.''

They left, and I set about fixing supper. Meal preparation was one advantage to having an absent husband. My culinary skills had diminished to nonexistent once my children's vocabulary expanded to include the word *Yuck.* That had been my son's first word. At least with Jim gone I didn't have to witness his attempts to mask his disappointment over dinner.

We ate pork chops, macaroni and cheese, and lime Jell-O so I wasn't depriving my children of their greens. As I ate, I sketched an idea for an employee-departure card: a cigarette-smoking black cat wearing a collar labeled Socks, his white paws banging away at a typewriter as he thinks, "I'm at *least* as talented as the former First Dog." The caption read: Best of Luck in Your Future Endeavors.

Nathan balked at the idea of going to Rachel's house a second time in the same day, complaining the girls always played Barbie and he was sick of the role of Ken. Karen promised this time they'd play Mommy, Daddy, and Baby Trucks, and that won him over.

I wasted my hard-earned "unwind" time grocery shopping. While struggling to learn the layout of the unfamiliar store, I stumbled upon the greeting card section. Time to play the plagiarism game, a monthly exercise in self-torture to find out if I'd accidentally copied someone's design and was about to be sued. My technique was to scan the cards while squinting, to check for any designs that looked like mine without actually reading any.

That accomplished, it occurred to me that inviting my old school chums for dinner was a good way to squish myself out of the Carlton grapevine and get a feel for who might be my one-way poisonous pen pal. I decided to stock up with manicotti ingredients for a dinner party.

During the short drive home, it hit me that school started in the morning. My youngest child would be going to kindergarten. Only yesterday he was a chubby, giggling baby. My eyes instantly misted, blurring my vision.

At the turn onto Little John Lane, something was wrong. This couldn't be Lauren's house. Had I taken a wrong turn? I slowly realized my mind wasn't accepting what I was seeing.

In Lauren's driveway were two police cars, lights flashing.

FOUR

Into Each Life...

THE FIRST PERSON I saw as I burst into Lauren's house was Carolee, our neighbor from across the street. "Everything's fine," she gushed. "The burglar alarm went off. Someone tried to break in by prying open a window in back."

I leaned against the wall momentarily, trying to force my breath and heart rate into some semblance of normal. "Where are the children?"

"With Lauren in the basement. She took them down there to keep them away from all the excitement. Steve's out back with the officers."

I nodded, grateful that Lauren's parenting instincts matched my own.

"Maybe you should sit down." Carolee reached for my wrist, and I could tell by the way she was aiming her thumb she was hoping to check my pulse. Once a nurse, always a nurse.

I held up my palms. "I'm fine. Thanks." Her blond hair was neatly curled and she wore her usual perfect makeup. Her new, white tennis shoes had green markings. She must have run across the lawn to get here.

We heard a dull scrape as someone opened the sliding glass back door. "...probably spotted the computers through my office window," Steve was saying.

Steve and Tommy Newton rounded the corner, followed by two uniformed officers. "We meet again," Tommy said, grinning at me. "Can't remember the last time I've taken two calls in the Sherwood Forest subdivision the same day. Must be havin' you back in town, huh, Moll? Brought us some excitement."

Carolee laughed as if Tommy's greeting were witty. She seemed to be eyeing him with considerable interest. No accounting for taste. Tommy touched the brim of his hat and smiled at her, to acknowledge a mutual interest perhaps. Like me, Carolee was in her mid-thirties. She was very attractive from the waist up, but had the skinniest legs imaginable, now hidden in aqua-colored sweatpants.

Steve said, "It's nothing, Molly. Some creep tried to break into my office. He ran before we got a look at him, but there are crowbar marks on the windowsill. I'm sure whoever it was just figured he could sneak in and out of my office window and not get caught. Probably assumed we didn't have an alarm or wouldn't have it activated when we were home."

Steve's suggestion made sense. His office was stocked with the latest in expensive equipment, including notebook computers that could be swiped swiftly. Yet my intuition wasn't buying a word of it. Death threats followed by an attempted break-in at the house where my children were. What the hell was going on?

Steve wasn't meeting my eyes. There was something he wasn't telling.

MY SLEEP THAT NIGHT was troubled, interrupted by nightmares and fears that every little noise might be a prowler. Even the serenade of crickets and katydids sounded ominous. Morning finally arrived. That meant the first day of school.

My daughter, Karen, had thus far been blessed with exceptional teachers and wonderful school experiences. Her luck was still holding, for she was in Rachel's class and Lauren had assured me their teacher was the best in the entire school. Karen insisted on taking the bus with Rachel.

That allowed me to wallow fully in my apprehensions for Nathan.

He didn't say a word during breakfast and barely touched his Rice Krispies. I suggested he wear his bright green baseball cap, which was his personal security blanket. Between that and his yellow T-shirt and purple pants, he was at least going to be easy to spot.

We drove to the school. Nathan's silence was killing me. I spewed so many positive statements at him I sounded like a videoed aerobics instructor. We pulled into the lot and got out of the car. His warm little hand held tightly to mine as I led him across the kindergarten playground toward his classmates. They were lined up against the outside of the brick building behind their white-haired teacher.

The teacher greeted Nathan warmly and instructed him to take his place in line, and asked me to join the group of wan-faced mothers a short distance away. Then she started the line moving into the building. The sight of my little boy trying to be stoic, his protruding lower lip trembling as he followed his classmates, was gut-wrenching.

Just as he was about to enter the room, he turned and yelled, "I wanted to ride the bus, Mommy!" Then he disappeared inside.

A couple of mothers laughed.

"My son loves public transportation," I said to no one in particular.

I went home and tried to concentrate on the newspaper.

There was a lengthy obituary for Phoebe Steinway Kravett. She had no children and her husband had died five months ago. The only survivor listed was a sister in Seattle. The funeral was scheduled for tomorrow afternoon.

Now I was thoroughly depressed.

I decided to use my current emotional state to design a cheer-up card. The major market for faxable greetings is businesses, so notices about changes in address and office parties are in demand. With the proliferation of computers and fax machines, there was also a market for faxable friendship cards, which I was trying to tap.

My new design showed people at a bus stop staring at a woman in their midst being drenched by her own personal rain cloud. The caption was: Into Each Life…a Little Torrential Rain Doth Pour.

Later, I joined the anxious mob of mothers outside the school, automatically standing in the same spot the teacher had assigned to us at the start of the day. Nathan was the tenth child out the door, his cap now in his hand. I knelt and he rushed into my arms crying, "Mommy." He wrapped both arms and legs around me, and I reveled in the warmth and scent of his little body.

Unfortunately, he was closely followed by his teacher, who did not look happy. She narrowed her eyes at me. "Are you Nathan Masters's mother?" Her voice was thin, worn out from years of making herself heard.

My first impulse was to point out that Nathan didn't call me Mommy for nothing. But I smiled up at her and said, "Yes, I am." As Nathan released me from my hug, I told him, "Sweetie, show me how well you can go down the slide while I speak with your teacher for a moment."

Nathan peered suspiciously at both of us, handed me his cap, then slowly walked toward the slide.

"How did things go today?" I asked.

"He wouldn't say a word, even to tell me his name. So I decided to let him choose the first animal during 'Old MacDonald.'" She paused and grimaced.

"And did he say anything?" I waved at Nathan at the top of the slide.

"Oh, yes." She sighed. "But instead of naming an animal, he said, 'Poop.' It totally disrupted the class. All the children started laughing."

"That's wonderful," I said with feigned enthusiasm. "I was so worried. He can be so shy sometimes. What a fabulous job you must be doing to draw him out like that. Thank you so much."

You can't be a parent for seven years without learning a few skills of manipulation.

She smiled slowly. "You're welcome. Though you may want to explain to your son that the lyrics are supposed to be farm animals, not BMs."

Nathan finished his ride down the slide and made his way toward us. The teacher was charming as she said good-bye to Nathan and told him how glad she was to have him in her class. Hmm. So she was humorless, but warm. A reasonable trade-off.

Once in the car, Nathan asked, "Now that I gone to kindergarten, can I stay home?"

"You're not done with kindergarten. You have to go back again, you know."

"I do?" he cried in abject horror. "How many times?"

"One hundred and seventy-nine."

"I'm never going to school again!" he wailed. "I'm running away from home!"

"Tell you what. To celebrate your first day of school, I'll take you to lunch. Where would you like to go?"

"McDonald's," he murmured. Then he sang quietly, "Old McDonald had a cheeseburger."

I joined him, and we sang the entire menu en route.

THE AFTERNOON PASSED quickly. I didn't receive any faxes, which was bad news for my business but good for my nerves. So when I saw an incoming fax after we'd returned from meeting Karen at the bus stop, my heart thumped until I saw the message line and recognized Lauren's number. In childish scrawl, the fax read:

Dear Karen,
Daddy sho me how to use the fax. Can you?
Love Rachel

I quickly typed:

Dear Rachel,
 I'm sorry, but we only have one computer and one fax machine. I don't let Karen use it. Thank you for your message. I'll give it to Karen. Can your Mommy please call me?

Love,
Molly

I faxed the note to the Wilkinses' house, and within five minutes the phone rang. No one responded to my hello. I could hear what sounded like a child's quick breaths.

"Is this Rachel?" I asked.

"Are you mad at me for sending Karen a fax?"

"Of course not, sweetie. I just don't let my children

use my computer because they get the keyboard sticky.''
That was partly true. Because my business, meager as it
was, depended entirely on my computer, I was overly
possessive. ''Is your mom there?''

She paused, probably trying to decide if I was going
to tattle on her, but then said, ''I'll get her.''

Lauren and I chatted for a while. She accepted my
dinner invitation for Friday night and repeated her offer
to watch the kids while I went to the PTA meeting tonight.

A couple of hours later, I drove to the meeting, mentally attempting to sort my thoughts. Was it really possible that Denise was so jealous of her husband she'd try
to frighten me into leaving for fear that I was available?
Could she hold a grudge against me for my immaturity
regarding Mrs. Kravett seventeen years ago? It all seemed
totally absurd and very unlike levelheaded, play-by-the-
rules Denise Meekers. Then again, people change.

Maybe Stephanie Geist Saunders was the culprit. We
didn't get along from the start. She'd moved into the
district in the seventh grade. Once, in tenth grade, we
were changing in the girls' locker room, and Stephanie
struck a chesty pose beside me. She said to her almost-
as-well-endowed audience, ''Hard to believe Molly and
I are the same species, isn't it?''

In my fantasies, her bra straps now serve as suspenders
for those 38-D cups she was so proud of flaunting.

I parked, then headed down the wide hallway toward
the cafeteria, battling a sense of déjà vu that made me
half expect some hatchet-faced teacher to put me in de-
tention for roaming the halls without a permission slip.
The double doors to the cafeteria were open. This one
building housed all thirteen grade levels when I was in
school, before the junior high and high school building

were added. The far wall still sported the twenty-year-old colorful but inept painting of a cougar that was the school mascot. It looked like a buffalo.

Inside the large room, fifty or so women were standing in noisy groups behind rows of folding chairs that faced two lone chairs by the cougar/buffalo's snout. I overheard the name Mrs. Kravett numerous times. I scanned for Denise Meekers, but didn't see her. There was a small table near the door with a full pitcher of iced tea. Drinking some gave me the opportunity to survey the room while feeling less conspicuous for being alone.

A tall man with an inch-long ponytail strode into the room and turned toward me.

He grinned. "Molly?"

"Jack?" Good thing Lauren had forewarned me that Jack Vance had changed. That allowed me to maintain a sincere smile. Those broad shoulders of his had sagged, taking his chest with them and leaving a roll of flab around the waistline of his black Dockers. His face had paid the price for too much time in the sun and was lined and blotchy. His salt-and-pepper hairline was receding.

"I heard you were back, and that you enrolled your children here," Jack said. "Are they excited about school?"

"Oh, definitely." Nathan's threat to run away from home rather than return to school certainly counted as excited.

"Good. Good. Let me give you an agenda, hot off the press." He handed me a sheet of paper and said, "Say. Would you like to have dinner with me sometime? We can get caught up and talk about old times."

"As a matter of fact, I'm having Lauren Wilkins over for dinner Friday." Jack brightened so noticeably at the mention of Lauren that I added "And her *husband.* I'm planning to ask some more of our former classmates as well. Would you join us?''

He accepted, claiming that thanks to his divorce, it had been a long time since he'd had a home-cooked meal. He wandered away and shook hands with one of the three other men in the room. His bureaucratic grin never faded. That change in him was more disturbing to me than his flab. He had always had such an unforced, effervescent personality. He'd gone from champagne to ginger ale.

Jack held out his hand toward another man, who abruptly turned his back and crossed the room. Curious, I watched him. He was strikingly handsome with silver hair and a trim build that made him look as if he should be carrying a tennis racket.

People began to take seats, and I caught sight of a woman in a tailored fire red dress suit. As if she felt my eyes on her, the woman turned. Her hair was in a perfect pageboy, and her face, though heavily made up, looked youthful and stunning.

Stephanie hadn't changed as much as I'd hoped.

She came toward me, flashed her Miss Universe smile, and held out her arms, though I knew I was in no danger of being hugged. "Why, Molly! You haven't changed a bit!" She was staring at my chest as spoke.

"Thank you." Matching her eye level, I added, "You seem to be holding up well yourself."

She gave me one of her tittering giggles. "Oh, Moll, Moll. Sorry your husband deserted you. How are your kids handling it?"

Her blatant nastiness struck me as funny and I laughed heartily.

A skinny, nerdish-looking man stepped up beside Stephanie. His slicked-back hair emphasized his cone-shaped head. I held my breath, hoping Stephanie would say that this was her husband.

"Hello. How are you," he said to me. He had a deep, disc-jockey voice.

"This is Denise's husband, Sam Bakerton. Sam, this is Molly..."

"Masters. Nice to meet you. I have a bowl from Denise. I meant to bring it back tonight but forgot."

He smiled. "She can stop by and pick it up sometime, I'm sure." Though just a snap judgment on my part, he didn't strike me as the philandering type. For one thing, his eyes didn't roam toward Stephanie while speaking to me.

Stephanie's vision *had* started to wander. No doubt we'd bored her. Because my plan for an insightful dinner party required me to do so, I invited her, plus Sam and spouses, to dinner Friday. Sam said he'd check with Denise, but thought they were free. Not surprisingly, Stephanie wouldn't commit and said she'd get back to me.

Jack cleared his throat, and all but the front row of seats filled rapidly. I wondered if that was some throwback from school days when there were so many valid reasons for avoiding the front seats. Stephanie said, "If you'll excuse me, I've got to sit next to Jack, after I get my husband situated." She giggled. "I don't know *why* he insists on coming to these things."

Stephanie rushed over to plant a peck on the cheek of the handsome silver-haired man, then took the seat next to Jack. So the man who'd deliberately turned his back on Jack Vance was married to Stephanie. And I'd invited them all to dinner. Oh joy.

Thirty minutes later, we were still apparently on the first item of the agenda, which read: "Introductions: Five minutes." Estimating six times the projected time allotment for each time, we'd be here for the morning bell. I scanned the remainder of the agenda, half expecting to find: "Balance the federal budget: Ten minutes."

Oddly, Jack spoke for less than a minute about Mrs. Kravett's death. This for a woman who'd worked at this school since before most of us in the room were born. He did at least announce that the funeral was tomorrow afternoon.

I'd had a few too many iced teas and excused myself. When I returned, Stephanie led the room in a round of applause. Not a good sign.

"Congratulations, Molly. You've been elected the new secretary-slash-treasurer."

A hundred *buts* popped into my head. Scanning the down-turned faces while making my way back to my seat, I knew there was no point in objecting. I'd been outfoxed.

"Don't worry," Stephanie cooed. "I'm sure we can find you a helper."

"A helper? Great. To serve as the secretary, the treasurer, or the slash?"

She ignored the crowd's titters. "Do we have any volunteers?"

Nobody raised a hand. A middle-aged, curly-haired woman leaned toward me and said, "Now you know why nobody drinks the iced tea at these meetings."

"Well," Stephanie said, smiling at me benignly, "we'll find someone to work with you. Eventually."

Was it Will Rogers who'd claimed he never met a man he didn't like? If so, he hadn't been to many PTA meetings. Let's just see how charitable ol' Will would've been were he elected PTA secretary-slash-treasurer during his momentary absence. Perhaps the operative word in his assertion had been *man*, but even so, there were four men in the room. None of them were jumping up and down crying foul on my behalf.

To my surprise, Stephanie suddenly announced that she needed to pick up her daughter from a soccer game, and Jack ended the meeting almost an hour early. Even more surprisingly, though several people started to stand, they hesitated and sat back down. It was as if they were stalling, waiting to learn if they'd won a door prize.

I looked toward the exit and saw why nobody was leaving. Sergeant Tommy, in full uniform, was standing in the doorway, watching me. No one said a word. I inwardly groaned, but crossed the cafeteria toward him, having learned from all those years as a student that the floor never caves in when you want it to.

"Hey, Moll. Something's come up. Mind gettin' into my car with me for a moment? Got somethin' to show you."

I glanced back. Everyone was watching us, in total silence. Feeling recalcitrant, I called out, "Good-bye. It was nice meeting all of you."

There was at least one advantage to being escorted from a PTA meeting by a uniformed officer: maybe they would unelect me as treasurer.

He led me to a blue police cruiser parked directly in front of the entrance and opened the passenger door. With visions of being whisked off to the penitentiary, I remained on the sidewalk. "What's this about, Tommy?"

He rounded the car and got behind the wheel, shutting his door. It seemed unlikely this was the procedure he'd use if he were about to arrest me, so I got into the passenger side and shut the door.

"Your questions 'bout Mrs. Kravett's death got me to thinkin'. Went back over there today. She died at her desk. Neighbor, all set to drive her to a doctor's appoint-

ment, found her. So I went through her desk. This was
the top sheet in the center drawer.''

He handed me a piece of paper that looked as if it had
been printed by a laser printer. It read:

I hate you, you Miserable Bitch! You destroyed my
life! All you ever cared about was crushing your
students, making sure they felt as worthless as you
yourself are. I tried to warn you when I wrote that
poem about you, but you didn't stop, did you? After
all the lives you've ruined, now you think you can
just retire in peace and quiet. Well, I've come back,
Bitch, for one purpose only. I'm going to make you
pay for each and every student you hurt. Not a minute goes by when I don't think of how much pain
you'll feel! I'M GOING TO KILL YOU!!!

You Were Expecting Maybe
Betty Crocker?

MY STOMACH knotted as I read the message. *Nobody could possibly think I wrote this. It's all one long paragraph, caps are misused, and it ends with three exclamation points.* I glanced at Tommy. He wouldn't understand that we former journalism majors have hyperactive internal editors that kick in at inappropriate times.

"Maybe..." My voice sounded weak. I cleared my throat and tried again. "Maybe someone wrote a second poem about Mrs. Kravett."

He shook his head. "Know how I said that threat was the top sheet in the drawer? This was the second sheet." Tommy pulled another piece of paper from his back seat and handed it to me. Though I recognized it instantly, I read:

"Where's your homework? Let me have it,
or else you flunk," cries Mrs. Kravett.
"How dare you think my class is boring?
Yes, that's right, I heard you snoring.
Like with Lauren, I'll smack your face.
This class is an utter disgrace.
Now shut up and stay in your seats
while I recite this never-ending poem by Keats.

You, too, would be constantly crabby
if you looked like me, so short and flabby.
You students are the worst pains in the necks
I've known in the twenty years since I've had sex.''

It was the poem I'd written, neatly clipped from the school newspaper before being photocopied. ''Not exactly Emily Dickinson,'' I mumbled. My face warmed. The shame I felt now was a fraction of what I'd experienced when I'd first seen that particular edition of the school's *Gazette*. With that shame came the anger, again, at Stephanie, who'd defied me and published my words without my permission.

She had also printed that paper without getting approval for its new front page from the staff advisor...Mrs. Kravett.

I recalled that day so clearly, even after all those years. We'd been in study hall when I wrote the thing, angry and vindictive toward Mrs. Kravett for having embarrassed my best friend an hour earlier. Lauren had fallen asleep in class, so Mrs. Kravett threw a chalkboard eraser. The eraser hit Lauren's desk, where it was aimed, awaking her with a start amidst a cloud of chalk dust. Yet my claim that it was her face sounded so much more dramatic. Plus *face* was much easier to rhyme than *desk*.

I'd passed the poem to Lauren, who'd laughed. She passed it on to her boyfriend, Howie, who handed it to Jack. I'd been so pleased with myself, watching my classmates laugh and smile at me with, I thought, new respect. Denise, however, looked appalled when she'd read it, but dutifully passed it to Stephanie.

She had laughed openly, and the study hall monitor almost caught her with it. Stephanie was editor of the paper that year, an attempt to make herself sound well rounded on her college entrance applications, since she couldn't attach an eight-by-ten glossy of herself in a swimsuit. As soon as the bell rang, she was at my desk, pleading with me to let her publish it. I refused and asked her to give it back. She said she had one friend she wanted to show it to first. The next morning, there it was on the front page.

I cleared my throat again and shifted positions in the car seat, watching people file out of the building. "Did you find any other threats in Mrs. Kravett's desk? Anything that might give a clue as to who sent these?" Other than indicating *me*, I silently added.

He shook his head.

Just then, Stephanie and her elegant husband left the school building. Stephanie's attempts to watch me surreptitiously as she walked past the car were almost comical. I rolled down the window. "Don't forget to get back with me about dinner Friday." I closed the window without waiting for her response.

"Y'all are having dinner?" Tommy asked.

"Yeah. Dinner is something I do almost every evening."

He raised an eyebrow at me, then looked away.

"Sorry for my sarcasm." I sighed and glanced into the back seat. Tommy had removed the papers from a khaki-colored folder. The tab was unreadable from my angle. Was my name now on a police file? Hoping the action appeared casual despite my trembling hands, I lifted the front of the folder and replaced the two papers, straining to read the scrawled tab. I couldn't, and the next sheet in the folder was facedown.

"You could have called me or shown me these in private. You didn't have to come get me out of the PTA meeting. What's going on, Tommy?"

"What do you mean?"

"Whose reactions are you testing? Mine? A former classmate's?"

He stretched and yawned, his face blank. "Got any ideas 'bout who coulda sent these messages to Mrs. Kravett?"

I let out a sigh of frustration. "No, though I sure know *I* didn't. Whoever sent them must be the same person sending me threats. Does Mrs. Kravett have a computer?"

He shook his head.

That wasn't surprising. Mrs. Kravett had raved about classics and ranted that electricity was responsible for the downfall of our society. "How did she get the messages?"

"Don't know for sure. There was an empty, unmarked envelope on the desk. Someone coulda slipped it under her door."

"Did you check the pieces of paper for fingerprints?"

He snapped his fingers and his eyes flew wide. "Shucky darn. Why didn't I think of that?"

Despite my anxiety, his antics amused me sufficiently to smile. "No prints?"

"Nope." He eyed me at length. "So. Got anything you want to tell me 'bout Mrs. Kravett?"

"Yes. I want to tell you that I'm being set up. And I want you to find whoever is doing it. And I want that person arrested and kept way away from me and my family. And no fax machines allowed in their itty-bitty prison cell far, far away."

"Uh-huh. You got nothin' to tell me that might help me figure out who that person is?"

I combed my fingers through my hair. With luck, Tommy didn't know me well enough to realize that gesture was a sure sign of my inner turmoil. There was no way I would mention my concerns about Denise, who'd merely made a couple of off-the-cuff remarks. Stephanie, as much as I disliked her, had given me no reason to suspect her.

I shook my head.

"Uh-huh." He got out of the car, trotted to my door, and opened it with a flourish. He glanced around at the empty sidewalks with exaggerated care. By now, the other PTA members had left. "Coast is clear. I'll escort you to your car."

"Thank you." His gentleness brightened my mood, and I could almost see why Carolee, as a single woman, might find him attractive.

We reached my car, one of the few remaining in the lot. "Somethin' I want to ask you." He paused. He was staring straight ahead, and despite the dim lighting of the darkening sky, his cheeks appeared to redden. His attitude made me edgy. He reminded me of an adolescent about to ask for a date.

"Go ahead."

"Er, your neighbor lady last night."

"Lauren?"

"No, the blonde. What was her name?"

I smiled to myself, anticipating what was coming next. "Carolee Richards."

"What's her story?"

His wording momentarily distracted me. It had valentine possibilities: *Our lives are unfinished novels, waiting to be read by the right person.* "She's a nurse at the hospital in Schenectady. She's single. I don't think she's seeing anyone in particular."

As I spoke, Tommy pushed a pebble in the parking lot with the toe of his black leather shoe. He nodded and still didn't meet my eyes. "Sounds like you know her fairly well. Ever have her over for dinner, that kinda thing?" He put his hands in his pockets and rocked on his heels.

I decided to take his hint. It was agonizing to know that someone, perhaps an old friend, was making it look like I had a hand in Mrs. Kravett's death. My mood would brighten considerably if I could do at least one good deed for auld lang syne.

"Would you like to come over for dinner Friday, Tommy? Jack, Lauren, and Denise are coming. Stephanie might, too. Around seven o'clock. I haven't asked Carolee yet, but I will tonight." Carolee, I thought, might feel a bit out of place with all those Carlton alumni, but the spouses would be in the same boat.

Now he met my eyes and smiled. "Thanks, Moll." He waved as he took a couple of backward steps toward his car. "I'll bring wine. Red okay?"

"That'd be great." I watched him do a skip-hop pivot as he headed to his car. His excitement was so...cute, for lack of a better word. Watching him brought back memories of my feelings when Jim and I first started dating: unbridled joy, as if he had suddenly switched on the sunlight, and the world was so much brighter and lovelier than ever before. Still, Tommy's happiness was for a semiblind semidate. And I hadn't even asked Carolee. Her work hours at the hospital were irregular. She might not be free.

On the drive home, I was relieved to see no police cars in neighbors' driveways. I went to Carolee's. She swung open her door so quickly when I rang, she must have been standing by it. She wore her same aqua sweatsuit as last night, yet was once again sweatless.

"Molly! Hello." Her voice sounded unnaturally high. "Is everything okay?"

"Relatively speaking, yes. Why?"

"No reason. Just a little jumpy, I guess. I watched you drive in and noticed your kids weren't with you."

"They're at Lauren's."

Carolee nodded, still maintaining her post middoorway. My children had taken to Carolee almost immediately, which was unusual, and Lauren considered her one of her best friends. I trusted their opinions. Yet all our conversations at Carolee's home took place on her doorstep. It made me feel like a Jehovah's Witness. She'd been in my house several times in the past three weeks, though.

"Before I forget," Carolee began, "Lauren said you were both going to Mrs. Kravett's funeral tomorrow afternoon and asked if I could watch the kids since that's my day off. I'd be happy to, so pass that on to Lauren. I had told her I'd think about it, since I needed to decide if I wanted to go to the funeral myself."

"You knew Mrs. Kravett?"

She nodded. "I work in the oncology outpatient unit. I get to know the families of my patients pretty well. Her husband had lung cancer. He survived for four years after the initial diagnosis."

"Why don't you come with us to the funeral? We'll get someone else to baby-sit."

"I've seen more than my share of death. Besides, funerals are for the sake of the living. Relatives and friends. I didn't know any of Mrs. Kravett's people, except Lauren." She paused. "And now you."

The way she studied my eyes as she spoke the last phrase bothered me. Maybe it was just the wording. Strange to be termed one of my old teacher's "people."

Carolee continued, "Why don't you bring your children over around four?"

"Okay. Thanks. Also, are you free for dinner at my house Friday? Lauren and Steve will be there, plus a few former classmates."

"Your former classmates?" She winced slightly. "Gee. I don't know."

"Sergeant Newton is coming, and I'm quite sure he's hoping you'll be there."

She smiled broadly. "Oh. Well. In that case, what time?"

THE SECOND DAY of school was wonderfully uneventful. Both children took the bus there and back without a hitch—except for one frightening moment when the kindergarten bus arrived at the stop and Nathan didn't emerge. I promptly charged onto the bus. He was playing hide-and-seek with me under his seat. I pretended to be amused, then carefully explained that Mommy didn't like to be scared and warned him I'd get angry if he ever did that again.

Later that afternoon, Carolee met Lauren and me at the door and said a brusque good-bye to us as the children obeyed her instructions to go downstairs to the rec room.

En route to the funeral in the BMW that Steve normally drove, I mentioned how awkward it felt that Carolee never invited me inside her house.

Lauren shrugged. "I've known her since she bought that house six or seven years ago. For the first few months, she never asked me in either. She just isn't much of a housecleaner. It takes her a long time to feel comfortable enough with adults to let them see her house in its natural state."

"We're not talking toxic-waste sites or anything, are we? I mean, you trust having Rachel there, right?"

Lauren chuckled. "Absolutely. I've been in her house many times. Believe me, there are no health hazards."

"What about childproofing? She doesn't have children herself, and she's a nurse. Are there unlocked cabinets filled with drugs?"

"Yeah, but don't worry. The kids'll have to climb over the open tar pit and the high-voltage wires to get at them."

I laughed.

Lauren asked, "Have you gotten any more threats or bizarre faxes?"

Last night, I'd filled Lauren and her husband in on my encounter with Tommy Newton. "No, though I'll certainly be watching to see which of our former classmates attend Mrs. Kravett's funeral. Somehow I hope to spot some face at the funeral that'll let me make sense out of all of this. Maybe someone wearing a button that reads: Have Fax. Will Send Death Threats."

We turned at a busy intersection, and it occurred to me how unfamiliar I was with this town. Most of my world had consisted of the ten-or-so-mile bus route I'd ridden so many times, so many years ago. The scenery was lovely; lush hillsides, enormous oaks and maples. Alongside the main roads were stately, century-old homes meticulously maintained. In Boulder, those would've long since been turned into bed-and-breakfasts. Loyal as I am to Colorado, the color spectrum of autumn leaves in the nearby New York Adirondacks is breathtaking, whereas the Rocky Mountains' aspens turn yellow. Not unlike comparing Beethoven's Fifth Symphony to "Chop Sticks."

Yet even as a child, my life here felt like one big

what's-wrong-with-this-picture game. I was the object that didn't belong. I was never sure why that was so.

We parked and got out of the car. We took a couple of steps toward the church. Lauren paused and said, "Hang on. I need to set the car alarm." She pressed a button on her keychain, then shook her head and added, "Men and their toys."

"Really. You know the invention for a car *I'd* like to see? A child-sized chute that goes from the house straight to the back seat. Kids would have a blast going down it. We wouldn't have to spend twenty minutes telling 'em to get in the car every time we have some five-minute errand to run."

"That'd be wonderful. But it's the men who design these things, so it'll never happen."

"True. They give us such so-called time-savers as self-cleaning ovens. Who cares? Where's my self-cleaning bathtub?"

Lauren laughed. It was a marvel how our childhood friendship had defied distance and time.

We sobered the instant we got in line to enter the church. As we slowly moved forward, a sense of revulsion mingled with macabre curiosity; our line led to a room that held a coffin, then into the main room for the service. My mother having had an aversion to taking children to funerals, I had never seen a dead body before. Curiosity won out, and I kept my place in line.

I peered into the coffin. It struck me as almost obscene to gaze down at my once feisty teacher this way, lifeless and waxen. She should open her eyes and say, "Stop daydreaming, Molly, and get to work!"

We walked slowly toward the main room. Lauren whispered, "It seems strange to see her without a piece of chalk in her hand."

"Really. She's barely changed in seventeen years. Except for now being dead, that is."

Lauren elbowed me, and we both fought off a fit of nervous giggles. The pews were crowded, and it soon became obvious that Mrs. Kravett had touched many lives.

Denise and her cone-headed husband were there, as was Jack Vance. In his tweed jacket he looked professorial—as opposed to principalial, I suppose. Tommy, in uniform, was seated in the back, and feigned indifference as we entered.

Stephanie, dressed in black but wearing model-like makeup, was seated in the second row. She spotted us as we took our seats near Tommy, smiled, and mouthed a big "Hi," accompanied by a happy wiggly-finger wave that seemed more than a tad inappropriate, given the setting.

Jack Vance gave a touching eulogy. At least, I assumed it was touching, because frankly, I struggled so hard not to make any noise while crying, I barely listened. My regrets and guilt about Mrs. Kravett had hit me full force.

Just after graduation, my parents purchased their condo in Florida. It had been more fun to visit them there than in New York. I'd been so cavalier about the passing of time. As an indirect result, Mrs. Kravett died not only before I could apologize for my poem, but thinking I was a homicidal maniac out to avenge her strict teaching methods. Someone, probably sitting in that same church, had set me up. No one, aside from Lauren, knew me well enough to realize how bad I'd felt about that poem.

At one point midproceedings, Lauren reached over, squeezed my hand, and whispered, "She was a teacher. She understood teenagers. She forgave you. Let it go."

That made me cry all the harder. Lauren could well be right about Mrs. Kravett's forgiveness. Yet a hateful threat that may as well have had my name on it was likely the last thing she ever read.

Though I stared through my blurred vision at each former classmate, I still had no clue. My emotional state made me all the more determined to eventually confront whoever had done this to me.

After the service, Stephanie, her handsome husband in tow, sashayed in our general direction. She was probably going to use the opportunity to RSVP about my dinner party. Overcome by anger and remorse, I blurted, "Why did you do it, Stephanie? Why did you publish my poem in the school paper without my permission?"

Her jaw dropped. Before she could collect herself and respond, Lauren grabbed my arm. "Molly," Lauren said sternly. "This isn't the time or the place. Come on."

She was right. I allowed her to lead me away. In the parking lot, I glanced back. Stephanie had attracted quite a crowd, several of them nodding as they listened to her. She gestured at me as she spoke, no doubt identifying me as the villain in her damsel-in-distress routine.

"Are you all right?" Lauren asked, once we'd reached the privacy of her car.

I nodded, but felt unable to master the lump in my throat. "I know I'm just looking for a scapegoat. But I'm still angry at Stephanie for printing that poem in the paper. She'd asked me if she could publish it, and I told her no. Remember?"

Lauren looked at me sympathetically, but said nothing as we pulled out of the lot.

I glanced at Lauren in profile. She was chewing on her lip. The last time she was doing that, there was palpable friction between her and her husband. At length, I asked, "Is everything okay between you and Steve?"

"Um, sure. Sort of. Actually… Let's talk about that some other time, okay?"

Uh-oh. We drove home in silence, reclaimed our children, and went inside our respective houses. Though I could relate to Carolee's cleaning inadequacies, I set about taking my frustrations out by scrubbing. The odor from the bathroom almost brought tears to my eyes. Nathan had been doing his hula-dance-while-peeing routine. I used an ammonia-based cleaner to combat the problem, which struck me as redundant. Good thing I write greeting cards and not advertising copy. I doubt that "Smells Slightly Better than Urine" would be a popular advertising slogan for a household cleaning product.

Later, I began to fret as I concocted some sort of dinnerish thing for myself and the kids. Someone who hated me enough to send me death threats might *act* on those threats. Here I was, possibly inviting him or her to my house for dinner. Talk about a social engagement with a hidden agenda. "Raise your hand if you'd like to kill the hostess."

As I envisioned the potential fiasco, I sketched a cartoon. People sitting at a table are staring in dismay at the bedraggled woman who's emerged from the kitchen. Her clothing is splattered and torn, flames are coming from the doorway, and she's carrying a charred and smoking platter. She says, "You were expecting maybe Betty Crocker?" Though there was little faxability potential, I might be able to freelance it as an apron design to a company that sold self-expression products.

I returned to my cooking. All the while a feeling of doom threatened to engulf me. Karen came into the kitchen and poured herself a glass of milk. I said, "Why do I feel like I'm about to make the biggest mistake of my life?"

"I dunno, Mom." She smiled up at me. As if guessing the answer to a riddle, she said, "Because you are?"

SIX

Stop Playing with Your Food!

STEPHANIE NEVER CALLED to say how many of herselves and kin were coming to dinner. After our little scene at the funeral, I couldn't really blame her. By 6:50 on Friday evening I had dinner in the oven and was busily cleaning the kitchen counters and floor. I measure ingredients by default: whatever makes its way into the pot I cook and whatever spills I sweep up later. It works well in terms of flavor, but I have a heck of a time whenever someone requests one of my recipes.

Lauren, Steve, and Rachel arrived first. Though Rachel had a hand of each parent, they acted like stone bookends. Within moments, Rachel dashed off with Karen and Nathan, and Steve immediately took a seat on the couch. That had been my father's favorite position. It must have masculine cushion dents, for Jim was always drawn to that spot as well. Both my father and my husband are thin, though, so with Steve's polar bear body, he sank deeper into it.

I complimented Lauren on her emerald-colored dress. She brushed aside my remarks and offered to help me in the kitchen. This was, of course, one of the social graces we women all learn. But let's face it. If you're having a formal dinner party and you truly need help in the kitchen from your guests, dinner is in jeopardy.

The doorbell rang. Lauren swung open the door and cried, "Jack! How are you?"

Jack Vance stepped inside, giving Lauren a partylike kiss of greeting. I felt a shade uneasy as I said hello, still unable to completely reconcile this average-looking middle-aged man with the Adonis of my memory.

Steve groaned, but I wasn't sure if that was due to his wife's being bussed or his having to get to his feet again so quickly. Jack crossed the room and pumped Steve's hand vigorously.

"You two know each other?" I asked, needing to work my way into witty repartee gradually.

"Sure do," Jack said. "The district hired him to establish software security measures. He's been teaching me a lot, let me tell you."

I grinned, nodded, and said, "Oh," my mind racing to come up with some follow-on that could make me seem at least vaguely interested in school-district software security measures. Yet another area where I missed my husband. He had an incredible knack for acting fascinated with the most painfully mundane topics. Provided, of course, that his *wife* wasn't the one speaking. "So. What kind of computer records do you need to keep secure?"

"You'd be surprised, Molly. We have student-at-risk listings, the status of various grants, funds, teacher ratings, PTA activities, results of various surveys, the finance committee activities, of course..."

"Of course," I agreed. I'd been bobbing my head like a dashboard trinket. I looked at Steve, expecting him to add something, anything, to the conversation, but he was staring off into space. Lauren, too, seemed to have fallen asleep, eyes open. The doorbell rang, and Lauren, Steve, and I simultaneously cried, "I'll get it."

It was Denise and her husband. His hair had yet another layer of grease gluing it onto his oddly shaped skull. Perhaps he'd had a particularly large head at birth that had never rounded itself out. He wore a checkered bow tie, white short-sleeved shirt, and green corduroy pants. I'd forgotten his name and hoped Denise would use it soon so I wouldn't have to ask.

"So, Molly, you met my husband the other night." Denise's light blue dress suit made her look particularly petite under all that fabric.

"Yes. Nice to meet you again." I wasn't worried about catching his name. After all, there were other people in the room Denise would introduce him to.

"Steve, Jack. How are you?" he said.

Steve, Jack, and X launched into an animated discussion about baseball. Compared to most women, I'm a sports nut. However, the action of an entire three-hour baseball game can be shown in a single highlight clip. It's a fine time-saver to watch the clip on the news, groan or cheer once, then get on with life.

"Can I get anyone something to drink?" I asked.

I took the men's orders, but Denise and Lauren insisted on helping. We got as far as the front door before Tommy arrived. He scanned the room with the desperate look of a lost child. "Uh, hi, Molly. Got the wine, like you asked."

I thanked him, and as we chatted, Carolee climbed the front steps. I invited her inside and noted Tommy's gleeful expression as their eyes met, followed by the slight look of surprise when he lowered his vision to her swizzle-stick legs.

"Let me introduce you to everyone." I scanned the room and realized I was in trouble. The only people she didn't know were Denise and X. "This is my neighbor Carolee Richards. You remember Tommy Newton, of course," I stalled, but Mr. Denise's name was still a blank.

Carolee nodded shyly. "Hi. Nice to see you out of uniform."

Tommy's grin was so wide he had a pair of dimples on each cheek that looked like quotation marks for his lips. We turned toward the living room. "And this is Denise and her husband. Denise and I went to school together for thirteen years. We were even in the same kindergarten class."

Carolee shook hands with Denise, then stepped toward X with an outstretched hand.

"Sam Bakerton," he said.

Sam. Nothing like Sam Malone on *Cheers,* I thought, as a memory device.

No sooner had we gotten drinks and taken seats in the living room than the door opened, and a female voice cooed, "Knock knock."

Stephanie entered. She was wearing a strapless black taffeta gown. Yikes. In my cotton paisley A-line, suddenly I was underdressed for my own party. There was no violin quartet or diva following her through the door. Nor a spouse. Perhaps her husband had decided not to come, anticipating Jack's presence.

Stephanie held out a covered platter toward me and said, "Darling. You were so out-of-sorts at the funeral. It's nice to see you back in one piece. I know this is a surprise, but I brought dessert." She scanned the faces of her captive audience. "Some of the men in the room probably haven't heard this story, but Molly started a fire in home ec. Not just once, but twice. The first time, she burned chocolate chip cookies. What was the other? Oh, yes. It was *supposed* to be a chocolate marble cake. By the time Molly was through with it, it was marbleized upside-down cake. She not only burned it, she dropped it on the floor.''

I gritted my teeth but managed a smile as I stepped toward her. "Yes, well, it's baking-impaired people like me who inspired the invention of ice cream."

She handed me the platter as if it were Waterford crystal. "This is cheesecake. I made it from scratch. I was going to bring cherries jubilee, but I wasn't sure I could trust you to set my dessert on fire."

"True. I would've asked you to hold it while I lit the blowtorch."

"Oh, Moll, Moll. Such a kidder."

I balanced the platter on my fingertips. "Just how much scratch goes into a cheesecake anyway?"

Lauren whisked the cake from my hand. "Let me set this in the kitchen for you, Molly."

Stephanie's husband stepped unannounced through the front door. He was wearing black slacks and a white long-sleeved silk shirt.

Stephanie said, "Oh, Preston, there you are." She took his arm and looked at me, her face expressionless.

"Hello. I'm Molly."

Preston Saunders. Now *there* was a yuppie name. I wondered what could have taken him so long to reach the front door from my short driveway. He reached out his hand, and as I shook it, the lingering smell of cigarette smoke on his clothing answered that question.

Preston glared at Jack Vance, now standing by the guacamole bowl. In a caricature, the two would have lightning bolts shooting from their eyes.

Sam broke the silence. "Shame about Mrs. Kravett isn't it, Jack?"

"Sure is. You knew her?" Though the question hinted

at nonchalance, Jack sounded all too aware that Sam had known her.

Sam said, "She did the proposal for the grant that my company...that Preston's and my company awarded to Carlton Central."

"That's right," Jack said. "I'd forgotten." Yet another lousy acting job. I looked at Preston. He was staring at an oil still life over the couch, pretending not to listen. That educational grant might have been the source of contention between him and Jack, but I'd put bigger money on Stephanie's flirtations as the cause.

"Mrs. Kravett started the student internship program at your company, too," Steve said. All three men looked at him in surprise, and he added, "The interns' schedules were in the school's data base. You'd be amazed how much I learn about people during the course of my job." He looked at Jack. "Though it would have made my job easier if Mrs. Kravett had shared her password with someone before she died. Now I have to work Sunday and take the whole system down to get at it."

The muscles in Jack's jaw tightened and his eyes flashed in anger. There was an awkward silence.

Everyone in the room was probably thinking, How long till I can make a graceful exit? That was certainly *my* thought pattern, and I lived here. Preston put his arm around Stephanie.

"So, I take it you didn't bring your children," I said.

"Good heavens no," said Stephanie. She flicked at me with a manicured paw that sported a wedding band and a diamond so large she must have listed to the left. "We'd owe my daughter another trip to Disneyland to reward her for having to come *here* tonight."

I turned a growl into a clearing of my throat. "Think I'll go see where Lauren's putting that cheesecake."

"Need any help in the kitchen?" Stephanie called after me.

"Yes, as a matter of fact. Mind helping me whip up a main course?"

She blinked, then said, "You *are* kidding, aren't you?"

I pushed through the kitchen door, letting it swing shut behind me. Lauren was leaning against the counter, gulping a glass of burgundy. She looked a bit sheepish.

"Don't get the wrong impression." She lifted the bottle. "I just get nervous at parties and need to toke up. Want some?"

I shook my head. I'd learned my lesson from a painful alcohol-related incident years ago, and now rarely drank even socially. "Lauren, there's something I've wanted to ask you. Is it just me, or is that woman a bitch?"

She didn't need to ask which woman. "It's her all right, but you bring out the worst in her."

"How? What is it about me that makes her act like that?"

"Maybe she's jealous of you."

"That's ridiculous. Nobody's ever been jealous of me. Except maybe my mother-in-law, for stealing her only son." That reminded me. Jim was supposed to call at eight tonight, Fridays and Saturdays being the rare days that the considerable time difference was workable. With any luck, I could play up his phone call to let it be known that I did indeed have a loving husband.

Lauren turned, studied my face, and said wistfully, "We can never see ourselves as clearly as we see others. That's why as friends we hold up a mirror. And I see so much beauty in you."

I was taken aback by her words and muttered through

my embarrassment, "Jeez, Lauren. You're getting philosophical on me."

She smiled slightly and blushed. "You wrote that in a letter to me seven years ago." I looked at her in surprise and she continued, "I'd sent you pictures from our tenth reunion and was obsessing about my weight. Remember?"

I did, vaguely, but we were soon deluged with party guests, who'd swamped into the kitchen. I should've known how guests gravitate there if the hostess leaves them unattended for any length of time. Lauren helped with my hostessing duties and we were soon actually eating at the dining table like real adults.

Our food was not the disaster I'd envisioned. The stuffed spinach-and-cheese manicotti was moist, the salad crisp, and even the garlic bread was just the way I liked it, crunchy on the outside and soft on the inside.

My daughter, Karen, self-appointed hostess of the basement party for the younger set, kept periodically moaning that the pizza'd better arrive soon or she'd starve to death. It did, and she didn't.

Lauren continued to hit the wine as we ate, matched in pace only by Tommy, who acted truly smitten by Carolee. She kept excusing herself to "check on the children." I wasn't sure how much of that was sincere interest and how much was an attempt to impress Tommy with her mothering skills. In any case, it was a wonderful convenience for me.

On a final trip up the stairs, carrying an empty pizza box and paper plates, Carolee announced, "Rachel just did the cutest thing. She showed your children how to use the fax machine."

I tensed. I'd deliberately turned off my machine that evening. A subscriber to Murphy's Law, I'd wanted to avoid the possibility of an obscene fax arriving, to be read aloud by Karen to our dinner guests. "What did she send?"

"Oh, just some little doodles she drew."

"Excuse me. I don't want my children to figure out that they can use the fax machine to send messages to my husband while he's in the Philippines. Our phone bill's high enough already." Forced to reveal my possessiveness about my office equipment, I might as well get in some plugs for my marriage.

As I headed down the stairs, an idea for a humorous nonoccasion card came to me. After chasing the three children out of my office, I made a quick sketch so I wouldn't be mulling it over during dinner. It was a drawing of a mother and son in a kitchen. The mother's back is turned while the boy fearfully duels a live swordfish. The mother is saying over her shoulder, "It's called sushi and it's good for you! Now for the last time, stop playing with your food!"

I heard angry male voices and rushed back upstairs. It was obvious the party was not going well. For one thing, now *no one* was speaking. Much as I'd like to have attributed that to my good cooking, no one was eating. All three Wilkinses looked upset; Rachel had come upstairs and was standing near the table, kicking at the carpet.

Steve threw his linen napkin on the table. "I will *not* sit here and be accused of overcharging my customers. I work my tail off for you people." He rose. "Lauren. Rachel. We're leaving."

"Don't go." I felt desperation, bordering on panic, as I scanned the faces of my guests. Stephanie looked oblivious, but Preston was red-faced, as were Denise, Sam, and Jack. Carolee and Tommy had rotated in their seats and appeared to be watching with curiosity. I put my hand on Steve's shoulder. "What's a party without a good-spirited debate, right? Talk about overcharging! Has anyone seen the tax tables for this year?"

Actually, *I* hadn't seen them, but surely the IRS was one enemy everyone had in common. Steve ignored me and headed to the door. "We've got ice cream and a whole cheesecake in the kitchen," I called after him. "Made from scratch." *What the hell had I missed?*

"Sorry, Molly," Lauren muttered. "Steve isn't feeling good all of a sudden." She glared at him. They were soon gone, leaving only a trail of apologies behind them.

Still, no one at the table was speaking. Preston shot an angry glare at Sam, who quickly looked away.

"Did I miss something while I was downstairs?" I asked as casually as I could.

Jack stood up. "Great dinner, Molly. I'd best be going."

"It's only eight o'clock."

"Yeah, we'd better shove off as well," Preston said. "Why don't we just take your cake with us, sugar, and we'll have some at home."

"Good Lord," I said. "Did a stink bomb go off up here while I was downstairs?"

Denise, Stephanie, spouses, and cheesecake promptly left. I escorted them to the door, but the instant they were outside, I locked the door and whirled toward my lone remaining guests.

"Tommy. Carolee. Neither of you is leaving this house till you tell me precisely what went on while I was downstairs." At least I'd managed to suppress the wagging finger that would've punctuated my words had I been speaking to my children.

Carolee and Tommy exchanged a look of shared perplexity. Tommy shrugged. "Beats me, Molly."

Carolee said in wide-eyed innocence, "Steve was sharing some anecdote about a computer job or something. I wasn't listening because Tommy was telling me about his sons. Then Preston said something and Jack said something, then Steve said, 'Oh you think *so*, do you?' And, well, next thing I know, there was this dead silence, and you came upstairs and Steve said they had to leave."

"No offense, Carolee," I said, "but that story seems to have lost a lot in the translation."

Tommy held up his hands. "Like Carolee said, we were talking to each other at the time. Didn't hear what was bein' said at the rest of the table. What kinda ice cream you got?" His lopsided smile warned me that he was not entirely sober.

TOMMY AND CAROLEE left together a half hour later. I called Lauren's house, but got their machine. I left a message to please call me back and tell me what was going on. I glanced through the window. The house lights were on and I could see an adult-sized shadow move across the drawn curtains in their kitchen window.

When my phone rang later, I rushed to it, hoping it was Lauren.

"Hi." It was Jim. "I called late on purpose. Your fax said you were having a dinner party tonight, and I didn't want to interrupt it."

"That was thoughtful." Next time I wanted witnesses when he called, I'd better clue him in first.

I told him about my teacher's heart attack, but suddenly decided not to tell him about the threats. It felt as if telling him about them would make my peril real. We chatted for a while, and I put the kids on the line with him before getting them to bed late, but allowing them to talk with their dad was more important than a little extra sleep, especially on a weekend. Then I decided to tackle the kitchen.

After loading the dinner plates into the dishwasher, I started on the remaining cooking utensils. I soon discovered something strange. After a few minutes, I checked the dishwasher, then every drawer and shelf in the house.

The search only verified my fear: someone had stolen my carving knife.

SEVEN

Finally. Some Shade!

AN EMPTY CAR was in my driveway. That had to be Sergeant Tommy's. He must have walked Carolee home and stayed for some tutti-frutti.

It was almost eleven at night. I parked myself on my doorstep and waited, calculating that he would either stay overnight at Carolee's or leave soon, but in any case, he would not leave his car in my driveway for everyone to see much longer.

The missing knife was just plain weird. I mentally sorted through my party guests' appearances. Who might have been able to sneak out a heavy knife with a nine-inch blade? Nobody had worn a coat, but at one point three purses were behind the stuffed chair close to the door. Whose were they?

"Ouch!" I slapped a mosquito on my arm. Talk about sharp blades. The mosquitoes were out in force. We have mosquitoes in Boulder, but the ones in upstate New York can be mistaken for hummingbirds.

Stephanie hadn't brought a purse. Hers would have been some tiny gold or silver clutch to match the outfit, and I'd have remembered it. She had that covered platter, though, large enough to have hidden my knife. So all four women could conceivably have gotten the knife out of the house. A man could simply have stashed it inside his shirt or pants leg. Which was not to say he'd want to run a marathon that way.

What if the cutlery thief had slipped it out the window, planning to go back for it? I raced across my lawn to the kitchen windows to see if that was feasible. It wasn't. You would have to slit or remove the screen, and they were intact on both windows. However, the sliding glass back door was directly off the kitchen. Perhaps the knife was still hidden outside. My back porch light was on. I made a quick search, but found nothing.

As I circled the house, I spotted Tommy crossing the street. His gait looked so carefree he was practically skipping. He passed below a streetlamp. He wore a dopey expression that made me suspect some love song was playing in his head.

"Tommy."

I startled him so badly he jerked his arm back as if to draw an invisible gun. He covered for the motion by scratching himself. "What are you doin' out here in the middle of the night? Catchin' lightning bugs?"

We met in my driveway. "I'm really worried. My carving knife is missing."

He stared at me and blinked slowly. He seemed half asleep and perhaps a little inebriated. "Carving knife? You mean like a knife you whittle with?"

"No! Carving knife as in carve the turkey. Kitchen knife. My kitchen knife is missing."

He grinned and unlocked his car. "Some guest prob'ly washed it. Put it away in a different drawer."

"I already thought of that. I've searched the entire kitchen. It's been stolen."

"Uh-huh." He glanced at his watch, then apparently unable to read it, opened his car door and angled his wrist under the overhead light. "Next time a unit's in your area, I'll have 'em come do a stolen-property report. Must be one hell of an expensive knife, since you're so worried."

Unable to keep the exasperation from my voice, I said, "It's not the knife itself that worries me. Somebody sent a death threat to Mrs. Kravett that implicated me. The way things are going, I'm afraid my knife will show up in somebody's back. And I want to go on record now as saying that I didn't put it there!"

He held up his palms, reminiscent of a parent attempting to mollify his child. "Maybe you should check your drawers again."

"Never mind!" I whirled on a heel and stormed into my house, letting the screen door bang behind me. "But if someone *does* get stabbed with my knife, I'm telling you now that I didn't do it."

"Uh-huh. I'll tell 'em you said so. Night. Nice talkin' with you. And...uh, thanks again for dinner. Check downstairs. Maybe the kids took it to cut the pizza."

Sputtering belated comebacks to Tommy's suggestion that I'd let seven-year-olds use a lethal weapon to cut pizza, I ransacked the house. There was definitely no knife. My check of the dishwasher and cabinets verified something else rather odd. I'd either lost a cup or gained a saucer. The cups had been on the counter in anticipation of the dessert that only Carolee and Tommy had experienced.

"Hey diddle diddle/A cat with a fiddle/My cup ran away with my knife/Run for your life." Nice rhyme, lousy meter. No sense reporting this second theft. No one ever got cupped to death.

Though it was late, I called Lauren's house again. The lights were still on, but their recorder answered. I left a message for them to call me, to please tell me what had gone wrong during dinner. I deliberately spoke slowly, but no one picked up.

Tires squealed. I raced to the window. A car zipped out from the Wilkinses' driveway. In the bad lighting I couldn't be sure, but it looked like Lauren, with the top of Rachel's head just visible in the back seat. It was half past eleven. Only horrible explanations for Lauren's great haste in leaving with her child at this hour came to mind. She and Steve had a terrible fight. Rachel had a medical emergency.

My personal problems paled in comparison.

The lights in their house went out. Then a second car pulled out of the driveway. This car passed directly underneath the streetlamp. It was definitely Steve driving. He turned the same direction as Lauren, but was moving considerably slower. My stomach knotted.

Unable to sleep, I went downstairs to work. My mind was on Lauren. The only scenario I could concoct for the two cars was they'd had such a bad fight that Lauren got Rachel out of bed and drove off, perhaps to some hotel. Steve had thought about it for a minute or two, then drove off after her, hopefully to convince her to return home.

Thinking of our friendship, I designed a silly card of two men dragging themselves across a desert. Overhead is an enormous buzzard, casting a shadow on them. As one man looks at the buzzard in fear, the other says, "Finally! Some shade!" The caption reads, Thank You for Helping Me to Look on the Bright Side.

A fax came in, and once again the tag line had been suppressed. I sat there frozen, willing myself not to read it. Finally my curiosity overcame my better sense, and I snatched it from the tray.

> Your husband is cheating on you.
> Serves you right. If you were any kind
> of a wife, you'd be with him right now.

I crumpled it, cursing rabidly, wanting to cram it down the sender's throat. I flung it into the rubber trash can, then kicked the can. It banged off the far wall. "Yes, damn you. If I were a better wife, I'd be with him. But my husband *is* faithful to me. I know that. Not because I'm a perfect wife, but because he's such a good, decent man."

After taking a few calming breaths, I realized this was a clue. The sender knew *me*, not my husband. Not much of a clue, though, on second thought. *No one* here knew Jim, except for the kids and me.

I glanced at my watch. It was after midnight. I tried to figure out the time-zone conversion. It was about 1:00 p.m. Saturday in Manila. I called my husband's hotel. In a thick accent, the receptionist said, "One moment please," then put me on indefinite hold. A minute later I tried again and got a busy signal. Next, the line disconnected during my ensuing conversation with the same receptionist. I was in no mood to risk a fourth call, at which point I'd be so edgy if I ever did get Jim, I'd greet him with tears or shouts—probably a combination of both. He deserved better than that.

If only I knew everything was okay with Lauren. This was getting to be too much for me to bear. I dashed upstairs and looked out the window at the Wilkinses' house. It was dark, deserted.

THE NEXT MORNING I awoke with a headache. The children were already downstairs, watching cartoons. I got them breakfast and battled an inexplicable but overwhelming urge to check my fax machine. I went down-

stairs and felt a tremendous sense of relief to see nothing
in the tray. Just as I was leaving the office, the motor
made its high-pitched whir. I dashed over to it and
watched as a message dropped down. The tag line indicated it had been sent from the Wilkinses' house. Written
in childish print was:

```
Molly,
HELP ME PLES
HELP
 Rachel
```

My heart drumming wildly, I called the Wilkinses'
house. Their machine was on. Dear God. What if Lauren
and Steve were having a violent argument? I raced upstairs. The children were still in front of the set.

"What's wrong, Mommy?" Nathan asked. Karen, too,
turned and looked at me.

"I don't know what to do." I combed hair back from
my face with both hands. *Call 911 and stay put. But
Rachel might need instant help. Or she might just be
playing a childish joke on me. I should at least knock on
their door before I call.* "Goddamn it!" Oops. "Don't
repeat that."

Normally I wouldn't worry about leaving my children
to run next door for a few minutes. This was not a normal
situation. I clicked off the TV.

"Karen, Nathan, we're going to play a game. A...spy
game." I grabbed the portable phone, which had an intercom button. I stretched the phone cord till the base of
the phone sat on the floor between them. "I'm going to
go next door to Lauren's house. We'll see if we can use
the phone like a walkie-talkie. Okay?"

"Cool!" Nathan cried. Karen, though, was studying my face. She didn't buy my play-a-game routine.

What if I got in there and Steve was totally out of control? "One more thing. This part is very important. Karen, if you hear me say the word *Oklahoma*, that means I want you to call the police."

"But *you've* got the phone, Mom," Karen said, sounding alarmed.

"I know. Just go right away to the kitchen phone. Do you remember what number to call?"

"Nine-one-one."

"That's right. And tell the police to come right away to the Wilkinses' house at twenty-ten Little John Lane. Nathan, Karen, stay right here and listen to me over the phone, all right?"

Before they could get more curious, I ran over and pounded on the Wilkinses' door. No answer. It was completely silent inside. If a violent struggle *had* taken place, it was over. Too bad there were no garage windows for me to look through and find out if their cars were inside.

"Can you hear me?" I said into my phone.

"Yeah, Mom. Nathan spilled some milk on the carpet."

"It was your fault!" Nathan cried.

"I'm going to call someone on this phone for just a minute or two, then I'll put it right back on so you can hear me again. Okay?"

I called the police and asked for Tommy. While waiting, I remembered Lauren once told me Carolee had a key. I ran across the street and rang her doorbell. No one was home. In the meantime, the receptionist told me Tommy wasn't there. She asked if I wanted to speak to another officer. Undecided and not wanting to leave my children incommunicado, I just told her to have him call me ASAP and hung up.

I pressed intercom and ran into Lauren's backyard. Steve had once shown me their alarm system. It consisted of sensors on all the windows, set in such a way that the alarm would sound only when the glass was broken or the window was opened by several inches.

The first window I looked through was Rachel's bedroom. Her pink chiffon curtains swayed in the breeze, her window open a crack. I called for Rachel a couple of times. The house was completely still.

If the alarm was set, opening the window farther would trip it, signaling the monitoring company to call the police. That was fine by me. If the fax was just a joke, I could call the police immediately and tell them why I'd deliberately tripped the alarm. If Rachel was in there alone needing help, I didn't want to wait for the police to arrive to get to her.

I lifted my phone. "...telling Mommy you did that on purpose!"

Still arguing about spilled milk. "Karen and Nathan." Silence. "I'm going to crawl through the window into the Wilkinses' house."

"Cool!"

"Remember our code word to call the police?"

"Oklahoma," Karen said in her you're-boring-me voice.

I angled the screen off the frame, then dropped my phone through the window. Judging by the clatter, it landed on top of wooden furniture. As I forced the window open, an alarm went off. Over the noise, I yelled, "Rachel? Lauren? Anybody home?" No answer.

Getting up high enough to stuff myself through her little window was no easy task. I felt buffoonish as I hooked my forearms along the inside walls and catwalked up, no doubt leaving footprints on their white siding. Then I balanced on my stomach and pulled myself across her student desk, knocking over pictures and knick-knacks. I wondered how cat burglars did it. They must keep in shape through specialty aerobics classes...B&E 101.

I called hello a couple more times. "What, Mom?" I heard Karen shout.

"Not you. I'm seeing if the Wilkinses answer me."

Where to put the phone while I looked around? My baggy cotton pants had deep pockets. I slipped the phone into one of them.

Except for the alarm, the house was silent and felt unoccupied. Nothing seemed amiss as I went through the hallway into the kitchen. The Wilkinses' phone rang. I answered.

A man with a Bronx accent said, "Security Systems. What's da password?"

"I don't know. I'm the neighbor. I broke in."

"You shouldn't a done that, ma'am. Now I gotta call the police."

"Good. But give me a couple of seconds before you do. I have to call them, too, and I don't want their lines tied up."

"Huh?"

I hung up and called 911. I told the woman who answered I was a friend of Sergeant Newton's, that I'd just tripped the alarm, gave the address, and explained about the help message.

"Where are you now?" she asked.

"I'm on the phone in the kitchen."

"You need to stay put. We've got a unit coming to that address. What's your name and address, ma'am?"

I answered, and she asked me again what room I was in. The kitchen. Could I see the front door? No. Did everything in the kitchen look in place? She intended to keep me on the phone till the police arrived.

Rachel's black-and-white cat appeared from somewhere in the house. Missy ran from me to the doorway, back to me, then to the doorway. This was a feline version of Lassie. She wanted me to follow her. Were cats that smart? Maybe not, but Missy was more fun to communicate with than the woman on the phone.

I'd committed at least two crimes I could think of off the top of my head. The least I could do was make sure Rachel wasn't in Steve's office. Instead of answering about my relationship to the child who'd sent the fax, I said, "Oh. Just a second. I think someone's at the door," and hung up on her.

I pulled my own phone out of my pocket. "Can you still hear me?"

"Yes," Karen said. "What did you say about Rachel?"

"Nothing important. She was probably just playing a joke. I'm sure she's fine." The Wilkinses' phone started ringing. No doubt the police dispatcher was trying to get me back on the line. I ignored it.

Missy was running back and forth in front of the double oak doors to Steve's office.

The answering machine came on.

Not wanting to leave prints, I pulled the bottom of my pink T-shirt free from my waistband and used that to try the doorknob. It turned. I swung open the door slowly, but stayed in the hallway.

The venetian blinds were down and the lights off. The air smelled stagnant. I could hear the faint hum of his computer and a monotonous, periodic beep. The screen put out a bluish light, outlining Steve in the chair. He was slumped over, facedown on his keyboard.

Please, God. Let him be asleep.

By now, the dispatcher was yelling at me through the answering machine. Her stern voice was demanding that I pick up the phone immediately. I ignored her.

"Steve?"

"Mom?" Karen's voice called.

"Uh, Karen?"

"Yeah, Mom?"

"I may need to hang up here. If I do, don't worry about me. Okay?"

"Steve? Are you all right?" I had my thumb right over the intercom button, prepared to press it and cut Karen and Nathan off instantly if this was what I thought and I did something that might scare them. Such as scream.

I took a step closer and saw something in his back. A knife handle. I closed my eyes. I felt dizzy. I heard myself say, "Oklahoma."

EIGHT

I Want My Mommy

MY HEAD POUNDED. All I wanted to do was go back to sleep.

Tommy Newton was in my bedroom and he wouldn't stop talking to me. Someone was putting a cap on my head. There were other people in my room. Strangers. Police officers. This wasn't my bed. Someone was touching my face, shining a flashlight in my eyes.

Oh, God. I remembered. I tried to sit up but my stomach lurched and the hardwood floor swam. Two men in white uniforms were near me. One leaned back away from my face. Two other men were near Steve Wilkins, still slumped over in his chair. Tommy Newton, in uniform, was the only face in the room I recognized. I muttered the word that popped into my head, "Oklahoma."

"Sorry, Toto. You're still in New York." Tommy moved next to the men in white, one of whom pocketed his penlight. They must be the paramedics. Or were these the men in white coming to take me away? They were directly in front of me, blocking my vision.

"Steve. Is he…"

"Yeah," Tommy said. "He's dead. Looks like you fainted and clonked your head pretty good."

I struggled to rise, but Tommy held up a palm. "Don't get up just yet. Have any idea where Lauren is?"

"No." The back of my head smarted. I touched the

sore area with my fingertips. *A lump the size of a grape-fruit! My hair! Where was my—* Oh. It was a bandage. I groped my head and realized there was a pad of some sort on the back of my head, held in place by what felt like a headband. A tourniquet for my head.

"Leave that on," a baby-faced medic told me. He and his partner set a cot next to me. "We need that to keep pressure on the wound to stop the bleeding. We're going to take you to the hospital now."

"No!"

To my surprise, the paramedics backed off and quietly conferred with one another. The phrase "not life-threatening" reached my ears. Always nice to know. Maybe they weren't allowed to take me to the hospital against my wishes.

How could I have hit the back of my head? Still groggy, I looked behind me at a puddle of blood.

"Lie back down," Tommy said.

"I'm fine." The black old-fashioned iron Steve had used as a doorstop was now on its side. Next to that was my phone. "Oh, my God. My children," I cried, snatching up my phone. How long had I been out? What had become of my babies?

"They're fine," Tommy said. "A woman officer's with them."

I pressed the page button, which made a loud beep at the phone base that could be heard from any room in my house. "Karen? Nathan?" I had locked the front door to our house. Had the children let in the officer? Or was my front door kicked in, my children in a state of panic?

Physically unable to stand, I scooted my legs toward the doorway, hoping to inchworm myself into the kitchen. There I could look out the window that faced my house.

"Mommy," said Nathan over the phone. "Where's the comb?"

Thank God. Nathan was all right.

Tommy said to me, "They've got to take you to the hospital."

"The comb? It's in the bathroom."

"You've had a concussion and need to be examined."

"No, it isn't! I looked there!" Nathan was in one of the volatile states he gets into whenever his hair gets too curly for Dippity-Do to flatten it.

"Plus, you're going to need a couple of stitches."

"Look again. Where's Karen? Are the police with you?"

"But, Momm-m-myyy, I need the comb!"

"I can't help you find the comb right now, Nathan. Put Karen on."

"But I need—"

My chest started to tighten from my growing anxiety. *Where was Karen?* "I'll tell Karen how to find it. Put her on. Now."

"This is Officer Black. Who is this please?"

"Officer, I'm—"

Tommy pried the phone from my fingers. "Officer Black, this is Sergeant Newton. The paramedics have to take the kids' mother to the hospital. Take the kids in the…"

He turned and spoke quietly into the handset, covering his free ear. Steadying myself against a wall, I got to my feet. The baby-faced paramedic grabbed my arm.

"Let go of me! I refuse to go with you!"

He released his grip and looked back at the second, older paramedic, who scowled at me as he told his partner, "We can't take her without her consent."

I staggered toward the front of the house. I had to get

home. The door was wide open and badly damaged. Only the screen door was between me and my escape. Tommy put a hand on my shoulder.

"Please, Tommy. I have to—"

From outside, a deep voice hollered, "Lady, this is a secured area! Now get back before—" Tommy brushed past me to the front door. I followed him out to the porch.

Stephanie stood on the Wilkinses' front walk, hands on hips, attempting to stare down an officer. He had just begun the process of unrolling a reel of yellow-and-black plastic police tape cordon. On the sidewalk behind her stood a teenage girl who, except for her gypsy-bright clothing and half short, half long hairstyle, could have been Stephanie at that age. There was one patrol car in my driveway, three in Lauren's.

Stephanie eyed Tommy and me and said, "Hello. I'm sorry we ran off so fast last night."

"You're concerned about last night's etiquette?" I asked. "Now?"

"I was going over to your place, to cheer you up after that fiasco of a party. I spotted all the police cars and thought Lauren might need me." She flicked a hand over her shoulder. "This is my daughter Tiffany."

"Hello," I said automatically. "Nice to meet you."

"Mrrph."

"We need to clear this area, Steph," Tommy said.

The paramedics came through the doorway. They appeared to have packed up. The older one said to Tommy, "She won't consent to..."

I headed down the steps and said to Stephanie, "My children are home and I need to get out of here, so—"

"She's had a head injury," Tommy said to the paramedics. "I'll assume full responsibility."

During my short descent to where Stephanie stood, I

heard a clang as the legs of the cot were snapped into place. Before I could say, "Hide me," I was swept off my feet and placed bodily onto the cot. "No! I don't need—"

"Lie still. You've lost a lot of blood, lady."

I rolled to my side, hoping to swing my legs off the cot, but was quickly strapped down, flat on my back.

Stephanie gasped. "Oh, for heaven sake, Molly!" She shielded her eyes. "I faint at the sight of blood." She faced me, her eyes covered by her hand. "Those stains will come out of your clothes if you soak them in cold salt water."

As they wheeled me past Stephanie's daughter, she said, "Mom, like, can we go now?" looking at her mother.

Still keeping her hand over her eyes, Stephanie asked, "Are you being arrested again, Molly?"

"I have to get home. My children are—"

The young man opened the ambulance doors. They pushed me inside. I felt as if I were being shoved head-first into a tomb.

"I'll ride with her," Tommy said to a police officer who started to step up into the van. The other officer stepped back, and Tommy climbed in with me. "We can't do anything at the premises till we get a search warrant. I'll take her statement at the hospital."

Just as they started to shut the doors, Stephanie's daughter leaned in. "Hey. Could you use a baby-sitter? I don't, like, do diapers, you know. I'll charge you...five dollars an hour."

Blam! The first door was shut.

"Please, Tommy!" I cried. "I'll go to the hospital. Just let me see my children first!"

"Hang on a sec," Tommy said. The paramedic

stopped and let the second door to the van drift fully open. Another officer began talking to Tommy, and the paramedic glared at them impatiently.

"Stephanie! Help me!"

Stephanie leaned into the van, a broad smile on her face. *My* asking *her* for help made her day, big time.

"Come here. Please," I whispered, doing an impression of a dying person's last request. She grudgingly got in and duckwalked toward me.

I grabbed her arm. "Please. Bring Tiffany and my children to the hospital." The nearest hospital was in Schenectady. I would be in for at least a twenty-minute ambulance ride.

She extricated her arm from my hand, checking her sleeve for stains.

"So you're going to, like, be sure and pay me for watching your kids in the waiting room, right?" her daughter called from outside.

Dizziness overwhelmed me. I closed my eyes. I felt myself dozing off again.

Moments later, I awoke. The ambulance was in motion. Tommy was watching my face intently, so I shut my eyes again. I didn't want to give a statement now.

Everything sank in during the ride to the hospital. I'd been so fixated on seeing my children, I'd missed the crux of the matter. My best friend's husband was dead. Murdered. In the house next to mine. Rachel had no father. Lauren was a widow. What would they do? Who was going to tell them, and how?

THEY GAVE ME a local anesthetic at the hospital. A pretty doctor who looked no more than twenty-five told me I had a concussion. She gave me eight stitches. She seemed to have an easier time with my scalp than I did sewing badges on Karen's Brownie sash. Hopefully her stitches would hold better than mine. As the doctor was working on me, Tommy stayed out of the room, but came back in with Tiffany just as the doctor was clipping the ends.

Tiffany said, *"Eeew,"* then calmly asked if I still wanted to see my children. My obvious answer was followed by, "So. Did they shave the back of your head?"

"No, but I had them tattoo a New York Giant's insignia back there just for the heck of it."

She snapped her gum, whirled on a heel, and left. Moments later she brought in Karen and Nathan. Tommy gestured to Tiffany and said, "We'll give you a minute with your kids. Be out in the hallway."

The doctor told me I was all set, but to stay put. On her way out, she paused, put her hands on her knees, and said to my children, "Your mother's going to be just fine."

"Did you sew my mommy's brains back in?" Nathan asked.

She smiled. "It was nothing that serious. Just a little boo-boo." She winked at me and left the room.

I assured my children that I was fine, but told them that Steve Wilkins was dead.

Karen said, "We already heard that from that pretty friend of yours. Tiffany's mom. Why don't you wear makeup like that, Mom? Tiffany's mom said she could teach you how."

Tommy entered, carrying my purse, which he explained the officer had retrieved from my house when she locked up.

"How did Officer Black get into my house in the first place?"

Tommy didn't answer. He ushered the children out of the room, saying he needed to speak with me alone for a few minutes. While Tommy was doing so, it occurred to me that one of my children had to have opened the door for the police; if an officer had kicked it in, Officer Black wouldn't have been able to "lock up" my house after getting my purse.

I wanted to ask Tommy who had told Stephanie about the murder, but Tommy didn't give me the chance. His first words to me were a gruff "Tell me exactly what went on, from the moment I left your house last night, till you came to after knockin' yourself out."

I recounted everything, to the best of my ability, giving him the approximate times of the two cars' driving off last night. I ran circles around myself explaining why I had left my children unattended. Before he had the chance to criticize, I told him I regretted waiting so long to call the police. Admittedly, that should have been my very first action, but I wasn't used to getting faxed help messages...only death threats.

Tommy was more concerned with what had gone on in the Wilkinses' house, my sensations as I'd lost consciousness. He told me an officer had found the original help message in the tray of Steve's fax machine.

That gave me a frightening thought. "The killer probably sent that after Steve was dead to lure me over there. Maybe he was waiting for me and hit me in the head."

Tommy showed no reaction to my suggestion. He asked me to describe the knife missing from my kitchen, which had a shiny black handle and a heavy, nine-inch blade.

"Sounds like the murder weapon, all right. Okay. So. Mind if we take your fingerprints?"

"They'll be on the knife. I used it to cut up mushrooms for last night's dinner." *There* was a disquieting thought; last night's dinner utensil, today's murder weapon.

"Course your prints'll <u>be</u> on the knife. That's why we need to print you. So we can rule 'em out and identify other prints on it."

"Oh. That makes sense. I just don't want…" I let my voice fade away. This was such a nightmare. My stomach lurched. I felt queasy. I might be accused of murdering my oldest friend's husband!

"See anyone at the party use the knife?"

"Not that I can say for sure. It's possible any of them could have. There was that time all of you were in the kitchen. But I really can't remember anyone touching the knife. Before the party started I had washed it and put it in the butcher-block knife holder.

"Where's that kept?"

"Right on the counter. Next to the sink."

"Tell me how well you knew Steve."

"Not very well." This subject made me nervous. The only thing my relationship with Steve could indicate was whether or not *I* had a motive to kill him. "I met him for the first time almost four weeks ago, when my family first got here. Both families had dinner together twice that first week. We talked quite a bit then."

"'Bout what?"

"Just…trivial stuff. Small talk, mostly. Sports, computers. I told him about my concept for Friendly Fax, the name of my company. He helped me get my computer set up. Then, for the next couple of weeks, I saw him only occasionally, coming or going from his home. The next time I saw him was when he came over and took a look at my threatening faxes."

"He helped you set up your fax machine?"

"He helped install my software."

"Did you show him the threats you got on your fax?"

"Yes, but not the one I got last night. That said, 'Your

husband is having an affair. If you'"—I paused, remembering the wording.—"'It serves you right. If you were any kind of a wife you'd be with him.'"

"Know how long the Wilkinses been married?"

What a weird question to ask me *now*. I answered slowly, "Ten years."

"Go to their wedding?"

The question brought back a sad memory. I shook my head. "I had plane reservations and everything. I was pregnant. The week of her wedding, I had a miscarriage. I canceled my trip."

"Seems to me, she was pretty serious 'n' all 'bout that captain of the Carlton football team. Remember? They announced their engagement at our graduation party."

"Howie Brown." I fidgeted with a torn cuticle, to disguise my growing agitation. This time I had no doubts: Tommy was playing dumb. He had known Howie well in school. Tommy had been the equipment manager for the football team. During time-outs he used to run out on the field and squirt Gatorade in everyone's mouths. They'd reward him by spitting on his shoes.

"Why'd they break up?" Tommy asked.

I met his gaze. He was watching me, his expression blank, as if he didn't already know the answer to this question, as if the answer were unimportant. I cleared my throat. My mouth was dry. "He was cheating on her."

"She ever tell you who with?"

"What's this all got to do with—"

"Ran into her a few months after graduation. She was pretty broken up about it. She kinda…dropped outta sight for a while. Just like you did."

He paused, but I kept silent.

"Glad to see she was married at our tenth graduation reunion. Course, *you* didn't go to the reunion."

"I want to go home," I murmured, thinking about Boulder.

"Were the rumors 'bout you 'n' Howie true?"

"What rumors? About the graduation party?"

Tommy kept his face still. He stared straight into my eyes, unblinking.

"I was drunk," I blurted. "It wasn't my fault."

"Uh-huh."

"Lauren knew it wasn't my fault. I explained it to her. She believed me." My vision blurred with tears. This was dredging up such horrible memories. *Eventually* she had believed me.

Or had she? During the past seventeen years, each time something questionable happened between Lauren and me, I asked myself that question. Such as last year, when her parents died in a car wreck and she didn't contact me till a month later. "Oh God," I whispered to myself.

Thankfully, we were distracted as a male doctor entered, ignored Sergeant Tommy entirely, and shined a penlight into each of my eyes to check for pupil dilation. He then proceeded to examine my head wound, all the while asking for my medical history, despite the fact that this was the third time I'd given it and he had my chart. Maybe he was checking for consistency. I suppose short-term memory loss is a symptom of a concussion.

Finally, he finished. He stood in front of me, smiled with what looked like practiced sincerity, and said, "Well, Molly. I'm afraid you have a concussion."

He let that sink in much longer than necessary, since despite whatever memory loss *he* might have anticipated, this was not news to me.

Then he said, "I think it would be best if we keep you overnight for observation."

"I *can't* stay here." My chest again started to tighten.

Another anxiety attack. "I've got two young children. I've got no one to watch them. My husband is in Manila."

"He makes envelopes," Tommy interjected with a wry smile.

The doctor raised an eyebrow, but said nothing. "Just the same, it—"

Carolee, I thought with relief. "A nurse lives across the street from me. Carolee Richards."

"Carolee?"

"She works here. I think she said in the…cancer ward." The correct term had slipped my mind. Was it ornithology? No, that had something to do with birds. Medicine had so many multisyllabic words that made everyone in that field sound so much more intelligent than, say, someone who wrote greeting cards. "Maybe she can check in on me a couple of times tonight."

"I'll have someone track her down for you, and we'll see what we can work out."

He left, and only then was I aware that Tommy was still watching my every move. I dearly hoped he wasn't going to arrest me. "Whatever happened to Howie?" I asked. "Do you ever hear from him?"

"He died. Eleven years ago. One-car accident. Hit the tree at Kinns Corner. His blood-alcohol was point-one-six. I, uh, was a patrolman then. Took the call."

The door swung open, and Tommy's face lit up so quickly I didn't have to look to know it was Carolee. They stood staring at each other, eyes locked. I could be wrong, but I got the impression she'd given him more than ice cream last night.

The pager on his belt beeped and he immediately said, "'Scuse me," and left the room.

Carolee turned to me and gripped my hand. "Hi. How are you feeling?"

Her words were spoken with such empathy, I had to look away for fear I'd start whimpering. "Fine. It's nothing."

"How did this happen?"

"I fainted. You did hear about Steve, didn't you?"

"Steve Wilkins?"

"Somebody stabbed him to death in his office. I fainted when I saw him."

She gasped. Her face paled. "Oh, dear Lord. Poor Lauren. And Rachel. I've been on shift all day. Dr. Mitchell just told me you had a concussion. He didn't say anything at all about anyone...getting killed. How's Lauren taking this?"

Tommy poked his head into the room. "Gotta go. Lauren and Rachel just got home."

"Could I go with you?" I asked. "I want to be with Lauren."

Tommy shook his head. "Sorry. Police procedures."

I stood up, feeling as wobbly as the last time I'd given birth. "Can I leave?"

"Officer Redding will take you down to the station house for fingerprints, then he'll drive you home."

"But Lauren's going to need someone to help her. She might need someone to watch Rachel."

"Have to insist. Sorry. Police procedures. I'll give her your condolences."

I glared at him and he added, "We'll be contacting other immediate family members. She won't be alone."

Carolee agreed she'd check in on me once or twice in the next twenty-four hours, then said she had to get back to work. In the lobby, Preston now sat with Tiffany. I had to stifle a gasp at the sight of my children. Nathan's

air was plastered down with something that made it look
as fake and shiny as a Ken doll's. Karen was wearing so
much makeup, she looked...I didn't want to think about
what she looked like.

Tiffany glanced up at me unsmiling, snapped her gum,
gestured at the children, and said, "Check it out. I got a
real knack for this. When I get out of school, I want to
be a cosmologist."

"Cosmetologist," I corrected. Though, judging by my
children's appearance, perhaps she *did* mean she wanted
to be a star gazer.

Preston gave me a somber nod. "I can't believe all of
this. My God. We were eating dinner with him just last
night."

"Did Stephanie leave?"

"She had some errands to run. I came to take Tiffany
home."

"Look what Tiffany bought me." Nathan held up a
black comb.

"There was a machine in the lobby," Karen explained.
"She says you owe her a dollar."

"You owe me twelve-fifty for lunch, too," Tiffany
said.

"You should rethink your career choice. You might
make a successful lawyer." I handed her two twenties.
"Keep the change." Now I'd be forced to bring my children to the police station. With our makeup and hair-
styles, we'd make quite a trio.

BY THE TIME we got home from the police station, it was
late afternoon. Two police vehicles were parked in Lauren's driveway and the house was circled by police tape.
There was a message from Jim on my answering machine. He was going to visit a manufacturing plant on

another Philippine island, where he'd be until Thursday. He told me the city and hotel name, but though I played it back twice, a blip on the tape rendered Jim's voice unintelligible.

I supervised the children's baths, necessary to get their faces and hair restored to their natural state. At some point last year Karen had decided she hated bathing. She often came up with excuses for why she shouldn't have to get into the tub. This time she told me she didn't need baths because she sweated water, which washed her. Even in my emotionally drained state, I recognized a good try when I heard one and told her so.

As the children were drying off, I called Lauren. No one answered, but I left a message that I was here for her and wanted to help in any way I could.

Not only did I wish Jim were here to help me and Lauren through all of this trauma and tragedy, I wished my mother were here. To cheer myself up, I sketched myself in a kitchen. In my drawing, the phone rings off the hook, pots boil over on the stove, toys are scattered across the floor, and Karen and Nathan are running in circles around me as I cry in frustration, "I WANT MY MOMMY!"

After completing my doodle, I stared out the window at Lauren's house, trying to fathom what she must be going through, and realizing how unimaginable that really was. My mother once told me she would rather die herself than have anyone else in the family die. A teenager at the time, I'd thought she was nuts. Now I suspect motherhood naturally turns the sanest of us into martyrs. Though I could not begin to fathom the emotional agony that Lauren was currently experiencing, I knew that much of her pain was not derived from her own terrible loss, but from that of her daughter.

To my surprise, I saw her and Rachel leaving the house with an officer. Even from this distance, I could see her shoulders shaking with sobs as she and Rachel got into the back seat of the squad car. The sight was heartbreaking, and I started to cry as well.

Karen skipped into the room. "I've got to help Nathan," she said, giggling. She grabbed the blunt-tip scissors.

"Wait," I said. "Why do you need scissors?"

She charged back up the stairs and called behind her, "His new comb is stuck in his hair."

NINE

Welcome Home

MRS. KRAVETT used to read us poetry. Almost all those poems I've long since forgotten, along with the poets' names, but one line that stayed with me was Carl Sandburg's allusion that fog comes on little cat feet.

This night plodded by on elephant's feet. Carolee had checked in on me at my home twice. I told her I felt physically exhausted but doubted I would be able to sleep. She told me, as I'd already assumed, that it wouldn't be wise to take sleeping pills on top of my concussion. So I'd suffered, listening to a distant thunderstorm, counting the car lights that passed my window throughout the night.

Earlier I'd managed to get the comb out of Nathan's hair. The result had been wild, unmanageable curls on the top of his head, which made him miserable. So in the morning, Sunday, we went to get his hair cut. Afterward he seemed satisfied with his close-cropped hair, though he still spent a good half hour in front of the mirror trying to decide if one ear or the other needed to be lowered.

When we returned, the police tape around Lauren's house was gone. I spotted her through her kitchen window. After phoning a few times and getting no answer, I needed to go over there and speak to her, if only for my own peace of mind. That meant hiring a baby-sitter, and Carolee had already mentioned she was working today. I got hold of Tiffany and she gleefully agreed to baby-sit once again. Her mother was going to drive her to my house. I successfully battled the urge to spruce up in her honor.

Stephanie accompanied her daughter to the door. They wore matching mother/daughter reflective Ray-Ban sunglasses. ''Knock knock,'' she said, after I'd already answered the bell. ''Just had to tell you what a delightful time I had yesterday talking to Karen at the hospital. God sure smiled on you the day she was born.''

He also had a belly laugh the day Nathan was born. I kept my thoughts to myself, suspecting that Stephanie wouldn't understand that I loved my children equally, despite Nathan's more challenging personality. We made arrangements for me to drive Tiffany home later, then she gave me one of those wiggly-finger waves I so hated and left.

After muttering a few instructions to Tiffany, mostly about not altering my children's appearances, I walked next door.

Lauren was home, but didn't answer the door. I rang the doorbell incessantly, figuring sooner or later she'd look through the window and see it was me. Cracks and dents along the jamb were plainly visible, as if the door had been hastily repaired after the police kicked it in yesterday. It could probably now be opened with one good push.

Finally I heard the metallic click of the deadbolt, and the door creaked partway open. It was Rachel. Her hair was uncombed. The hollowness in her eyes and sallow expression reminded me of how Karen looks when she's got a fever. One hand tugged on her plain pink turtleneck as if searching for a blankie. She sucked on three fingers of her other hand. Her magenta stretch pants were wrinkled and rode up one calf. She stared at me.

I instinctively bent down to her eye level. "Hi, sweetie. I'm so—"

"Rachel," Lauren yelled, "don't open it."

"It's me."

Lauren rounded the corner. She looked like Bette Davis in *What Ever Happened to Baby Jane?* I had to bite back a gasp.

"I don't want company. Not even you. I'm sorry." She gripped the edge of the door with both hands as if fully intending to slam it in my face. Rachel disappeared inside.

"I just wanted to tell you how sorry I am. Can I bring over dinner for you tonight or—"

"I can still cook and take care of myself."

"I'm sorry. I didn't mean..." My throat ached as I battled my emotions. Why was she treating me like this? What could I say? "Is there anything I can do? Can I watch Rachel for you, or—"

"No. Thanks. Good-bye." She shut the door.

I went back to my house, utterly dismayed and hurt. I tried to tell myself I shouldn't take it personally; who was to say how I would treat Lauren had our positions been reversed? Yet this was so unlike the Lauren I thought I knew so well. Something was very wrong.

A question tormented me. Did Lauren think *I* killed Steve?

As soon as I opened the door, Tiffany said, "Hey, you're, like, back early. You've only been gone five minutes. That'll still be five dollars, you know."

"All right, then. Since I've hired you for an hour, I may as well use it. I'll be back in fifty-five minutes." I grabbed the phone book, planning to use the map inside for ideas as to where I could go and return in less than an hour.

I started my car and paged through the phone book for inspiration. Mostly out of curiosity, I looked up Mrs. Kravett's address. She lived just a block beyond a road I remembered from my bus route. I had probably passed her house every school day and never realized it.

With no real sense of purpose, I drove toward her house. As I matched the address, I stopped the car and stared. Incredulous, I double-checked the phone book.

Mrs. Kravett's house was a mansion.

How could a teacher afford a home like this? This wasn't the sort of humble abode that would have gone without teachers' and students' mention. How did she escape the rumor mill during my high school years?

I got out of my car, still gawking. Two stone lions on either side of the driveway stood sentinel. An iron gate was open between them. At the top of the driveway was a white, three-story house. There were at least twenty windows on the front of the house alone, two private balconies on both the second and third floors. The property was the size of a nine-hole golf course. Time to leave; somewhere there had to be a guard ready to accuse me of trespassing.

I jumped at an electronic hiss from the lion to my left. Then came an old lady's voice from the statue. "Are you Molly Peterson Masters by any chance?"

Scared witless, I almost shrieked. For all the world, that voice sounded exactly like Mrs. Kravett's. "Um, yes. I... That's right." I glanced around me, trying to find the camera lens. Something that could have been a lens in the lion's mouth was aimed right at me. Also could have been the barrel of a shot gun.

"I'm Phoebe's sister. Are you here for the reading of the will?"

"Will? What will?"

"Didn't you get the notice? It was sent three days ago."

Frankly, I felt stupid talking to a lion statue, but I didn't know where else to look, so I stared at his old, chiseled features and said honestly, "I'm sorry, but I have no idea what you're talking about. I didn't get any notices about a will."

"Hang on a minute, dearie."

The lion stopped hissing. I glanced at my lowly maroon Corolla and played with the idea of getting into it and driving away.

At length, I could see a short, squat, white-haired lady make her way down the driveway toward me. At this distance she looked just like a living version of the body I'd recently viewed. I didn't know the proper protocol, but decided to walk toward her to spare her the footsteps.

We met a third of the way down the driveway. She studied me at length, then said, "Hello. I'm Ellen Steinway, Phoebe's sister. I must say I'm confused. The reading of the will is in two hours, yet you say you haven't been notified. So my questions are, why not, and what are you doing here?"

This was spooky. She not only looked and sounded like my former teacher, she talked like her. Just as I had in class, I found myself befuddled and apologetic. "My notice about the reading of the will must have been delayed in the mail. I was just driving by, realized it was her house, and stopped. I've been out of town for a number of years."

"So I've heard. Since you're here now, come on in."

I followed her into the foyer and looked around. "This

is palatial." The remark was not unlike saying, "This is a big car" while stepping into a limo.

"Phoebe used only a couple of the rooms. The rest...well, you can see for yourself." She opened a carved oak door and I peeked in. The room was dark, the furniture covered with dustcovers. It appeared to be hunkered down for a sleep, Rip Van Winkle style.

"I'm amazed by all of this," I said. "When she was teaching, I had no idea she lived in a place like this."

"Oh, she didn't, dearie. The money was Bob's, and they had been saving it and investing. Guess you could say he had the Midas touch. Four years back, when his lung cancer was diagnosed, they realized the time had come to spend some. They bought this old mansion."

I'd heard of saving for a rainy day, but if the house was any indication, we were talking Noah here.

"So you live here now?"

"Oh, my goodness, no. I'm going back home to Seattle as soon as the estate is settled." She shuffled through the arched doorway into an enormous room that housed a grand piano and sat down in an antique ladder-back chair. Though I followed, I felt too edgy to sit.

"What will become of the house?"

"It's going on the market. Some investor will buy it." She crinkled her nose, and added, "Who'll probably flatten the house and put in a hundred condos."

"Why did you think I was here for a will reading? Surely *I'm* not in it. I was just one of her students, from a long time ago."

"Won't you be surprised, dearie." She had a wheezy little laugh, at my expense, apparently. Then she cleared her throat and said, "About a month ago, when Phoebe heard you were coming back, she made out a new will. We discussed it over the phone many times, so it's no surprise to me. She left a sizable portion to me, as her only survivor. The bulk goes into a scholarship program in her husband's name.''

''That's wonderful. But what—''

''Don't rush me. I'm getting there. A committee of teachers will choose student candidates each year. They supply that list of candidates to one person, who has the final say and handles the dispensations. You.''

''Me? But that's absurd! Why on earth would she pick me for such a role? She doesn't even...we hadn't seen each other in seventeen years. She didn't even like me!'' *Not to mention my accidentally launching a school-board investigation over the false charges of her striking a student!*

Ellen Steinway laughed, which caused a brief coughing fit. ''That's just what Phoebe said you would say.'' She led me to an oak rolltop desk against the far wall. With the toe of her orthopedic shoe, she tapped a large cardboard box next to the desk. ''You may as well take all of these papers with you. They're copies of legal documents, and reports and work from current deserving high school students.''

The papers in the box would fill a file cabinet. Perhaps Mrs. Kravett had chosen me for the job to avenge my poem. This must be what Mrs. Kravett had wanted to discuss with me just before she died. ''I have a friend who's a lawyer in Denver. I'll call him and have him contact Mrs. Kravett's lawyer and see if they can get this resolved.''

''Oh, dearie. There's nothing *to* be resolved. It's all set and everyone's quite pleased.''

''Everyone?''

''Except maybe you, Molly, but you'll get used to the idea. This has all been rather sudden, I suppose.''

That was an understatement. Her observation reminded me of a question I'd meant to ask. "How did you know my name?"

"Oh, I spotted you leaving the funeral, and asked a woman who you were. She told me your name."

"What woman?"

She looked reflective for a moment. "The name escapes me. She was pretty, a couple of years older than you, wears lots of makeup."

"Stephanie Saunders?" I grinned, loving the idea of anyone thinking I looked younger than Stephanie.

"That's the one." She put her hands on her ample hips and narrowed her eyes at me, a pose straight from her sister's repertoire when appraising an uncooperative student. "Are you a writer?"

"No, well, not exactly. I write greeting cards."

"Aha. I recently sorted through my sister's desk. She kept a file of predictions for her former pupils. Would you like to see your class's?"

"I'd love to."

She unlocked the rolltop and stared. "I don't remember leaving this in such a mess. I must just be getting old."

She flipped through some papers till she found the ones she wanted. She gave one to me and waved several papers folded together. "There's a copy of the will here, too. I'll just drop it into your box in case you'd rather not come back for the formal reading." She tottered over to the box and flipped the will into it.

I scanned the list for my name and read Mrs. Kravett's prediction. She had me down for either a newspaper columnist or a television sitcom writer. I continued to read the predictions. Stephanie's was fashion model or politician's wife. Denise was listed only as a future house-wife. That surprised me.

"She hit the nail on the head about that Tommy Newton. He's your backup if you refuse to lead the scholarship board."

I fought back a smile. I had an out! Tommy had teen-agers of his own. He'd be great at selecting scholarship recipients!

She narrowed her eyes at me and added, "Though I'm sure you won't let my sister down by backing out on her like that."

"Oh, well, I..." Damn. She was right. I couldn't let Mrs. Kravett down. Again. "No, I won't."

She glanced at the paper in my hand and chuckled. "That boy Tommy's a sly one."

I referred to his name. He was down as an accountant or a policeman. Those two fields seemed completely in-congruous to me. "What makes you say that?"

"He figured out she'd given up on life after Bob died. Nobody else in this town did. Certainly that rotten boy Jack Vance didn't realize it. Of all the people to wind up *her* boss!"

"But he's the *elementary* school principal."

She pursed her lips. "He must have changed jobs. He ran the high school for five years."

As she was speaking, I looked up his prediction. In-surance salesman.

"Teaching was all she had left. She put her heart and soul into her classroom. When Bob died last April, I came out to stay with her for a couple of weeks. She let her nurse go, the housekeeper, started closing up all the rooms. Just kept one gardener."

"What did the nurse look like?"

"Black woman. Middle-aged. Why?"

"I was just wondering if she was someone I knew, that's all."

"I had a devil of a time, getting her to take her medication. Had to have the doctor threaten her with hospitalization."

"Was she on a lot of medication?"

She took digitalis once a day, and Lasix every third day. Course, I only remember that because I was with Sergeant Newton when he took the pill bottles, and he asked me about them."

"About whether she'd been taking them?"

She nodded. "He was asking me all about Phoebe's medication. The prescription bottles from the bathroom are the only thing the police took with them, at least in my presence."

I tensed. Maybe Mrs. Kravett was murdered, after all. "I wonder why he took those."

"He asked for my permission to do an autopsy, and I said that was fine as long as he gave me the results. They discovered the medicinal levels in her bloodstream weren't right. That boy Tommy asked me if it was possible she'd stopped taking her pills on purpose." She snorted. "Of course it was. Her husband died. She had no children, no family 'cept me. And look at me. I'm seventy and have only one lung left. Once that rotten school principal railroaded her out of her job, what did she have to live for?"

I DROVE HOME, the box of files in the passenger seat. My head was spinning, more from confusion and surprise than from the minor pain I still felt from my injury. As I turned onto Little John Lane, Carolee was right behind me. She waved and pulled into her garage. After a moment's debate I parked, then went to her door.

As usual, she greeted me in the doorway and made no move to allow me inside. She corrected my assumption that her work shift already ended; she was actually *leaving* for the hospital in a half hour.

"Carolee, I want to ask you something. Do you know what Mrs. Kravett was suffering from?"

"She died of congestive heart failure. That's when blood sloshes back into the lungs, preventing the lungs from filling with air."

"She was on two types of medication. Digitalis and…" Drat. I'd forgotten the name of the second medication. "Something else."

Carolee leaned against the doorjamb. Her features were tense. "The digitalis reduces the heart rate and increases the contractility of the heart muscle. She probably would have also been on a diuretic. Lasix, perhaps."

"A diuretic?"

"That's a medicine that decreases blood volume by increasing urinary output."

I involuntarily grimaced. "So she'd take both of these medications daily?"

"She might take digitalis up to three times a day, Lasix every other day or every third day. Cardiology isn't my specialty, though, so don't quote me on that."

"Would it be possible for her to get her pills confused?"

"Sure, it's *possible*. Unlikely, though. They're both small white pills, but patients who've been on medication for a period of time certainly know one pill from the other."

"Her husband had died recently, and she was under the stress of being forced to resign from teaching. Also, she used to have a private nurse. So maybe she wasn't used to giving herself her pills. In that scenario, would it be more likely for her to get her dosage confused?''

"You sound like a lawyer," Carolee said. "I met her nurse, Susan Jefferson. She brought Bob Kravett into the oncology unit sometimes. She was efficient, but neither Bob nor Phoebe liked her very well.

"Still, even if Phoebe had gotten confused and taken the wrong pills, all heart patients are monitored closely. She would have had blood tests taken at least every two or three weeks." She smiled. "You must have been talking to Tommy, right?"

"What makes you say that?"

"He asked me those same questions last night."

That was interesting. No doubt Tommy was interviewing the neighbors after Steve's death. Yet he'd taken the time to be asking Carolee about Mrs. Kravett's medication. Maybe I could get information about Mrs. Kravett from the pharmacist. "How do you spell *Lasix?*"

"I'll write it down for you." She led me into the kitchen and grabbed a sheet of a notepad by the phone.

A few dirty dishes were stacked by the sink, but the house was far from the disaster area I'd envisioned. My vision focused on a familiar-looking cup near the sink. It was gray with a brown rim, markedly different from the blue flower pattern of her other dishes. I picked it up. "Um, isn't this my cup?"

"Oh. I, uh...collect cups, and I just borrowed this. I meant to bring it back."

That excuse had more holes in it than a pincushion. I'd never heard of anyone collecting *borrowed* items. I was maintaining an idiotic smile, mostly out of embarrassment for Carolee. "It's no problem." I set my cup back on the counter. "If you want the saucer, too, I can bring it over."

Her eyes grew fierce. "No. Here." She thrust the cup at me. "Take it. Want to look around? See if there's anything else you think I've stolen from you?"

"Of course not, Carolee. I understand. It's just a cup, for heaven sakes. You...wouldn't happen to have borrowed my knife, would you?"

"Certainly not. If your knife is missing, I assure you, I don't have it."

I made a hasty retreat. No wonder Carolee was so reluctant to let people into her house if she'd lifted items from them.

These were very expensive homes, and Carolee had apparently purchased hers on a nurse's salary. Hmm. Had Tommy considered the fact that Carolee, as a nurse, could have been the one who dispensed those medications to Mrs. Kravett? Perhaps she'd deliberately swapped prescriptions. But what could she possibly have to gain by Mrs. Kravett's death?

My thoughts were interrupted by the sight of Denise and Sam Bakerton walking up the driveway toward my parents' house. Their Chevy Suburban was parked in Lauren's driveway. Once again, teenaged feet protruded from the rear window, this time sporting women's black shoes.

"Denise. Sam," I called from Carolee's front steps.

They turned and waited for me. Denise had a casserole dish. They were formally dressed, as if they'd come straight from church. Their faces looked pale and somber. Before I could ask the reason for their visit, Sam said, "Preston called yesterday. We were so shocked to hear about Steve. We tried Lauren's door first, but there was no answer."

Somehow that didn't surprise me. "Well, she..."

"Is Lauren accepting visitors?" Denise asked.

"No. She's distraught, of course." I opened my door. "Do you want to come in?"

They exchanged glances. "Only for a moment. We're on our way to church, and our daughter is waiting in the car."

They followed me inside and Denise handed me the dish. "I made Lauren a chicken dinner. Could you give it to her for me, next time you see her?"

"Sure," I said, though I wondered if Lauren would once again find offense in the gesture. "That reminds me, I have your bowl around here, someplace."

"No rush. Maybe you should put it in your freezer. That way she can defrost it at her convenience."

I assumed Denise meant the dinner, not the bowl. "By the way, what happened Friday night? Why did everyone run off like that?"

Denise sighed. "Out of the blue, Steve took offense at a harmless remark of Sam's."

Sam blurted, "All I said, as a joke, was that our company was fortunate to be having such a good month so we could cover his bill. Steve turned it around so that it sounded like I was saying he overcharged. Afterwards, I wasn't going to sit there and let Preston chew my head off. Alienating a consultant who can manipulate the software that runs your company isn't wise."

Tiffany skipped down the stairs. She blew out a pink bubble, snapped her gum, then said, "The kids are playing in Karen's room. That'll be ten dollars. You were gone over an hour."

I set Denise's dish on the table and grabbed my wallet. "I'm writing you a check for seven-fifty."

"Hello, Tiffany." Denise had again donned her Binky-the-Clown voice. "I didn't know you were here. We go right by your house. Can we give you a ride?"

"Sure. Whatever." She held out her palm for the check.

"Just to let you know, if you ever choose to baby-sit for my children again, I'll pay four dollars an hour."

She snatched the check from me and let the screen door bang behind her.

Sam and Denise said again how shocking Steve's death was and how sorry they were. Moments after they'd shut the door, there was a quick knock, then Denise popped back inside. She gave me a nervous smile. "I keep forgetting to bring this up. Sam told me about your being railroaded into being PTA secretary/treasurer. That's so awful of Stephanie. So I've been thinking about it, and I'll take over as treasurer, anyway."

"Oh, great. Thanks. I'll just call Stephanie and—"

"You don't need to do that. I'll tell her myself. Just give me the records and checkbook, and I'll take it from there."

"I haven't gotten the treasurer's stuff yet."

"You haven't?" She paused. "So you haven't even *looked* at anything yet?"

"Not yet." I didn't understand Denise's reaction. She looked relieved. "*Should* I have?"

"No, absolutely not." She made a dismissive gesture with one hand. "The financial statements for the PTA are so complicated. If you can just pass everything to me the moment you get them, I'll take over for you."

"Why don't I just call Stephanie and have her give them directly to you?"

"No, no, no. She won't like being usurped like that. I was thinking *you* can be the treasurer of record, I'll do the actual work, and everybody's happy."

"So you want me to *pretend* to be treasurer? But give you the actual control of the PTA's money?"

"In a manner of speaking." A car honked from nearby. Denise leaned out the door and hollered, "Just one second."

Maybe it was merely a by-product of my bashed head, but none of this made sense. "We can't *do* that, Denise. If my name is on the PTA accounts as treasurer, I'm ultimately responsible for what happens to their money."

"Fine. You don't trust me." She threw her hands in the air. "I try to do a friend a favor, and you insult me. Never mind. Forget I said anything."

HOURS LATER, my head injury was throbbing. Though I leaned back against an ice bag as I watched an NFL game, the pain was omnipresent. Watching men hit the poop out of one another probably didn't help.

Lauren had not returned my call about my having a dinner from Denise in my freezer. After the game ended, I sketched a nonoccasion card. A woman is sitting on her front steps. Behind her an enormous tree has fallen onto her house. A man in a business suit is looking at the house in horror, as she says, "Welcome home, dear. Have a nice day at the office?"

Later I thrilled Karen and Nathan by ordering pizza for dinner. Partway into our meal the phone rang. I answered brusquely.

"Molly. I need...You've got to help me."

The voice was so strained with emotion, it took me a moment to recognize. "Lauren? What's wrong?"

"I'm at the police station. They've arrested me for murder."

TEN

No Time for Wrappin'

LAUREN GAVE ME little information in her phone call. I didn't know why the police had arrested her. Maybe she'd even confessed, out of some sense of panic or guilt. In any case, she told *me* she was innocent, and I believed her.

I offered to take care of Rachel, but Lauren said she wanted Rachel to stay with Steve's sister in Potsdam till the funeral. I volunteered to call the sister. Lauren said Tommy was already making those arrangements; she just needed my help in getting her released on bond.

This was not my area of expertise. My one experience with a bail bondsman thus far had been years ago in Denver when I'd wandered into a shabby little business to ask for change for the parking meter. In the lobby of fake mahogany paneling sat a large, dark man with a dozen gold chains around his neck and gold rings on every chubby finger. He'd chuckled at my request, but took my dollar and gave me four quarters. In a voice badly damaged by God knows what, he leered at me and said, "Usually deal wit' larger amounts. Pleasure doin' business wit' ya just do same." I'd vowed then and there to avoid any future dealings with anyone in that particular field.

Instead of breaking that vow, I phoned Stephanie, whose continuous brushings with rich and famous folk could, for once, come in handy. I asked her who the best criminal lawyer in town was. She gasped, then said, "Oh, Moll, Moll. Now they've arrested you for Steve's murder!"

"Yes, well, I try to stay busy. Can you please just give me the name of a good lawyer?"

She gave me a name, said, "You can trust me to keep this quiet," and hung up. The lines all over upstate New York were no doubt abuzz with the news that I'd been charged with Steve Wilkins's murder.

I called and explained the situation to the lawyer's wife. She muttered, "Why did your friend have to get arrested on a Sunday? That's the only day Mike has off." I managed to keep my voice calm as I apologized on Lauren's behalf for ruining her day. Numerous phone calls later, I'd been assured Lauren would be out on bond by tomorrow afternoon.

OVERNIGHT, the weather turned chilly. Monday morning I packed my children off on the school bus. Now if I could just arrange to have all of my daily crises occur between the hours of 8:00 a.m. and noon when kindergarten was in session. I waved good-bye to my children, then headed to the Carlton police station.

A female officer pointed me toward Sergeant Newton's tiny office. If the door had opened in instead of out, it would have banged into his desk. I marched in and shut the door firmly, fully determined to make Tommy suffer for my pent-up hostilities.

"Hey, Moll." He gestured at the folding chair across from his desk. "What's up?"

Because standing and looking down on Tommy put me in the power position, I remained on my feet, on the lone unoccupied square foot of linoleum. "You arrested

Lauren for murder, that's what! You arrested an innocent person.''

''Think so?''

''I know so! Why don't you?''

''Why don't I what?''

''Why don't you know that Lauren Wilkins is not a murderer!''

''We got some evidence here 'n' there.''

''What evidence?''

''With all due respect, Molly, that's for the judge to learn about at her preliminary hearing.''

''For God's sake. We went to school with this woman. You've lived in the same town with her for thirty-plus years. You, of all people, should know she's not capable of murder. She's a mother. How could you do this to her?''

''A policeman's lot is not a happy one.''

''Give me a break.''

Tommy held up a hand in unspoken apology. ''You don't believe your friend is a murderer. That's understandable. Wouldn't have expected you to waltz in here 'n' tell me your best friend is a killer, but a good person in every other way.'' He paused, then furrowed his brow. ''But see, when we make an arrest, we don't use such things as woman's intuition. We go by probable cause.''

Woman's intuition? Now he had my dander up. ''That's probable cause, as in whatever made you arrest Lauren Wilkins was probably caused by someone's screwup.''

''You're accusin' the police of screwing up?''

I nodded. My knees felt weak. When I stood for long periods of time, my head wound started throbbing. I sat down on the folding chair. From this vantage point, I could see a photo on his desk of two redheaded boys.

Between them stood a dark-haired, pleasant-looking woman. I had to look away, or my righteous indignation would be lost. I wanted Tommy to tell me what evidence they had against Lauren, so I could help her disprove it.

"I guess, then, hand in hand with that little accusation is the idea that you know better than us dumb ol' police-folk. Who do *you* think killed Steve Wilkins?"

"I have no idea, Tommy. I'm not a criminal investigator."

His smug smile infuriated me.

"But if I had to say right now, I'd say it was your girlfriend, Carolee Richards."

That certainly caused the smile to leave his face in a hurry. "Carolee? Why?"

"Because she's one of the few people who would've known how to kill Mrs. Kravett and make it look like an accident."

"Mrs. Kravett? What makes you think Mrs. Kravett was murdered?"

"I talked to her sister. She told me about the pills."

He leaned back in his chair. "You're tellin' me Ellen Steinway *knew* the pills had been switched?"

"So someone *did* switch the digitalis with the Lasix. She was taking three times the normal dosage of Lasix, and a third the dose of digitalis. And that led to her heart failure."

"All right, Molly. A little knowledge is a dangerous thing. 'Sides, I don't want you mouthin' off your theory 'bout Carolee, 'cause you're way out in left field. I'll tell you what I can."

He leaned forward and rested his elbows on his desk. "Those prescriptions were filled by the druggist downtown. Nothin' to do with the hospital where Carolee works. Further, given the blood test results, the pills had to have been switched 'bout a month before her death. I was at Mrs. Kravett's barbecue in July. So was Lauren. *Her* fingerprints were on both bottles, not Carolee's.''

"That doesn't make sense. Those bottles were handled by Mrs. Kravett a hundred times after the barbecue. How could the prints have stayed on the bottles that long?''

"Just bad luck for Lauren. We got a partial of a thumb on the bottoms of both bottles. Most times when someone grabs their pill bottle, that's not where they touch it."

"But...I found my cup in Carolee's house. Maybe she's a thief. Maybe she'd been stealing and Steve found out so—"

"Lemme get this straight. You think Carolee killed Steve Wilkins to keep him from revealin' that she took your cup?''

My face warmed. I was beginning to wish I could leave, come back, and start this conversation all over again.

Tommy was fighting back a smile. "That'd be quite a drastic reaction. Wouldn't you say?''

"So you've charged Lauren with killing Mrs. Kravett, too?''

"Not enough evidence. Yet. 'Sides, her death isn't officially murder.''

"Why not?''

"Because it's possible it was accidental. The pharmacist could've mislabeled the pills when Mrs. Kravett got her prescriptions refilled. I talked to the druggist and he denies it, but we can't rule it out as a possibility. Good defense lawyer'd hop all over it. Reasonable doubt.''

"And you're sure it was Mrs. Kravett who picked up those prescriptions, no one else?''

"Yep. Signed for them. Got her signature on record. Yet those pills are definitely in the wrong bottles. Lauren's fingerprints on 'em. Nobody else's. 'Cept of course, Mrs. Kravett's.''

"Who else was at the barbecue?"

"Lauren. She claimed Steve was working. Denise and her husband...I can never remember his name."

"Sam Bakerton."

"Right. Also Jack Vance and his date. She looked like a high schooler. Stephanie and Preston Saunders. Plus a batch of people from other graduatin' classes."

"You said you had a *partial* thumbprint. Couldn't it have been someone else's?"

"They're hers. More importantly, her fingerprints were also on the knife."

"She could've used that knife at the party. She opened that bottle of wine you brought. She probably used it to cut open the metal wrapper on the cork."

"That's what *she* says happened. But things don't look so hot for her. Got a hotel clerk who says Lauren was all set to sign in, near hysterics, Friday night. Steve shows up and says she can't have Rachel, 'n' grabs her. Yells that if she wanted custody of her daughter so bad, she shoulda been more careful 'fore lettin' Rachel see her own mother in bed with another man."

I had to grip the edges of my chair; otherwise, I might have fallen from my shock. "With *what* man?"

He ignored my question. "Steve was writin' Lauren a good-riddance letter when he got stabbed."

Dear God. "I don't believe any of this, Tommy. Lauren's a good mother. She would never—"

"She admits to most of it. Says she didn't stab her husband, though."

I stared at my knees, embarrassed, angry, hurt. Why hadn't she told *me* about this? It felt as if Lauren had betrayed me, as well as Steve. I asked quietly, "Where's Rachel now? Can I talk to her?"

"She's on her way up to Potsdam with her aunt. She'll be all right."

I glared at him. "If you were seven and your mother was accused of murdering your father because of something you'd witnessed, would you be all right?"

He winced. He looked at the photograph of his children and their deceased mom.

I stood up, grabbed the doorknob, and headed out, my senses reeling.

"Take it easy," he called after me.

I got into my car and started the engine. I was now on a mission, to clear Lauren's name, for Rachel's sake. I smacked the steering wheel and said to myself, "I'm not going to let Rachel go for one extra minute thinking she's in any way responsible for her father's death."

I drove to the only drugstore downtown. The pharmacist looked just like he should: tall, white-haired, wire-rim glasses, white lab coat. He smiled down at me, leading me to wonder just why it was that every drugstore counter I've ever seen is built on a platform. Is that to make us all feel like helpless children when we ask for drugs? Or are would-be robbers supposed to trip on the steps?

"May I help you?"

"I have some questions about medications. I'm Molly Masters. Maybe you know my parents, the Petersons?"

"Ah. Molly. You're their oldest daughter. How're your sister's allergies?"

"Uh...much better."

He chuckled. "Pardon me. It's a professional liability. Just as bartenders remember regulars for what they drink, I remember people by their medications."

I forced a smile, but that was an unsettling concept. It was one thing for a bartender to look at you and see a gin and tonic. Quite another for a pharmacist to see hemorrhoidal ointment.

"So, Molly, what can I do for you?"

Adopting my best just-curious voice, I asked, "Can you tell me what digitalis and Lasix look like?"

He tensed. "They're both little white pills. Why do you ask?"

"Mrs. Kravett was my teacher a number of years ago."

His face instantly fell. He shuffled papers and became a whirlwind of activity as I continued. "I've heard a rumor that she accidentally took the wrong dosage of heart medication. She was so sharp, I find that hard to believe. Are Lasix and digitalis that similar-looking?"

"She wore trifocals. I cautioned her about the dangers of confusing her dosages."

"I heard the pills were in the wrong bottles. Did Mrs. Kravett always pick up her prescriptions herself?"

He slammed a notebook shut. "Listen to me, young lady. People's lives depend on my precision. I put those pills in the right bottles. Sergeant Newton says they're in the wrong bottles, so all I can say is they were in the *right* bottles when I filled her prescription. I would stake my life on it."

"Thanks. Have a nice day."

He turned his back on me without reply.

My stomach was in knots as I drove home. I've never been good at lying, especially to myself. It was painful to admit that I had serious doubts about Lauren's innocence. To top it off, I was getting a pimple on my nose. Apparently it wasn't enough that I was reliving the emotional anguish of my teen years. I was destined to regain my complexion as well. Nathan would be home in an hour. I went to my office.

My fax machine had a letter. I stood for a moment weighing my options, thinking that if this was one more threat about my husband's fidelity I'd fall apart. Finally I read the first paragraph:

Dear Ms. Masters,
 I really need your help. My best
friend is having a hard time with her
teenage children. I've been looking
for a card to cheer her up, and I can't
find anything that's right. I saw your
ad and thought I'd give you a try. Have
you written any humorous cards about
parenting?

"No, and I'm not up to being funny," I answered out loud. Then I went on to read the rest of her letter. She sounded like a nice person, sincerely worried about her friend. I wanted to give the job at least one shot.

I had little personal experience with raising teens. I thought about Tiffany and her outlandish outfits. Maybe I could do something about clothes.

Eventually, I thought about music and settled on humor about rap music, though the first time I did the design I spelled it *wrap,* which shows how "with it" I am. I drew a middle-aged woman in a miniskirt holding a transistor radio to her ear as she struts by a pair of obviously unimpressed teens. The woman says, "Sorry, kids. Got no time for rappin'. Got to go do my grocery shappin'." Picking a name at random for my fictitious character, the caption on the card below says, "Mildred

Langweiler makes yet another heartfelt, if ineffective, attempt to communicate with her teenagers.''

Then I sent a written description of the card to my potential customer and went off to meet Nathan's bus.

He, as usual, dismissed all my attempts to glean information about his school day with his two stock answers: "Fine" and "I don't remember." Then he stared at my face and said, "Mommy, is that big red bump on your nose a mosquito bite?"

"It's a pimple. And thank you for noticing."

I went downstairs at the first opportunity and grabbed a message from my machine. The customer was thrilled with the rap card and thanked me profusely, asking me to send the card itself immediately.

Apparently not everything could go wrong at once after all.

ELEVEN

Cindy, the Locked-Nest Monster

MONDAY AFTERNOON, Lauren called. She told me she was out on bond and would stay at a hotel till the funeral tomorrow. "I can't stand the thought of being in that big house by myself," she said.

As I listened, I battled a perverse urge to say, "Why? This is the perfect chance for you to be with your lover."

"You're kind of quiet, Molly. You're still upset about the way I acted the other day, aren't you. I know I was mean to you. I'm really sorry. I was so freaked out at the time, I—"

"It isn't that. I talked to Tommy Newton this morning. He told me why he arrested you. He told me about your affair. That Rachel had seen you with the other man."

There was a pause, then a meek "Oh."

I silently cursed at myself. This was going to hurt. One thing I've learned over the years is that keeping strong feelings to myself is worse than admitting them. "We've been friends for thirty years. I wish I didn't have to jeopardize that friendship now, but you know how lousy I am at hiding my feelings. What you do within the confines of your marriage is your own business. But allowing Rachel to see you with another man in...I simply *can't* sit back and pretend my learning about that from someone else hasn't affected me."

She sighed and, at length, said quietly, "I didn't intentionally let Rachel catch us together. She was supposed to go to a friend's house after a soccer game. She forgot and came straight home. It was the worst moment of my life. I knew I couldn't tell you, because I knew you'd react this way.''

"I can't help it. I'm a staunch believer in marital fidelity. So…'' I stopped myself. I was about to tell her to shoot me. "I know these things happen all the time. I just…never expected it to be you.''

She started to cry. "Neither did I. I never thought I'd be unfaithful to my husband. It just happened. But I didn't kill Steve. I need you to believe me.''

"I do.''

There was another pause as she tried to collect herself. "Are we still friends?''

"We're still friends. Mind you, I'll never come into your house without knocking, but you're the best friend I've got in the state of New York. That hasn't changed.''

"Thank God. I'll see you tomorrow.''

After we hung up, I struggled to come to grips with my ambivalent feelings. Was I being honest with myself and Lauren? What really bothered me more: that Lauren cheated on Steve, or that she didn't tell me about it? Would I have felt so betrayed by her actions if Steve were still alive?

And who was the other man?

ANOTHER FUNERAL. I kept the children home from school and brought them with me. Most of my parenting decisions are based on what feels right to me at the time. It felt right to have Karen there, for Rachel's sake.

Lauren had instructed the clergyman to announce that she did not want anyone to express their sympathy to her at this time. The kids and I sat at the back, where I hoped

Nathan could use the coloring book I'd brought for him without attracting attention. No one spoke as Lauren entered. Rachel was beside her, followed by a family of four. With the mother's white-blond hair, they could only have been Steve's sister and family.

As the service proceeded, I scanned the various backs of heads. Everyone from my dinner party last Friday was in attendance. For most of us, that had been the last time we'd seen Steve alive. Someone, though, had seen Steve at least one more time, and had stabbed him to death. My anger over that thought allowed me to stay dry-eyed throughout the service.

As we stood up to leave, Tommy Newton happened to look my way. He shook his head. Maybe he had seen the determination on my face and knew my mind was set on finding the killer.

Once we were all outside, Lauren seemed intent on leaving the scene quickly, but Rachel and Karen spotted each other. Rachel shyly said, "Hi." Karen said hi back and hugged her. It nearly broke my heart.

While I struggled to regain my composure, Stephanie approached. She looked from me to Lauren, put a finger to her lips, then pantomimed her condolences: She clutched her hands to her heart, closed her eyes, and hung her head. Then she snapped out of it, yanked a brimming folder from her enormous purse and thrust it into my arms, saying, "This is everything you need as PTA treasurer. Call me if you have any questions. Your name is already on the account. Toodles." She whirled on a spike heel and grabbed Preston's arm, and they headed to their Mercedes.

Lauren gaped at Stephanie, then chuckled in dismay. "My God, that woman's insufferable."

Glad to see a shadow of the Lauren I knew, I pounced on it. "Could you come for lunch tomorrow?"

"I'd like that."

We said our good-byes, then I took Nathan's and Karen's hands and headed toward our car. I spied Jack Vance and Sam Bakerton at the far corner of the lot. They were arguing. Jack and Preston didn't get along, but he and Sam had been friendly at my dinner party. Perhaps the problem lay in that grant their company had given to the school through Mrs. Kravett.

Carolee was standing near the parking lot, watching Lauren and Rachel in the distance. As we neared, she said hello to my kids and gave me a sad smile. "This is so hard," she said in a choked voice. "I can't stand to see Lauren this way. If I get too near her, I know I'll start blubbering and make a complete fool of myself."

"I know what you mean."

"My lunch break's over. I'd better get back to the hospital. If you..." She paused, then said, "Never mind," and got into her car.

"If I *what*?" I called after her. She didn't answer and drove off.

"If I *what*?" I muttered again to myself.

Karen and Nathan were watching all of this with interest. "Here's a suggestion for when you get older, guys. When you start a sentence, complete it, even if you wind up having to say something stupid. For example, 'If you...drive in the rain, your car gets wet.'"

"Do they make big towels for drying cars?" Nathan asked.

I rolled my eyes. "No, just extremely large blow dryers."

As I unlocked my car, I spotted Denise. She'd been sitting in her car nearby, apparently patiently waiting for her husband to finish his debate with Jack so they could leave. She waved, stood up, and called, "Molly, come meet my daughter."

I told her I'd love to, then let my children into our car and stashed my PTA treasury paperwork under my seat. For some reason, Denise was obsessed with the treasury account. I wasn't letting her *near* it till I had the opportunity to figure out why.

Denise met me a row up from her car and said under her breath, "We decided to take our daughter out of school today, too. Rhonda baby-sat for the Wilkinses this summer."

I nodded and watched Denise's car as we approached, curious to see what Rhonda looked like. All I'd seen of her so far was the back of her head at the service, and her feet sticking out the car window. She was petite, like her mother. A Walkman headset sat in the midst of all her wild, light brown hair. She had her eyes closed and was bobbing to her own tunes. She was very thin, with a nose that the rest of her features needed to grow into.

"Rhonda! Take those things off!" So much for the baby voice Denise used to address other people's children.

Rhonda shot her mother a dirty look, but followed her instructions.

"Say hello to my friend Molly."

"Hello." She smiled. Her mouth was full of braces.

"Hi. It's nice to meet you, Rhonda."

Denise put her hand on my arm. "Would you like to go out for lunch? Or have you eaten already?"

"No, and I'd love to, but I have the kids with me. Would you mind if—"

Before I could ask if she would mind bringing the children, Denise said, "Rhonda would *love* to baby-sit.

She's twelve and has been through Red Cross emergency training.''

Rhonda nodded enthusiastically. ''I'm a great baby-sitter. I love kids.''

Sam and Jack had parted company, and Sam approached, having donned a smile that was obviously forced. He greeted me, and Denise told him she'd asked me to lunch. Sam narrowed his eyes at her and said, ''Are you sure that's a good idea?''

''Absolutely,'' she answered. ''Rhonda's agreed to baby-sit. We'll take the kids to Molly's, and you can go straight to work from here. Molly can drop Rhonda and me off after lunch.''

Sam frowned, then studied me. ''Promise me you'll keep an eye on Denise. It's of primary importance.''

''It is not,'' Denise snapped. ''She can say no if she wants.''

He held up his palm. ''Denise, we've discussed this. So what's it going to be, Molly?''

I felt like one of Custer's men, with the general saying, ''Indians? What Indians?'' Something very weird was going on, but I was inclined to go along with it.

I now suspected that one of two things was happening: (a) Something in the water had gradually turned my former classmates into raving lunatics, or (b) there was an ongoing cover-up involving my classmates, and Steve and Mrs. Kravett had stumbled onto it. Multiple choice was never my forte, but if the answer was (b), lunch with Denise just might get me closer to unraveling the mystery.

We got into my car, with Rhonda immediately being as good with my children as any baby-sitter could possibly be. We dropped them off and gave Rhonda instructions for their lunch.

Denise said to me, "I know of a wonderful spot we can eat, though it's fairly remote. Mind going there?"

"Sure. Just be prepared to be the navigator. I have no sense of direction." That was an understatement. I can get lost in a dark closet.

By the time Denise had me make my third turn, I had no concept of where I was. She scooted the passenger seat forward so she could reach the radio and tuned in a talk show. A parenting counselor was telling some poor sap, "No child under the age of six should watch any TV. From six years and up, no more than an hour a day."

"That's why his talk show's on *radio*," Denise said.

"...should be doing something active with your children. Plant a garden, do crafts projects..."

"Oh, please," I muttered. "Next he'll talk about no sugar. Does this guy stay home twenty-four hours a day with his children, or does his wife? Just once I'd like to meet one of these perfectly raised children of parent advisors and ask what their life at home was *really* like."

Denise laughed, turning to a music station. We chatted, but Denise was tense and anxious. She kept turning to glance through the rear window, as if she expected someone to be tailing us. I dearly hoped she wasn't taking me to some remote spot where she would pull a gun on me and say, "All right. This is it. Let *me* be PTA treasurer or I pull the trigger."

We'd been driving for well over half an hour. "Just where is this place?"

"We're almost there."

"When you said it was remote, I assumed it was still in the state of New York. What does this place have to offer that warrants the drive? Nude waiters?"

"Where's your sense of adventure?"

"Back in my medicine cabinet with my Dramamine. I

can't take all these curvy roads. We've passed a dozen restaurants already.''

"Just up ahead. The place on the right." I put on my blinker and pulled into the dirt parking lot. The lot was filled with cars. I glanced at the restaurant. It was blue with red trim and had phony windows painted onto the cinderblocks. I looked up at the large white-and-black plastic sign.

"Jack's Inside Straight?" I read, incredulous. No wonder there were no windows. "This is a *bar*." I looked again at the building. The walls looked uneven, hastily constructed. "And a seedy one, at that." Denise hadn't even been drinking at my dinner party. Did she have trouble with alcohol? That would explain Sam's instructions for me to keep an eye on her.

She started to get out of the car, but I grabbed her arm. "I don't like the looks of this place. What does the name mean? Is Jack inside, a heterosexual? Are they directions, as in 'Yeah, Jack's straight inside. Can't miss 'im.'?"

Denise yanked her arm away from me and got out of the car. "They have sandwiches. You can get lunch." She slammed the door shut. I hurriedly got out of the car and blocked her path.

"What's going on?"

"Oh...uh. Truth is, I needed you to drive me here. Sam checks my mileage on the car each day, and if I'm over, he takes the car keys. I'm being held prisoner by my own husband. This is just limited-stakes gambling. It doesn't hurt anyone."

"Gambling?" I looked again at the sign. "Inside Straight. That's a gambling term, right? He should've called the place Flush It Down Jack's Toilet. Royally."

Denise pursed her lips and brushed past me. She was

a small person. I could possibly wrestle her back into the car.

"I get it now," I said. "All that baloney about your wanting to be treasurer. You wanted access to the PTA funds for gambling money."

Denise stopped and turned toward me. "Everybody's cut me off. Sam makes me answer for every nickel of grocery money. I was PTA secretary/treasurer for two years. I paid back every penny I borrowed. Stephanie fired me anyway. Imagine. Fired. From a voluntary position." She started to go inside. "Don't worry. I've only managed to scrape together twenty dollars."

"This is real cute, Denise. I'd say you owe me one, but you're way past that point already."

The interior had red carpeting everywhere, on the walls and floors. It smelled of stale bodies and stagnant cigarette smoke. The staff wore pseudo old-western saloon garb. Denise's face lit up like a slot machine hitting the jackpot. "I'm sorry about all of this. Sam thinks I have a gambling problem."

"You do."

"Only when I lose." She went to a counter, handed the cashier a twenty, and asked for two rolls of quarters, which she expertly broke into a plastic bowl. She gave me a friendly jab on the shoulder. "Don't knock it till you've tried it. Go ahead. Get some change. You might just have beginner's luck."

I got five dollars in quarters and allowed Denise to demonstrate video poker to me. The machine took up to four quarters a hand. The display showed the five cards you were dealt, and buttons under each card allowed you to choose which cards to hold when a second hand was dealt. A pair of face cards paid your four quarters back. A royal flush earned $2,500.

I played three hands, lost three dollars, and moved on to a slot machine next to Denise. I put four quarters in that machine and won eight. Whoopee. A dollar.

"Some fun, huh, Molly?"

"To tell you the truth, I'd have more fun dropping my money through a street grate. I'm going upstairs for a sandwich. Can I get you anything?"

She shook her head and continued her monotonous motions. Feed the money. Pull the arm. Feed the money. Pull the arm.

The red carpet ended at the top of the stairs. There it was met by unfinished plywood, littered with peanut shells. The rustic walls were decorated by various dead animals. Deer heads, bear heads, antlers, elk head, a deer butt wearing shades. Each corner had a large TV tuned to ESPN. The bartender called to me, "What's your pleasure?"

"Can I get a sandwich here?"

"Sure thing. I can make that right up for you here." He gestured at a meat slicer behind him, then slid me a menu. Judging from the wall hangings, I was expecting to see venison, but my choices were ham, turkey, or roast beef. Wanting to take the least chance with food poisoning from his less-than-spotless meat cutter, I told him I was a vegetarian and got a cheese, lettuce, and tomato sandwich.

Denise was still at the same slot machine when I returned. She slipped the last of her quarters into the slot and pulled the handle. "Damn." She grabbed her wallet. "All I've got is one lousy dollar. Get me some change, would you?"

I accepted the dollar from her, but took a step toward the cashier and stopped. I watched a fat woman pouring money into a slot machine. She'd melded with her machine.

"Give me my money!" Denise got off her stool. "I mean it! This machine is gonna blow! I can feel it!"

"But, Denise, you—"

I stopped when I noticed that, behind Denise's back, some grungy looking man had fed four quarters into the slot machine Denise had been playing.

Denise followed my gaze and whirled around. She shouted at the man, "Hey, get away from my—"

He pulled the handle as she spoke. "Yes!" he yelled, and quarters started pouring from the machine.

Denise gasped. She whirled toward me, her eyes brimming. She stuck her finger in my face. "I hope you're satisfied! Now you owe me two hundred and fifty dollars!"

"Here's your dollar." She snatched it from me, then started toward the cashier. I grabbed her arm. "Listen, Denise. I promised your husband I'd look after you, and it's time to go."

"So go. I'll get a ride home later on."

The clientele wasn't composed of anyone I would trust to give Denise a ride, even if I could trust myself to find my way home, which, of course, I couldn't. "You're coming with me. Now."

"Guess again."

"All right, Denise. Let's make a bet. If I win the bet, you come with me. If I lose, you stay. Deal?"

"Deal. What's the bet?"

"I bet I can make you say the word *no*."

"What? What kind of a stupid bet is—"

"It's just a joke. But I bet I can make you say no."

"Fine. You're on."

"Uh-oh. You've heard this one before."

"No, I—"

"We're out of here."

"That wasn't a fair bet."

"I don't care. Deal's a deal. Let's go."

Denise clamped her mouth shut but came without a complaint. As we drove home, she barked out a few instructions and eventually started talking with dreamy eyes of all the close calls she'd had on machines, and how she knew she was destined to win the big jackpot someday.

WHEN I GOT HOME, my fax machine had a message from a potential customer. If I was available and up to the task, she needed a greeting for a neighborhood block party by five o'clock, otherwise she'd go the conventional route and hit the card shops. This was not my usual mode of operation. I had maybe an hour to sketch something out. Still, necessity being a mother and all, it was worth a shot.

After free-associating on "meeting neighbors," I settled for the only one I could live with on such short notice, and rationalized that if she rejected the idea, I'd wasted only an hour. Using my paper trimmer, I cut a thick X from construction paper and temporarily fastened it over the drawing. That way she couldn't use it without paying me.

The drawing showed a skinny, monsterish woman with a huge, padlocked nest on her head. Beside her are her two strange sons, and she's greeting a couple standing in front of a house with a sign that read SOLD. She says to the couple, "Hi. I'm Cindy, the Locked-Nest Monster, and these are my children, Frank and Stein. Welcome to the neighborhood."

Moments later, my business line rang. The recipient

said, "My husband and I just love it. It's so clever the way Frank looks like a frankfurter and Stein looks like a beer stein. Was that intentional?"

I rolled my eyes, but said yes. The customer is always right, though not always intelligent. Hadn't she considered the odds against my having drawn characters named Frank and Stein that *accidentally* looked like a hot dog and a beer mug?

We arranged payment, and I told them to be sure to put in a good word about me to their friends.

The phone rang again. This could be the all-time fastest job referral.

"Molly. It's Sam Bakerton. Did…did you have a nice lunch today with my wife?"

"I'm not quite sure how to answer, but the phrase 'Ask me no questions, I'll tell you no lies' comes to mind."

"Uh-oh. You went to Jack's Inside Straight."

"Right." *And a fine time was had by all.*

"I'm sorry. I should've warned you. She *is* getting better. It's a slow process."

"Good luck." That was inappropriate, given her neurosis. "I mean, I hope everything works out for you both."

"Me too," he said. He hung up.

While the children watched television, I scanned the PTA treasury reports.

The bookkeeping records had either a very unfortunate coffee spill across last year's figures or a nicely placed one. Most of that year's accounting was illegible. At the start of the spill, the PTA had over ten thousand dollars, and just under nine thousand afterwards. I flipped through the carbon copies of checks written. Many copies had been removed.

I called the credit union and asked the teller to give

me the information about the missing checks. I was stunned to learn that they totaled over eight thousand dollars. After frantically explaining my situation as the New PTA treasurer dealing with a potentially bogus set of records, she put a manager on the line. Fortunately for me, the credit union did not use the same procedures as banks, which return the paid checks to the customer each month. So, after considerable groveling and cajoling on my part, the manager was able to pull the records and locate the actual checks. They had all been made payable to ''cash'' and were signed Denise Bakerton.

Eight thousand dollars! Denise had gambled away eight thousand dollars of the PTA's money! Was I going to have to announce this during my treasury report at the next meeting? ''According to my figures, I should have over ten thousand dollars in the account right now. Is that right?''

''That's correct.''

''So there was over eighteen thousand in this account at some point last year?''

''No, this past summer a deposit covered the exact total of those checks.''

I let out a sigh of relief. Denise had indeed paid back the money she borrowed. ''Can you tell me the name of the depositor?''

There was a pause, during which I could hear the soft sounds of paper being shuffled. ''Phoebe Kravett.''

TWELVE

Woe Is Me

AT FIVE AFTER EIGHT Wednesday morning, my children were on the bus. The weather was, to use a colloquialism, blechy. The rain clouds looked like dark, lumpy sleeping bags. Apparently they intended to stay for a while. There was no breeze, no break in the gray or the relentless patter of rain on the roof.

All told, it was a perfect day to solve a murder. Indoors, that is.

All the pieces of my puzzle were spread out on the plush gray pile in the living room: my PTA secretary/ treasurer's file, the box of papers Mrs. Kravett's sister had given me, my school yearbook, a legal pad, and a sharpened number two pencil. Wearing jeans and a CU sweatshirt, with a fuzzy purple-and-blue afghan around my shoulders and a cup of hot chocolate in hand, I sprawled out on the floor as well.

Atop my chocolate was a dollop of whipped cream. I've mastered the technique of sucking through my lips just the right amount of cool cream and steaming chocolate. I luxuriated in the experience as the warm blend slid down my throat, realizing this was as close to a sexual encounter as I was likely to come anytime soon.

Try as I might, I couldn't get the last thick dregs to dribble into my mouth. Since Karen and Nathan weren't here to see me, I licked up the last few drops. So much for romanticizing a beverage.

I set the cup on the coffee table behind me and rubbed my hands together in eager anticipation as I surveyed my stack of clues. *Start with the most unexplored...the box from Mrs. Kravett.*

I reread her three-page letter to me detailing how she'd envisioned the criteria for the scholarship program. Then I read the will. Then came the pile of students' "exemplary work" from the past three years, which, she'd explained in her letter, was when she first got the idea for someday having a scholarship in her husband's name.

This contained the schoolwork and personal histories of some forty-plus students. At first glance, there was nothing that could provide anyone with a motive for murder.

My interest perked up when I started to scan a report written by a student intern named Cherokee Taylor about Saunders and Bakerton Imports, the company owned by my classmates' husbands. The report touched on what the company did, gave a brief biography of its co-owners, and mentioned that the two men met through their wives, who had been good friends since high school.

Upon a quick read, the paper was not as well written as the others. It was merely a typical high school composition: messy handwriting, poor spelling, weak sentence structure, no plot. I could just imagine Mrs. Kravett handing this back and saying, "This is supposed to be an essay, not a grocery list. Give me something that elicits an emotional reaction."

Why had she even kept this? I set it aside for a more careful reading later, and pored through the remaining files.

This was getting me no place fast. I decided to jot down some notes of the clues and chronology of events.

At the top of the page I wrote, *Solution to a Dual Murder.* I decided to use Karen's "lost people" format. I put the names of my dinner guests on the left, and wrote *Motive* for the column on the right. I decided to dismiss the possibility that Steve Wilkins had stormed out of my house with my carving knife, whereupon some person unknown to me stumbled onto the knife and stabbed him with it.

A motive for Lauren was easy. Domestic violence was, sadly, a fact of life. All I could come up with for Jack Vance, Denise, Stephanie, and spouses was that Steve had stumbled onto something in Mrs. Kravett's data base. Some secret that the guilty party was willing to kill Steve over, rather than let be revealed.

But what type of secret?

Possibly the student intern at Preston and Sam's company *had* done a second report, one that turned up some dirt. This was especially feasible since there was all of that bubbling discontent between Jack and those two.

Mrs. Kravett might have had something on Jack that could oust him as principal. He had forced her to retire. Perhaps she'd gathered ammunition prior to acquiescing.

Denise's gambling debts were being covered by Mrs. Kravett. Steve could easily have stumbled across a memo to the effect that Denise was no longer allowed access to PTA funds. But that didn't seem like much of a motive for his murder, and Denise's golden eggs were lost upon Mrs. Kravett's death. Still, Denise was acting damned suspicious these days.

Try as I might, I couldn't come up with anything Mrs. Kravett might have had on Stephanie. I racked my brain for a connection between the two women. Stephanie's daughter was too young to have had Mrs. Kravett as a teacher. Seventeen years ago, Mrs. Kravett had ousted Stephanie as editor for printing the unapproved front page that contained my poem. But that had played right into Stephanie's hands. It turned her into an instant student celebrity and got her out of the job she hadn't wanted in the first place. All of that was such old trivia—pond scum under the bridge.

Stephanie was devious, underhanded, selfish. Anything *but* someone I wanted to write off as innocent. To uncover her motive, I might have to spend more time with her. I'd rather scrub bathtubs.

I jotted down that Carolee knew Mrs. Kravett and enough about medicine that she could have plotted her death. Maybe Steve had come across some evidence in Mr. or Mrs. Kravett's health history on the school computer that was incriminating to Carolee.

Last, it occurred to me that I could probably rule out the police sergeant entirely as a suspect, but Tommy won points as the only person at the party with absolutely no discernible motive—always the villain of TV murder mysteries. So I logged his possible motives as being in love with Lauren and mentally gonzo after the death of his wife, and/or hoping to glean control of Mrs. Kravett's money. I then double-checked the will. Sure enough, Tommy was first in line to take my place in the event of my death. That made *me* his likely victim, not Steve Wilkins, but there may have been some computer file that acted as a codicil.

The doorbell rang. I rose, draped the afghan to hide my project, checked the window, and saw Tommy. I glanced back, verified that the afghan had covered my notes, and opened the door.

"Hey, Moll. Thought I'd drop by."

"Really? Why?"

He shrugged. "In my line of work, you get used to readin' folks' expressions. Guess I was a little concerned 'bout what yours had to say at Steve's funeral. Mind if I come in?" He stepped in as he spoke and quickly shed his coat and hat. "Got any more threats lately?"

"No, thank goodness."

Though I tried to steer him past it, he eyed my suspicious-looking blanketed work.

"The house is a little messy. I was…with the rain, I thought I'd set up an indoor picnic for the kids when they get home."

"Rather lumpy blanket. Whatcha got under there? Giant ants?"

"What's a picnic without 'em, right?"

He headed straight toward the afghan. If I tackled him from behind, he'd know for sure I was hiding something.

"There's an Uncle Milton's Ant Farm underneath the blanket, box and all."

He tossed the blanket aside and shook his head. "Uh-huh. Stuff from Mrs. Kravett. Our yearbook. Just what I was afraid of. You're pokin' your nose into the murder." He folded his arms and glared at me. "Boy, Molly. Don't know what to do with you. Frankly, I should stick you in jail. For your own protection. 'Cept, knowing you, first thing you'd do would be to incite a prison riot."

"I resent that. Want a cup of cocoa?"

"Sure." He followed me into the kitchen, where I prepared another cup. Before I could finish, he wandered unsupervised back into the living room, then called, "Got any marshmallows?"

"Sorry."

"Rats. What's a cup of chocolate without marshmallows, right?"

That last remark cost him his dollop of whipped cream. I brought him the cup. To my chagrin, he was flipping through the files from Mrs. Kravett. Right beside the box of files, face up, lay the notebook that stated my thoughts about Tommy's motives for murdering Steve Wilkins.

"Got a search warrant?"

Tommy straightened. "Looked through this stuff over at Mrs. Kravett's house already. Sure am glad you're in charge of the scholarship 'stead of me. Bet it's lotsa work." He grinned. "Her predictions for our classmates sure was fun. Bet the sitcom she pictured you writin' was *Petticoat Junction*."

I smiled with a clenched jaw and walked toward him. If I stepped on the edge of the legal pad, it would flip over on the thick carpeting so Tommy couldn't read it.

One step away, Tommy held up his palm. "Careful." He bent over and scooped up the pad. "You almost stepped on this."

Damn! "Thanks. If you were Sir Walter Raleigh, you'd have just thrown your cape over it."

"Sir Walter Raleigh didn't have the option of picking up the puddle," Tommy deadpanned. He handed me the pad without reading it and took his cup of cocoa. "Mind if I take that 'Solution to a Dual Murder' back to the station house? The boys'll get a good laugh outta my bein' such a good suspect and all."

My cheeks warmed. I watched him gulp his chocolate. "Did any of those boys ever tell you your cap makes a dorky dent in your hair?"

"Yep. Got a dent in my head to go with it. So. Still think Carolee's a combination serial killer/cup thief, or you got some more hot tips?"

"Not really, though I did find out that Denise Bakerton has a—"

"Problem with gambling?"

"A daughter named Rhonda who's a really good baby-sitter. You may want to use her sometime."

Tommy raised an eyebrow.

"Oh, that's right. You said your boys were already teenagers. They probably wouldn't need a sitter." I brushed my bangs back. "Actually, my theory is that Steve may have stumbled across something in the school's data base that—"

"We had Jack Vance print us a report of Steve's system usage. At no time Saturday was he logged on." Tommy handed me his empty cup. "Notice I gave your cup right back. Seein' as you're so attached to 'em, and all. Guess so long as you keep your sleuthin' limited to within your own four walls, we'll be all right."

He headed toward the door and put on his coat and hat. As he turned the knob, he said, "By the way, I may have arrested Lauren, but you're still on *my* list of suspects."

He left. I sat back down on the rug. So. Tommy's visit had thrown some doubt on my best theory: that someone had killed Steve because he'd stumbled onto something about Mrs. Kravett in the school's data base. Before I ruled the theory out entirely, I needed to get a look at the school's computer records myself.

On the bottom of my notes, I doodled a little pheasantlike bird saying, "Woe is me." That gave me an idea for a card. I snatched up my drawing pad. Under a "What's My Line?" banner, I drew three identical birds, all claiming to be the real Woe.

The doorbell rang again. It was Lauren. She looked pale, her eyes puffy. I tried to ignore her appearance and said, "Hi. Come on in. I haven't started getting our lunch ready yet, but how about—"

She shut the door and leaned against it. "I saw Tommy's car in your driveway. I'm so scared. Molly, I don't want to go to prison."

I put my arm around her shoulders. We went into my living room and sat on the floor, where I told her my theory that Steve had discovered some volatile secret in the school's data base. "I specifically remember him saying something at the party about not having a password for Mrs. Kravett's files. Remember?"

Lauren's spirits rose a bit. She looked thoughtful. "I don't remember that, but maybe I wasn't in the room at the time. The important thing is, Steve might have been hooked up through his modem to the school computer at the time of his death. Maybe he was looking at the file with someone right then, not realizing *that* someone was going to kill him over it."

"According to Tommy, Steve wasn't working on a file from the school's computer at the time of his death."

"But the killer could have pulled up a different file, real quick, after erasing the one that incriminated him. Or her."

I shook my head. "My opinion of Tommy has changed. His nice-but-not-too-sharp routine is just an act. Computers automatically keep time logs of files and sign-ons. Tommy already checked those logs. He knows precisely what Steve was really working on when he died."

Lauren fidgeted with the nap of the carpeting. "Did Tommy tell you what that was?"

"He said it was a good-bye letter to you."

Lauren cursed under her breath.

It had already occurred to me that Steve's killer might be Lauren's jealous lover. I was dying to learn the lover's identity. Besides, it seemed absurd to be trying to solve this while not having such a potentially important piece of the puzzle. "Who's your lover?"

"I'd rather not say."

"It's going to come out during your trial, anyway."

She didn't look at me. "Not necessarily. It's over with. It never meant anything to us in the first place. He looked at it as extracurricular activity. I was lonely."

"Maybe you're wrong about what your relationship meant to him. Maybe he killed Steve to have you to himself. Or maybe they argued and he stabbed Steve in self-defense."

"In the back? While Steve was sitting in his chair?"

I shrugged. "Maybe during another burglary attempt."

"Burglary? There was no burglary. That was *him*."

"Who?"

"My lover. We never wanted anyone to see his car so he parked different places each time and came in through the back. Every Monday evening, while Steve was either working late or taking Rachel to her soccer practice. Trouble was, her soccer league ended the week before. I thought I told...my lover that, but...I always left the back door open, too, as another signal. I locked it. Who knew he'd try to open the window?"

"Are you sure it was him?"

She nodded. "While Steve was in the basement with the kids, thank God, the fool tried the back door. Instead of leaving immediately, he spotted me passing by the office doorway and tried to throw open the window to tell me the back door was locked. Is that stupid or what?"

Pretty darn dumb, all right. "But Steve said there were crowbar markings on the—"

"Steve had already found out about...him the week before. We had Rachel, Karen, and Nathan with us when the alarm went off. I had to act... I tried to pretend it was a real break-in attempt. Then, after the police had already been called, Steve put two and two together and confronted me. He put those markings on the windowsill himself before the police arrived, just to save face.''

While I tried to assimilate the information, Lauren burst into racking sobs. ''I'm getting what I deserve. I'm a terrible mother. I let my own daughter…my own…''

''You have to forgive yourself for that. You're still her mother and she needs you.''

''Steve was never there for me when I needed him. I felt so neglected. I just…I wanted to hurt him back. Deep down, I wanted Steve to find out about my affair.''

Truth told, I believe in monogamy, in loyalty to wedding vows. I couldn't pretend to support or vindicate Lauren, so I offered her tissues, waited until she'd collected herself, and changed the subject.

''Tommy told me your fingerprints were on the medicine bottles in Mrs. Kravett's house.''

''Huh? She had a heart attack. What difference does it make if—''

I shook my head. ''That's just what's been reported to the press. The police know that the pills weren't in the right bottles. Her pills had been switched, essentially giving her a toxic dosage.''

She let this sink in, then said, ''Oh.''

''So how did your prints get on those bottles?''

''At the barbecue in July, I went through her medicine cabinet.'' She said this matter of factly, then looked at me. ''Don't *you* do that?''

''Of course not. Why would I go through someone's cabinet?''

''Aren't you curious to see what type of medications people use?''

''No, not at all.''

She sighed and stared into space, chewing on her lip. "I checked out of the hotel today. We're back in my house again. I drove Rachel to school this morning. This is all so hard on her. I don't know what to do." She looked at me, her eyes again brimming. "I need your help. I can't face this alone."

THIRTEEN

Trouble Balancing the Books?

THAT NIGHT, I spoke to a potential customer about doing a flyer to advertise her bookkeeping company. The more input a customer gives me into a design, the longer the work takes me, and this woman had been very specific. I spent a couple of hours after the kids were in bed and a couple more the next morning. The caption read: Trouble Balancing the Books? The drawing showed a woman juggling hardbound books, one spinning on her nose. Below the drawing was the customer's address and phone number.

Afterward, I toyed with the idea of designing a business card for myself: Molly Masters. Owner of Friendly Fax, Inc. Mother of Two. Meddles in Murders in Her Spare Time.

By 10:00 a.m., my time was reasonably spare. This was an opportunity for me to visit Jack Vance at the school and try to get a look at the computer logs.

The more I'd thought about it, the more he seemed the likeliest candidate for being Lauren's lover. Steve had groaned when Jack arrived at my house. Lauren had had a major crush on him in high school, till Howie Brown came along. Jack had brightened when I first said she was coming to dinner. It all made sense.

I drove to school and entered the lobby. As I was already aware from my dealings during school registration,

Jack's office was guarded by a barracuda in a dress. This lady could scare off Dracula. She had permanent frown lines etched in her face, and the reading glasses on her nose were probably fake, worn just so she could scowl over them at those who dared to bother her. She sighed audibly when I asked if Jack was in, then snarled, "And *you* are?"

"Molly Masters. Mother extraordinaire." I gestured at the closed door behind her. "If you're too busy to get up, I could knock on the door myself."

She puckered her lips. For a second I thought she was going to spit on me, but then she punched a button on the intercom and leaned across her desk, keeping her eyes on me the whole time. "There's a Mrs. Masters here."

"Send her in."

Keeping my distance from his bodyguard, I entered. Jack looked genuinely glad to see me as we exchanged pleasantries. Then he asked, "Have you had lunch yet?"

I glanced at my watch in surprise. "It's barely after ten."

"Great. I had an appointment cancel on me, so let's go grab an early lunch."

Visions of Tuesday's junket with Denise haunted me. What if he was *the* Jack, as in Jack's Inside Straight? "You *do* mean at a restaurant, don't you?"

He chuckled as he rounded his desk and took my arm. "So, you've heard about my little hobby already."

Hobby? Such as gambling? Here we go again. Another visit to Jack the heterosexual. "I have to be back before noon to meet Nathan's bus."

"Don't worry. I can only take an hour for lunch. We'll be back by eleven."

At least that eliminated the possibility of our roaming the countryside for little hideaways. He drove us in his red sports coupe. Within two miles, Jack pulled into the parking lot of an entertainment complex that featured batting cages. "Here we are."

I glanced at his face in profile. He looked as excited as a little boy. He pulled a pair of tennis shoes from under his seat and kicked off his loafers. His left sock had a small toe hole. "School hours are the only chance I get to come here. You'd be amazed how fast the kids clear out of the place when I'm around. Nobody wants to have their principal near while they're hangin' out. The owners specifically asked me not to come after school and weekends."

We got out of the car. Jack adjusted the band on his ponytail, then pulled an aluminum bat out of his trunk. He went up to the vacant-eyed man at the counter and bought a handful of tokens. He faced me. "Would you like to take some swings? Here." He dropped a token into my palm. "Ten pitches per token. I've only got the one bat, though."

In my jeans, pullover, and sneakers, I was dressed appropriately. I chose a light bat from their selection, all of which were too shoddy for anyone to want to steal.

Having lived in Boulder, fitness-freak capital of the world, I'd played on many a softball team. But this ball machine had a perverse tendency to spit out a pitch just as I'd given up on it. It reminded me of the way my husband took photographs. He would say, "Smile" four or five times and wait until my teeth dried out and I blinked to finally click the shutter.

Thinking of my absent husband only made me lose power in my swing. He would be back in his Manila hotel sometime today. I should have called his office to trace down his temporary hotel and tell him about the faxed threats and the murders. What was I doing in some stupid batting cage, waiting on a ball machine with no arm? I should be with my husband. I should have gone to the Philippines. They probably even have Pizza Huts there, which would've appeased Nathan and Karen.

When I'd netted the tenth ball, I returned my bat to the counter and went to watch Jack in the fast-pitch cage.

He flashed me a quick grin. "See that last one, Moll? This pitcher's tryin' to brush me back. I may have to charge the mound."

I laughed and watched him clown, pointing à la Babe Ruth at where he was going to send the ball, playing announcer of the unseen game that always had him stepping up to bat at the bottom of the ninth, bases loaded. My, did he miss his fans.

My thoughts tumbled between new questions and old memories.

When at last he had finished, he buttoned his shirt and replaced his tie. His face was red and damp, his breaths hard. "God, that was fun," he said, beaming. He shot a glance at me as if he expected me to launch into some "Rah rah ree, Kick 'em in the knee." If so, he had the wrong girl. That was Stephanie's territory, then and now.

All those homecoming parade floats Jack and Stephanie had reigned on. When the cheers faded, so did their relationship. Lauren had informed me in a letter a long time ago that Stephanie dumped Jack their junior year in college, when he failed to make first string for the third straight year. Jack's athletic prowess in high school had apparently been largely due to his lack of competition among the small upstate schools.

"Can I buy you lunch?" Jack asked.

"No thanks. My stomach doesn't wake up till after noon."

Jack bought himself two hot dogs, nachos, and a cola.

We sat at a pea green, circular fiberglass picnic table cemented to the porch. As if anyone would actually want to steal it.

We chatted idly about our careers while he wolfed down his food. At the first opportunity, I asked, "Have you kept up with Lauren much over the past few years?"

"Not really. I heard about her arrest. Hard to imagine why she'd do it."

"There was a rumor she had another man in her life."

"Hmm." He grinned. "That's interesting. I wish I'd have known she was available. She was a four-star in my little black book in high school. If only Howie hadn't moved on her first, I might have had another notch on my belt. If you know what I mean."

Unfortunately, I did, and it made me tighten my fists under the table. "Tommy said you were dating some young woman at the barbecue last July at Mrs. Kravett's house."

"Jane is not all that young. Midtwenties. Anyway, that's over. Dropped me like a hot potato soon as she got her boyfriend suitably jealous."

"Least you got another notch on your belt."

He grinned, and I tried not to stare at a piece of hot dog stuck on his front tooth. He patted his rounded stomach. "Lately I've got to keep letting *out* my belts." He stared off into space. "I was the star of every sport in high school. Remember?"

I nodded, but he still had a faraway look in his eye. He was seeing remembered fans and victories, not me.

"You have no idea what it's like, Molly. To reach the apex of your life when you're only eighteen. What did Mrs. Kravett predict for me?"

"How did you know about that?"

"The detectives told me when they interviewed me

about Mrs. Kravett and Steve Wilkins. So what did she
say?''

I remembered well. Insurance salesman. After the job
description, Mrs. Kravett had written, ''Jack Vance
strikes me as a classic case of an ego that knows no
bounds in a boy yet to face any hardships. When the real
world intrudes on his image, he'll collapse.''

He read my face. ''Don't answer that. Phoebe always
hated me.''

''That's what I always thought she felt about *me*. Did
you hear about her decision to put me in charge of the
scholarship program?''

He ignored my question. ''But in *my* case it's true. She
lobbied like hell to block me from getting the position as
principal. She may have wasted plenty of breath claiming
it was nothing personal, that there were more qualified
teachers at Carlton than I, but it was obvious from the
get-go. She resented my success. She wanted the position
herself.''

''She did?''

''Absolutely. She made a big show of claiming her
heart problems made her ineligible, but that's all it
was...a show. Once I got the job, she never missed a
chance to humiliate me.''

''That must have made you angry,'' I said, prodding
the same way I did when Nathan was struggling to express himself.

''Of course,'' he huffed. ''But I certainly—'' He
stopped abruptly. He covered the pause by stuffing a drip-
ping nacho into his mouth. ''These are really good. Sure
you wouldn't like some?''

''No, thanks.'' Filling in the blanks, I asked, ''I heard
how dejected she was when she was forced to retire.''

He kept his eyes downcast and ignored me.

"That was *your* decision, wasn't it?"

He narrowed his eyes at me. "I was in charge of the high school at that time. I did what was best for the school. For my students. You parents wouldn't have me do any less. She was so absorbed when her husband got cancer, she made a mess of her class schedule. Sent her students out on stupid field projects, writing reports on businesses."

"What's wrong with that?"

"She taught *English.* She was supposed to be teaching the classics...reading for enjoyment. Instead, she...she was teaching them how to write office memos and technical jargon. She—"

"Mrs. Kravett was teaching her students technical writing? Are we talking about the same person here? The woman who used to preach about how much better off we'd be if we threw out our TVs and stereos and blenders?"

Jack snorted and nodded. "She even took some computer course at night last year. Claimed it was time English curriculum reflected the real world."

An overwhelming sense of sadness enveloped me. I could see her so clearly in my mind's eye. There she was at the blackboard, hands on her hips, frowning at us in our seats as she asked, "Haven't any of you turned off all that electric junk in your house, just once? Grabbed a good book, sat in front of the fireplace, and read aloud to a loved one?" After class, we'd snickered about how "out of touch" she was. Now, it felt so awful to know that even *she* had surrendered to some extent and had tried, at the last, to *get with the times.*

Jack continued, "The whole thing was just an excuse so she wouldn't have to grade book reports and give lectures anymore."

"Jesus Christ, Jack! The woman was sixty-six and she showed more guts and innovation than you, thirty years her junior!"

"I've got to get back to school." Jack rose. He didn't look at me as we walked to his car. I felt sure he wished my head was in the way when he flung his bat into his truck.

As we pulled out of the parking lot, I said, "Tommy Newton told me you showed him some computer records to determine when Steve had logged on. Could I look at them?"

Jack shook his head. "The police took 'em."

"Why didn't anyone know Mrs. Kravett's password?"

"Steve was wrong. She didn't *have* a password in the first place. She never used the computer."

"You're sure about that?"

He gave an angry shrug. "Unless she lied about it. We have forms for the staff to fill out that have them log their passwords, just in case they forget or…" Die an untimely death, I mentally filled in. "The forms are kept in a locked cabinet in my office. She wrote there that she didn't use the computer and didn't have a password."

"You can always get a password out of a system if you know what you're doing," I said. "I remember something in my computer training about a memory dump…getting a printout of storage buffers. And at my party, Steve said something about his plans to do that on Sunday." *Except he was killed on Saturday.*

Jack nodded. "He said he was going to shut down the system to get her password last Sunday. I already told him he'd be wasting his time, since she *didn't* have a password."

I clenched my jaw and looked out the window. We were almost at the school. If Steve said Mrs. Kravett had a password, she had a password; that's not a mistake a computer expert would make. Apparently Jack's arrogance made him oblivious to such an obvious conclusion. Regardless of what Jack had said earlier on the subject, he was also arrogant enough to assume that Lauren had locked her door by mistake and to set off an alarm trying to open a window to tell her so.

"Can I try something on your computer? It will just take sixty seconds, tops."

He raised his eyebrows, but before he could protest, I added, "It could have something to do with why Steve was murdered."

"So now you're Molly Masters, PI, huh?" We pulled into the school lot.

"Something like that."

We entered the front lobby. The barracuda was sitting at her desk. She peered over her glasses at me, then went back to work at her terminal. Behind her, against the wall of Jack's office, sat two girls who looked a year or two older than Karen. Both were whimpering. Their knees were scraped, their clothes muddy and tousled. Jack leaned toward them, hands on hips and said kindly, "Let me guess. You both got kicked off the chess team."

The girls looked at him in confusion and shook their heads.

"Football? Track? Bobsledding?"

The girls managed small smiles through their tears, finally realizing he was teasing.

"No? We'd better all step inside my office and see if we can get to the bottom of this."

Listening to him, I was relieved to see he was much better at dealing with children than with adults.

He glanced over his shoulder at me. "Molly, you can run your little experiment on Ms. Nelson's terminal."

By the gesture of his head, I took it to mean that Barracuda's name was Ms. Nelson. She turned her laser eyes to me. "Make it snappy."

"Can you log out of this program, please?"

She not only got out of the program she was running, she turned the computer off. I flipped the switch back on and got a screen asking me to sign on. I typed MASTERS and pressed enter. The screen returned a message: Unauthorized User. I entered KRAVETT and got the message Enter Password. So she had indeed used the computer and had established a password.

For password, I tried her husband's name, Bob, then Robert; then her sister's name, Ellen, and finally Steinway. Each time, the message Invalid Password flashed. I thanked Ms. Nelson and left.

I mulled over the events of the past few days. I had forgotten to ask Lauren an important question that might clear some things up for me. I had a few minutes to kill prior to Nathan's bus arriving, so I went to her house.

As soon as we were seated in her kitchen, I said, "I've been meaning to ask you something. What happened the night of my party? Why did Steve get so angry and everyone leave in such a huff?"

"That was all Steve's little smoke screen so he could get out fast while saving face. He picked an argument with Sam, Denise's husband. Steve pretended to be offended about a joke Sam made about how steep Steve's charges were. He *really* wanted to leave because of something Rachel said."

"What did she say?"

She blushed. The answer hit me a moment later, and I answered for her, "Rachel recognized your lover at the party."

She nodded. Her features tightened and she had to

blink back tears. "Back when the...when my lover was...testing the water with me, shall we say, he used to take Rachel and me out to the park for picnics. Having Rachel casually say hello to him would have been just fine, but I...winced. Steve was looking right at me. Our eyes met, and he knew. And *I* knew he knew—the pain was written all over his face. Once Steve made the connection, he wanted us out of there fast before everyone else realized what had happened." She took a halting breath and chewed her lip. "Hang it all. I'm taking up smoking again. If it shortens my life expectancy, hurray." She got up and snatched up her car keys. "Sorry to kick you out. I'm going to the store for a pack."

"It's time for Nathan's bus anyway. I'll see you later."

"Molly? I may as well tell you. You'll find out sooner or later anyway. My...lover? It was Preston Saunders."

FOURTEEN

Pay Your Bill

SHORTLY AFTER Karen's afternoon bus had arrived, Tiffany came to my door. She'd just gotten a new haircut. The left side of her blond tresses was decidedly longer than the right. It was a wonder her equilibrium wasn't thrown off. She was panting too heavily to speak, other than a breathy "Hi." I looked past her and spotted a bicycle lying on its side in my garden.

"Tiffany, are you all right? Did you crash your bike?"

"Bike? No." She fanned her face, then put a hand to her chest to emphasize her physical ordeal. Watching her, all I could think was that Stephanie should simply have had herself cloned instead of bothering with natural childbirth. The two women had the same delicate features—pretty little nose, big eyes, wide cheekbones. If Tiffany were a couple of inches taller and used a sober hairstylist, she and her mom would be dead ringers.

She took another gulp of air. "I don't have a kickstand on it yet. I didn't want to get it scratched up by leaning it against a rough surface."

"I see." Better my garden smashed than her precious bike scratched. She was her mother's daughter, all right. "What brings you here?"

"My boyfriend's birthday is, like, coming up, soon?" She blushed and continued, turning each sentence into a question. "And I need, you know, some cash? I thought maybe you could use a baby-sitter?'' She looked up at me hopefully.

"Gee, I really don't need a sitter right now. I wish you'd called first and saved yourself the trip.''

"My mom says it's harder to say no to someone face to face." She lifted her overplucked eyebrows into a pleading expression.

Her mother was right, in general. Unfortunately for Tiffany, this particular face looked like Stephanie's. And that was *one* face I *relished* saying no to.

"Sorry, but I don't need a sitter today.''

Her jaw dropped. "You mean I rode all this way for nothing?"

"It appears so."

"Could you give me a ride home?"

"No, I can't."

"But, like, you just said you weren't doing anything. That's why you don't need a sitter. So you can give me a ride, right?"

"Wrong."

She clicked her tongue, put a hand on her hip, and shot a disconsolate glance at her bike in the garden. Her shoulders sagged and her lip trembled. This was obviously an act, but it did cause me a pang of guilt. She was just a child, and she didn't have to pay for the sins of her mother. Granted, this was also a *spoiled* child. She would have benefited greatly from Mrs. Kravett's no-nonsense teaching style.

Decisions. "Tell you what. Come on in and I'll get you a snack to shore you up for the long journey home." I would have to look up the Saunderses' address. My bet would be that it was less than ten blocks away.

Karen, who'd been changing out of her school clothes, skipped down the stairs and said, "Yippee! Tiffany's here! Nathan, come on down and get your hair straightened!"

"No, Karen." I called back up the stairs, "Never mind, Nathan. Tiffany's just here to eat your food, not style your hair."

He raced out to the landing. "The snack cakes and powdered doughnuts are mine!"

Tiffany grinned up at him. "Could I have cookies and milk?"

He looked thoughtful. "Okay, but only four cookies."

I got her the requested fortifications, and we grabbed opposing barstools at the kitchen counter. In the adjoining family room, Karen turned on afternoon cartoons. Moments later, Nathan appeared. He did an obvious check to make sure he approved of her snack.

She tousled his hair, something Nathan despises. "Hi, big guy. How are you?"

He growled and raced back upstairs to comb out her finger marks.

"So, what's your boyfriend like?" I asked.

"Mom 'n' Dad say he's too old for me. He's a senior. His name is Cherokee Taylor." She giggled. "Isn't that just *the* best name you've heard?"

"He was in Mrs. Kravett's junior English class last year, right?"

"Yeah. How'd you know?"

"It's an eye-catching name." What did friends call him for short? Chair? Key? "Hang on a sec."

I dragged out the files and quickly found Cherokee's. "Mrs. Kravett kept a paper he'd written. It was about your father's business, Saunders and Bakerton Imports."

"Yeah. That's how we met. Me and Cherokee, I mean. Last year he came and interviewed Daddy." She peered over my shoulder at the report. "Oh. That's the old one.

Mrs. Kravett made him start all over again and write a new one.''

''How could you tell which version this was so quickly?''

''The final version had a different title. Something like 'Company Cashes In on Endangered Animals.'''

The title on *this* report was ''Local Company Proves It Pays to Import.'' That was one heck of a topic change. ''Endangered animals?''

Tiffany nodded. She jammed a chocolate cookie intact into her mouth.

''Tiffany, I'm no expert, but I would think you need to be careful about what you're saying. There are laws banning the import of products from endangered species. It sounds as if your boyfriend had implied that your father broke some of those laws.''

She rolled her eyes and nodded, a few crumbs spraying from her lips as she said, ''Tell me about it. My parents went nuts when Mrs. Kravett called and, you know, told 'em what Cherokee said in his report. Daddy said the whole paper was a batch of...stuff from the wrong end of a bull. That's the other reason why I can't, like, let 'em find out we're dating. It's not just that he's, you know, four years older than me. They hate him because of that report he wrote.'' Two more cookies went down the hatch.

''So what happened?''

She dabbed a napkin to her lips in a belated attempt at daintiness. ''He got an A.''

''No, I mean what happened after your father said the report was bogus?''

''According to Cherokee, the guy who gave him all the information was fired. Daddy says that was Sam Bakerton's decision. Daddy's partner is in charge of hiring and firing. He, you know, said it was because the guy was just, like, lousy at his job. Everyone had a meeting, and Mrs. Kravett insisted on giving Cherokee's paper to some...customs officer or something."

She paused long enough to guzzle her milk. "Dad said they investigated and...I can't think of the word but it means they couldn't find anything wrong. That was the end of it. 'Cept Daddy says if Cherokee so much as drives down our street, he'll shoot him. Daddy'd shoot Cherokee, I mean."

I hopped off the stool, excited at having finally heard what sounded like a very strong lead into the murder case. "Listen, I think I've changed my mind about needing you to sit for me."

"Great!"

"My only special instructions for you are Karen no makeup, Nathan no hair. And, again, I'll pay four dollars an hour. I'll be back before five."

I grabbed my usual cohort in crime—the phone book—and looked up the address for Saunders and Bakerton Imports. It was in Albany, which would take me the better part of an hour to reach. I'd have to drive fast to make a round trip in less than two hours. At least the trip there would give me time to formulate a plan.

Or not. When I pulled into the parking lot forty-five minutes later, I decided my snooping wasn't going to be all that easy. So far my plan was to ask Sam and Preston whether some of their products were illegal, they would say no, and I would leave, humiliated and perhaps a marked woman, just as Mrs. Kravett had been. This is what's known in academic circles as poor planning.

The company looked like a big warehouse, which, once I thought about it, was as it should look. The company received and then shipped products around the globe. An attractive woman sat at the desk in the lobby. Behind her, to my happy surprise, was a board that listed twenty or so names and whether they were currently in, and Sam Bakerton's read OUT. Now I could pretend to Preston that I had come to visit Sam. The receptionist asked if she could help me. I introduced myself and said, "I was here to see Mr. Bakerton, but I see he's not here."

She glanced back. "That's right, but he should be back any minute. Why don't you wait here?"

Drat. "Maybe Mr. Saunders could see me instead."

She buzzed him and gave my name, and moments later an impeccably dressed Preston Saunders emerged, grinning broadly. "Molly. To what do I owe the pleasure?"

"Actually, I was here to see Sam. He'd promised me a tour next time I was in the area, which happened to be now." Yeah, right. My tires were still steaming.

"I'd be happy to escort you."

He showed me his office and Sam's, which were equally large and posh, then took me into the huge warehouse. As we navigated the aisles, we managed to keep a patter of dull conversation going that would've made Jack Vance's PTA meetings sound lively. I finally got my opening when Preston showed me a stack of boxes he said contained African carvings.

"They're ivory carvings?"

"Oh, no. There are strict regulations controlling ivory trade."

"Government red tape, huh," I said in a How-'bout-them-Giants voice. "There're probably ways to get around that crap, though."

He shook his head. "As long as this company bears my name, we'll follow all the regulations. Wiping out elephant herds and whole species of animals just to decorate somebody's home just doesn't make sense."

"Really? I thought I read about an investigation of a company around here that was doing just that. Must have been your competition then."

Preston's expression instantly grew hostile. "We're the only large-scale import company in the area. Where exactly did you read that?"

"Must be my mistake. I probably read it in the newspaper back in Colorado and got my locales confused."

"I'd better get back to work. Let me show you out."

Preston walked me out so brusquely, all that was missing was a swift kick to my rear when we reached the door. I'd hit a nerve. Cherokee Taylor's report could well have divulged something that proved fatal to Mrs. Kravett and Steve Wilkins. If so, was the Taylor family in jeopardy?

I sped on the way home, though I slowed as I neared the police station. Despite this, a cruiser pulled in behind me just a mile from my house. I could tell by the red hair that Tommy Newton was the driver. I made a quick, unplanned right turn, hoping he hadn't spotted me and would go straight. He followed and put on his flashers. I pulled over, rolled down my window, and donned my innocent smile as I watched his approach in my side-view mirror. "Tommy. Hi. Just the man I was looking for."

"Uh-huh. Bet you thought you were gonna get ticketed."

I filled Tommy in on my conversation with Tiffany and my theory that Preston or Sam could've killed Steve after he'd stumbled onto Cherokee's story on disk, where Mrs. Kravett could have stored a copy for safe keeping. Tommy said, "Get out of your car."

"Why?"

"Just want to stop strainin' my neck to look at you."

I stopped the engine and got out.

"Molly, this is my last warning." He tugged on his sleeve. "This here is a police uniform. Look around. You see anyone else 'round here wearin' a uniform?"

My face warmed. "Is this a trick question?"

He blew out a puff of air. "I'll put it into a sound bite for you. Butt out."

"Yes sir." I got back into my car, indignant and hurt. For one thing, my information should prove helpful to him and had in no way muddled any evidence.

I waited behind my wheel until Tommy made a U-turn and drove out of sight.

I drove home, shelled all of my cash over to Tiffany, and agreed to give her a ride home. With Tiffany hovering nearby to offer such helpful advice as "Careful" and "Watch out," I removed the front wheel from her bike and angled the bike and its wheel into the trunk of my car.

Karen and Nathan sat quietly in the back. Tiffany, however, chattered mindlessly as we drove, though she did give me directions. She pointed at a ranch-style home ahead of us. "There's Cherokee's house," she said wistfully. A woman and a young man were tending the yard. "There he is! Stop! I gotta say hi!"

I pulled into the drive, and Tiffany rushed out and into Cherokee's arms. He looked a bit like a computer nerd, except for the hairstyle. His sandy-brown hair was wavy but closely cropped on the sides. A Cherokee in a Mohawk. He wore one dangling earring. The woman smiled at me and waved. I waved back.

"Is that Tiffany's husband?" Karen asked from the back seat.

"No, her boyfriend. They're not married."

"Do people tell lies in a library?" Nathan asked.

"What?"

"Why is it called a library? Why isn't it a book-berry?"

"I don't know."

His voice was tensing. "Do people *lie* down in lie-berries?"

Cherokee's mother strode up to the car. I rolled down the window. She said, "Hello, I'm Janice Taylor."

"Why is it called a lie-brary?" Nathan yelled again.

"Hello, I'm—"

"MOMMY!" He started crying. "I just want to know. Why is it called a—"

I turned and snapped at him, "Because it was invented by some guy in Philadelphia named Ralph Woodwin Library, that's why!"

Embarrassed, I returned my gaze to Cherokee's mother, but she gave me a smile that was mothers' non-verbal shorthand for "Don't bother to explain. I'm a mother myself."

"Nice to meet you. I'm Molly Masters. I was just driving Tiffany home." Tiffany and Cherokee strolled over, hand in hand.

"She and my mom are good friends," Tiffany said.

"I see." Her face fell.

For Tiffany's sake, I didn't want to blurt, "Don't worry. I can't stand the woman, either." So instead I asked, "Didn't I see you at Mrs. Kravett's funeral?" As if I could have seen *anyone* through all those tears, but it was a reasonable guess.

"Oh, yes. I remember seeing you now, too. That was so sad. She was quite a mentor to Cherokee."

"She could recognize honesty and artifice," I offered, hoping to elicit a response.

She studied my eyes. "So you know the story."

"Not really."

She said under her breath, "He'll get his. He may have escaped on a technicality, thanks to that spineless cohort of his, but he'll pay."

"Mom!" Cherokee snapped.

She whirled toward her house without another word, forcing me to choose between calling after her, "Who are we talking about?" and driving away. Cherokee looked at Tiffany with loving eyes as she got into the passenger seat, which quickly turned to an angry glare as he focused on me. I backed out of the driveway.

Cherokee's mother must have meant *Preston* would "get his" and *Sam* was "spineless," but I had a disquieting suspicion I would never know for sure.

"Turn left here."

Tiffany continued to give me directions. Granted, I have no sense of direction, but even *I* notice when I pass my own house. Tiffany navigated us back the way we came toward her house.

THE NEXT MORNING, I got word that my new bookkeeper customer wanted another fax designed for her business, a friendly payment-overdue notice.

I'd gotten into the greeting card business as a writer, not an artist. One thing I had learned about cartooning was to make as few lines as possible. A character defined with a few deft strokes could look humorous, the anatomical exaggerations intentional rather than the result of the inadequacies of a self-taught artist.

For this particular job, I could use the ultimate minimalistic approach. Because we were in noncompeting businesses with different client bases, I didn't need to do a new design; I merely faxed her the late-payment notice I use for my own customers. It showed a sad-faced man wearing pants with empty pockets pulled out and a T-shirt that read BILL. The caption read: Don't Forget to Pay Your Bill.

The entire transaction was handled before it was time to get the kids to the bus. I emerged from my office and swooped the mostly empty cereal bowls off my children's place mats. "Okay, guys. Time to get to the bus stop. Run upstairs and brush your teeth while I grab your backpacks."

The children obeyed me without complaint. They were all zipped into their coats and ready to go in record time. I felt like Supermom. She cooks. She works. She—

"Where's my lunch, Mom?"

—forgot to pack a lunch for her daughter. "You're getting a hot lunch today." She fakes it.

"No way! They're having beef awk juice today!"

"All right, all right. I've got ten seconds. No problem." I raced into the kitchen and flung open the pantry. "How about a can of tuna and a can opener?"

"Mo-o-omm!"

When Karen drags the word *Mom* into three-plus syllables, she means no. I grabbed a couple of slices of American cheese and an entire packet of soda crackers. "Here you go." I chucked them into her lunch box. "Buy milk to drink. Rip up the cheese slices and make your own finger sandwiches."

"But Mo-o-omm!"

"It's that or the beef awk juice. Your pick."

She grabbed the lunch box and frumped out of the house behind Nathan and me. I glanced back at her and tried to make her return my smile. She murmured, "Everyone else's moms pack *good* lunches."

We just made the bus. From the corner of my eye, I saw Lauren emerge from her house carrying two cups. She spotted me waving good-bye to some freckle-faced boy on the bus, since my own children didn't even look for me, let alone care I was waving.

"Brought you a cup of coffee."

"Thanks. You made my day."

We sat on the curb and sipped coffee. Though I filled her in on my suspicions about Preston and Sam, Lauren was skeptical that the two men would resort to murder to hide Cherokee's report. My theory was indeed something of a stretch, but Lauren's husband might have been about to stumble onto a document that could destroy Preston's company, *and* Preston was the rival for Lauren's affections. Perhaps two motives added up to one murderer.

Speaking of the devil, his spouse, Stephanie, called as soon as I got home. She asked me to meet her in the lobby at school, saying she wanted to go over my duties as secretary/treasurer with me. This would be interesting. I wanted to see what kind of a dance she would do when I pointed out the creative bookkeeping that Denise had done to cover her gambling problems. Stephanie suggested we leave right away and meet at the school in fifteen minutes. Knowing she would no doubt arrive late and keep me waiting, I agreed to do so, but didn't even leave my house for twenty minutes. She was just getting out of her car in the semicircle by the elementary school building when I pulled in. Her face fell for a moment when she spotted me.

Stephanie led me to a cozy room she claimed was time-shared by the PTA committee members and the school psychologist. Along one wall, a blue corduroy futon mattress adorned with fluffy yellow pillows was so inviting I wanted to curl up and take a nap, but we sat in standard-issue plastic-and-chrome chairs at a round table in the opposite corner. At one point, Stephanie paused from her homily about the virtues of our giving preference to team-teacher projects that benefited the most students. She leaned toward me and said in conspiratorial tones, "You really shouldn't wear that blouse. The color is all wrong for you. I do color charts for people, you know."

"Of course you do."

"That blouse sucks all the color out of your complexion."

"I like having a translucent face."

"Offhand, I'd say you're a winter. I'm, of course, spring. None the less, the blouse I have on would go much better with your colors than what you're wearing." She rummaged through her purse, roughly the size of a one-bedroom apartment. She removed a compact, opened it, and shoved it into my hand, mirror facing me. "Here. I'll hold my sleeve..." She held her arm out toward my face. Her wrists reeked of musk oil perfume.

I shoved her arm away. "Okay, you've made your point." I pulled out my shirttails and unbuttoned my top button.

"What are you doing?"

"Take your blouse off right now and give it to me."

"What do you—"

"I can't go one more instant with this washed-out face of mine. My reflection's starting to disappear. We're trading blouses."

"Don't be silly. Your blouse would be too tight across the bustline for me."

I gritted my teeth and counted to ten, to no avail. "Stephanie, has it ever occurred to you that I don't *need* you to criticize my wardrobe, along with every little thing about me? I have kids for that."

"I'm just trying to be helpful, Molly."

"No, you're not. You have a compulsive need to make yourself feel good by trashing everyone around you. The only reason I'm allowing my day to be ruined by being in your presence is to find out who killed Steve Wilkins."

Stephanie tossed back her hair. "Well," she sniffed, "the answer to that one is obvious."

"Oh? Who killed him?"

"Why, Lauren of course. Everyone but you can see that plainly."

"Why are you so sure? The police occasionally arrest the wrong person. That can happen."

She snatched up her compact and dropped it into her purse as she rose. "Never mind about your blouse. Your bangs need trimming. You've got a big blind spot where Lauren is concerned. If you knew her as well as I do, you'd have realized long ago exactly what she's capable of." She opened the door, then paused and looked at me. "And yes, I *do* mean she's capable of murder."

FIFTEEN

You Call That an Unhappy Childhood?

TO KAREN'S DELIGHT, Rachel and Lauren spent virtually the entire weekend with us. My stitches seemed to be dissolving nicely, and even if I was maimed for life, my hair covered the scar. No one arrested, no one killed, no one threatened. So according to my new criteria, it was a great weekend.

Although Jim and I *did* have a very brief but infuriating phone conversation. He was in a vile mood from the start, complaining about test failures, schedule delays, and some Asian stomach flu he was battling. He never asked about how things were going at home, just said he had to get back to the bathroom so give the kids a kiss for him, then hung up.

Now that my marriage had become intercontinental, I was experiencing the negatives of marriage with none of the positives. It was like getting food poisoning from an intravenous feeding.

Sam Bakerton appeared at my door unexpectedly on Monday morning. His hair was slicked back on his egg-shaped head, and his bow tie emphasized his sharp Adam's apple.

He smiled at me rather shyly from the doorway and said, "Hello, Molly. Preston Saunders said you were looking for me on Friday. Did it have something to do with Denise?''

"No, no, nothing like that.''

He stuck his hands into the pockets of his mud-colored suit jacket and stared at me. He expected me to expand on my answer. I was going to have to think fast to come up with some plausible reason for supposedly having driven to Albany to meet with him, a man I barely knew. "Come on in. Can I get you something to drink?''

"No, thanks.''

He followed me into the living room, sat down in the chair opposite mine, and watched me. He had the nervous bearing of someone applying for a job.

Maybe since *I* had no answers, I could keep *him* busy giving answers. "Why did you think my visit had to do with Denise? Is she all right?''

"She's fine. I just couldn't think of any other reason you'd come all the way out to visit me.''

His nervous demeanor gave me an idea for an excuse. "I came to your office because I was thinking of applying for a part-time job. Do you have any openings?'' *Please, say no.*

"What type of job were you looking for?''

"Something that pays well, is fun, and requires only three hours a day.''

He raised an eyebrow but nodded solemnly. "I see. What are your qualifications?''

"None, really. Unless you happen to be looking for a greeting card writer. You're not, are you?'' Yikes. What if they wanted someone to write advertising copy? "Not that I can write just *anything*. My abilities are limited to greeting cards. Sadly.''

"I'll check the job board, but that's a fairly unlikely scenario.''

"Ah, well. It was worth a shot." I smiled at him, bu
he made no move to leave. May as well check into my
lead. "I just met someone who worked for you. Do you
know Cherokee Taylor?"

"Sure. Nice kid. Sharp as a tack. Too bad he wa
willing to do anything for an A, including trying to send
my company down the river."

I was surprised he'd be this open about the subject
My face must have registered that surprise, for he added
"Preston mentioned you seemed rather curious abou
some of our import policies."

"That was quite an intriguing report Cherokee wrote."

"How did you read that? It shouldn't be—" He
stopped himself. "That report was libelous. The only rea
son Preston and I didn't sue him was because Jack Vance
agreed to silence it. Mrs. Kravett was going to print it in
the *Gazette*, for God's sake."

"What exactly was untrue about it?"

"We haven't shipped ivory for years. The governmen
policy had a caveat that ivory imported prior to 1990
could be sold. Cherokee stumbled onto an old shipmen
that we didn't sell because we felt, legal or not, it jus
wasn't ethical. So we kept it in the back of the ware
house. He managed to find the one drug addict we'd ac
cidentally hired, and the two of them concocted the whole
thing."

"Cherokee's source for this report was a drug user?"

"That's right. An addict *and* a habitual liar, as junkies
tend to be."

"So the ivory is still at your warehouse?"

"No, we unloaded it so we wouldn't have to run the
risk of any more scandals."

"Sounds like you were being more than fair. So why

is it that Preston and Jack are still carrying such grudges against each other?''

"Preston isn't one to forgive and forget. Besides, I'm sure I don't need to tell you that Jack and Stephanie used to date in high school.'' He got up. "It's time for me to get to the office. I'll check the job board for you, Molly.''

I thanked him and followed him out to the driveway. I spotted Lauren through the window. She held up a coffee cup, pointed to it, then gestured for me to come over. I smiled and nodded, then dashed over without locking my house.

We chatted for a while over coffee. She chewed on her lip from time to time and frequently ran her fingers through her brown hair. These small nervous gestures were, to my eye, the only physical signs of the enormous emotional pressure she was currently under. As I watched her pretty round face, thoughts of what Stephanie had said about Lauren's being in my blind spot kept nagging at me. Finally she asked, "Is something bothering you?''

"It's an old subject, really. Lately, though, my mind keeps going back to it.'' It was uncomfortable talking about this now, but I needed to get it behind me once and for all. "Did you forgive me for what happened between Howie and me?'' There was no need to be more specific. Lauren knew I was referring to the graduation party.

She widened her eyes, but said, "Of course. Eventually. Once I realized what an untrustworthy spouse he would've made. And I knew you hadn't intended for it to happen.''

"I was so naive. If I could have changed only one incident from my teen years, that would be it.''

She frowned and gazed into her coffee cup. "The

whole thing was partly my fault. He got the hots for you as soon as you wrote that poem about Mrs. Kravett.''

That was an eye-opener. It had been such a painful incident that after she'd supposedly accepted my initial apology, we never mentioned it again. ''You're not serious.''

''Believe me, that's what did it. Your line about the twenty years since she'd had sex was a turn-on. He started obsessing on you. He asked me if you were a virgin.''

''Oh shit,'' I blurted. ''Did you answer him?''

She nodded. ''Unfortunately. Then he must have decided he was just the man for the job.''

My face was so warm my cheeks must have been fuchsia. ''I told you the truth, you know. We didn't have sex.''

''Yeah.'' She gave me a sad smile. ''He told me *you* wanted to, but he refrained.''

Anger instantly overtook me. ''That's a—''

She held up her hand. ''I always knew that was a crock. Your version of the story was much more believable.''

The truth, as I'd told her then, was that I'd gotten terribly drunk and needed a ride home. I'd hoped Lauren, Stephanie, or Denise could give me one in Stephanie's car, but they weren't around. Jack and Howie were nearby and relatively sober. Howie said he'd give me a ride in his car, and I accepted.

He was nice-looking and had a good sense of humor, so when he'd first moved to Carlton as a sophomore, I'd developed an unreciprocated crush on him. I thought of Lauren as a sister, so when he fell for Lauren, he naturally slipped into brother-in-law status.

That night, he drove in the opposite direction of my

house, but told me we were "just taking the scenic route." Stupidly, I believed him. He pulled over at a deserted spot, neither of us knowing that Stephanie and Lauren had been in Stephanie's car toking up, saw us drive past, and followed.

Howie said he wanted to talk and told me how serious he was about being engaged so young. In my drunken stupor, I agreed that they were too young and hoped they would wait before tying the knot. My concern was for Lauren, but he chose to take it as flirtation. Next thing I knew he was kissing and groping me in a most unbrotherly manner.

The kiss was soon interrupted. He claimed whoever was in that car shining their brights at us and honking the horn were friends having a little fun. So hang on, he'd told me, and he'd lose them. A few wheel-squealing turns later, we'd left poor Lauren and Stephanie, unbeknownst to me, in our dust, and Howie was telling me he was taking me to a hotel where he "couldn't wait to finish what we started."

I told him to take me home immediately or I was going to throw up all over his car. He could see I was prepared to act on the threat, so he dropped me off at home without further ado.

The next morning, Lauren wouldn't take my calls. Nor the next day or the day after that. Denise told me why and filled me in on the rest of the night's events. Lauren and Howie had broken up when Howie returned to the party a couple of hours later. Stephanie and Denise had then comforted my nearly suicidal best friend for two solid days.

I studied Lauren's face. "You know, Lauren, I have to take back that statement about the one thing I'd change. The one thing really would be that damned poem. If I hadn't written the poem, Howie wouldn't have suddenly developed the interest in me. And I wouldn't have gone through all that humiliation with Mrs. Kravett.''

Lauren shut her eyes and rested her forehead against both hands as if she had a terrible headache. When I asked if she was all right, she said, "As long as we're coming clean here, it wasn't Stephanie who printed your poem in the school paper. It was me.''

"What? Don't kid me about—''

She scooted her chair back noisily, got up, and crossed the room to lean against the counter. Though she turned toward me, she didn't meet my gaze. "I wish I *were* kidding. In retrospect, I did it to get back at you because Howie was obviously so hot for you after reading it. All he talked about during lab that afternoon was you. I was jealous.''

Rage seeped into me. "How *could* you? You knew Mrs. Kravett hadn't really struck you, and that I'd never want my false accusation spread around. I had no idea Howie would react like that, and I certainly wasn't responsible for *his* reaction.''

"I know that. Now. At the time, it was like I couldn't help myself. I was Stephanie's assistant editor. We had the whole paper set up already, but Howie was the one who ran the copier after school to print it. I convinced him Stephanie told me to run the new front page. Then later, I convinced him it was just a misunderstanding on my part.''

"How could you *do* such a thing! And then let me go all these years thinking it was Stephanie?''

"You don't know how many times I tried to tell you. For a long time after Howie, our friendship seemed too fragile to withstand that. After a while, it just got harder and harder to broach the subject.''

That was absurd. It would have meant so much to me to learn that I wasn't the only one who'd made mistakes during our friendship. I grappled with my shock. It was like learning your favorite childhood present from your dearest relative had been stolen from a store. "Why didn't Stephanie tell me?''

"I don't know. I guess because she's not the horrid person you make her out to be.''

"So you pay her back by sleeping with her husband.'' Ouch. Would that I had a delete key for my mouth.

Lauren turned her back to me and gripped the edge of the sink.

"I'm sorry,'' I said. "I had no right to say that. It was a counterpunch.''

"You'd better leave my house.''

My cheeks burned as I got up and left silently.

I was in a lousy mood when I got home. I vented it in the only constructive way I could think of. I drew a man lying on a psychiatrist's couch. The man is staring at the psychiatrist in dismay as the psychiatrist tells him, "You call *that* an unhappy childhood? Ha! When I was two, my mother deserted me. Then when I...''

CAROLEE STOPPED BY, her day off. I'd more or less forgiven her cup thievery, having attributed it to an impulse she could not control. Nonetheless, I ran a quick visual inventory and planned to lock up any valuables. The coast was clear.

Carolee's blond hair was pulled back into a neat, bouncy ponytail and her face sported its usual carefully applied makeup. Her shorts revealed her skinny limbs, which, though I'd seen them dozens of times by now, I still found visually distracting. I offered her a cup of coffee, which she accepted, and, being caffeined out myself, made a cup of Lemon Mist tea. "Have you talked to Lauren today?" I asked as I wrung out my teabag near the sink.

"No, why?"

Because I'm curious to know whether she's talked to you about our argument. But even I am not *that* blunt. "No reason."

We sat at my kitchen table. She stirred two full teaspoons of sugar into her coffee. "I owe you so much for introducing me to Tommy. He's just wonderful, in every way."

"You've gone out with him again?"

"A couple of times. We'd see each other every day if it weren't for our conflicting work shifts." She grinned slyly. "He is *such* a gentleman."

"I'm glad you two hit it off. It wasn't really my doing, though. You met at Lauren's house after the break-in. So she deserves the credit. Actually, the…burglar does." That thought saddened me. There *was* no burglar. It was her lover, Preston. God. On top of all my other troubles, had I lost my lifelong friend?

I glanced at my watch. "Whoa. I don't mean to rush you, but I've got to get out to meet Nathan's bus."

She took one last long sip of coffee and set the mug down. "That's okay. I've got to run, too. Catch you later."

I walked her out, then jogged down the block just as Nathan emerged. Once inside, he proudly presented to me a would-be square made out of Popsicle sticks glued together and colored with markers. I handled it carefully. The glue job was tenuous at best and would shatter with a badly placed breath.

"Oh, Nathan, this is wonderful," I said. I ever so gently placed it on the counter, ignored the ink that had transferred to my fingertips, and gave him a big hug. My first handcrafted-at-school present from him. This was one for Nathan's baby book, if only we were keeping one. Now came the hard part: figuring out what it was. "This is a picture frame, right?"

"No. My teacher says you can put hot things on it."

"Hot things?"

"On the table. Instead of pot holders."

"Oh. Of course. It's a trivet."

"It was my teacher's idea," he said.

Just what I always wanted. A flammable, fragile trivet that stains surfaces. "Would it be okay if we used it as a picture frame anyway?"

"No! It's for hot things on tables!"

I promised him we'd use it as intended during dinner and decided to, first, covertly use our hot-glue gun to reinforce Nathan's handiwork. Why would a teacher send a student home with a gift that was obviously going to break apart when used? Didn't she realize how upsetting this would be for her students, not to mention their parents? I would have to be sure to design an appropriate thank-you card for his teacher. Perhaps one that spontaneously combusts.

I started to clear the table to get lunch prepared. I picked up the coffee mugs and the sugar bowl. Then I noticed something.

My sugar spoon was missing.

SIXTEEN

Fax Me Some Paper

THIS WAS the evening from hell. My children bickered relentlessly. A few minutes after six, I fried some ground beef, mixed it with boxed macaroni and cheese, and served a side dish of applesauce straight from a jar.

Karen and Nathan brought their foul moods to the dinner table and periodically reached over the table to smack each other. In the midst of battle, Karen suddenly asked, "Why don't we go to church when Daddy's not here?"

"Because your dad's Catholic and I'm not," I snarled.

"Why aren't you Catholic?"

"Because I believe you can be spiritual without being institutionalized." That didn't come out the way I'd meant it, but I was talking to my seven-year-old daughter and I was damned cranky.

"You never say grace, either. Aren't you graceful?"

"No, not during dinner."

"But we—Nathan! Stop it!"

"Mommy! Karen hit me!"

"He hit me first!"

Through my teeth, I said, "You want us to say grace? We'll say grace. God is great. The food is so-so. Don't hit your brother; that's a no-no. Amen."

Through the grace of God, Karen laughed at my ad-libbing. That got Nathan laughing as well, and it looked as though we would live through the evening after all. A small victory, but a victory nonetheless.

The phone rang while we were clearing the dishes. It was still telemarketing hour, so I hesitated before answering. An owner of an office-equipment store wanted to know if I could design a faxable advertisement for her business. I assured her she'd found the right person for the job, and two hours later eagerly fired up the computer the minute I had tucked Nathan and Karen in.

Eventually I settled for a drawing of a man behind the counter of an office-supply store. He's listening to a customer say over the phone, "Our fax machine is out of paper. Could you fax us some right away, please?"

Later, it took me a long time to fall asleep. I was excited about the job I'd completed and the inroads I'd made into establishing a viable business for myself. Maybe *inroads* was too strong a word, but definite in-paths were being built. The children were healthy and happy when they weren't beating on each other. Nathan was adjusting to school nicely, as was Karen. Considering that someone had been murdered next door and Jim had been gone for a month now, these were not small feats. Despite formidable challenges and obstacles, I was handling single-momhood just fine. I felt proud of myself.

I AWOKE to the sound of breaking glass. I bolted upright in bed. It was still dark. My heart beat wildly. I was afraid to breathe loudly. I hoped against logic that the noise had been dreamed.

The scrape of a window opening. A dull thud. A footstep in the kitchen below me. I grabbed the phone and dialled 911. A female dispatcher answered.

In a quaking voice just above a whisper, I said,

"Someone's just broken into my house. My children and I are alone upstairs."

"You're at twenty-twenty Little John Lane?"

"Yes."

"A patrol unit is on its way. Stay calm."

"I've got to get my children."

"No. Stay put and don't talk. Stay on the line with me till the officers arrive."

"But my children—"

"Listen to me. The worst thing you could do now is startle the prowler. Are you certain someone is still downstairs?"

I listened. My bedroom door was ajar, as always. There was another thud. I couldn't tell from which downstairs room. "Yes. Oh, God. Hurry."

"They're on their way. Just another minute or two."

I held my breath, listening to the noises in the house. A floorboard creaked somewhere downstairs. That did it. I couldn't wait any longer. I rose.

"I've got to get my children. I'll leave the phone off the hook." I dropped the handset on my bed, held my breath, raced to Karen's room, and swept her into my arms. She groaned. I whispered, "Mommy's taking you to her bed tonight." After doing the same with Nathan, I locked the bedroom door and got into bed beside them.

Then I heard a sharp metallic click. The latch on the sliding glass door. I grabbed the phone. "The back door. Someone just opened it. Tell the police to come to the back door."

Moments later, I saw the flashing lights of a patrol car through my curtains. I no longer paid attention to the dispatcher, but listened instead to the policemen's heavy footsteps downstairs. Then someone knocked gently on my door.

"Ma'am? This is Officer Galloway. Are you all right?"

I sighed, overwhelmed with relief.

"Yes," I said in a near whisper. "We're all fine." I carefully got up without waking Nathan or Karen. "Would you mind slipping your ID card under the door?"

He did so, and I slipped on some gray sweatpants that matched the T-shirt I'd worn to bed, then opened the door to Officer Galloway. A stocky, white-haired man, he bore the same stern expression that was on his picture ID. I returned the card and followed him and a second, younger-looking, officer downstairs.

"See anything missing?" Officer Galloway asked.

I made a quick visual check of the kitchen. One pane in the kitchen window was broken. The screen had been slit. Nothing else was out of place or missing. I checked the dining room. "Oh, no. The brass candlesticks are gone. They're family heirlooms."

"Can you describe them to me, please?"

I gave him as detailed a description as possible while I checked the hutch, where my parents stored valuable antique plates and glassware. Still there. He followed me into the living room. Nothing missing. I went into the family room.

"The VCR's gone." That would not be an insignificant item to my parents, especially to my father who'd spent hours customizing its operation, but my concerns were now on my office equipment.

Officer Galloway escorted me downstairs. All of my computer paraphernalia was in place, to my relief.

Later, while Galloway and I shared decaffeinated coffee, the other officer took fingerprints. The powder made my kitchen even messier than it already was. Powder on the twenty-seven-inch TV. ''Why didn't he swipe the television?''

''The set's too heavy to be stolen by a solo perp. You're lucky there wasn't a partner.''

''I feel lucky just because no one came upstairs.''

After the police left, I cleaned up the glass shards too small for them to take as evidence and duct-taped cardboard in place of the pane. This wasn't that much easier to break through than the glass, just quieter.

I spent what little remained of the night lying in bed between my children who would otherwise have come to blows even in their sleep. I finally fell asleep a little after six and was awakened minutes later when my daughter popped her head up and said, ''Hey, what are we doing *here?*''

''I moved you here last night. I wanted the company.'' I'd decided to wait until after school to tell them about the burglary.

Nathan groaned that he was sleepy and didn't want to wake up. My sentiments exactly.

My head was pounding by the time the kids were ready for school. I was spurred on by the thought that as soon as they were gone, I could go back to bed. I felt absolutely dog sick and had quite a case of the shakes. I fell into a restless sleep.

The doorbell rang. I was disoriented. The clock read 9:18. For a moment I had to think, a.m. or p.m.? As I stepped into slippers, I nearly passed out and had to grab the dresser for support. My legs felt leaden as I dragged myself downstairs. Going through a night with no sleep always made me feel queasy and gave me a headache. But this was monstrous. I must be coming down with the flu.

It was Tommy. I opened the door and muttered "Hello," adding, "I'm not feeling well."

"Don't look so good, either. I saw 'bout your break-in last night on the blotter." He stepped inside. "Jiminy. Your house is hot." He walked over to the thermostat. "D'ya always set this at eighty?"

"The kids must have played with it. I've been asleep...didn't notice. I feel...so groggy."

Tommy's eyes suddenly widened in alarm. He took off his coat and wrapped it around my shoulders. "Get outside. Now. And stay out." He pushed me onto the porch and waved me farther back. "Go sit down away from the house. Are your kids at school?"

I nodded. As I wobbled my way down the cement steps, my slowed mind finally realized what was happening. Carbon monoxide. I'd been inhaling it for hours.

I sat on the edge of the lawn, staring at the house. A couple of minutes later, Tommy emerged. His face was almost as red as his hair. He took deep breaths of the chilly air, then propped my door open wide. He crossed the lawn toward me. "It's okay now. Furnace vents were blocked. House'll air out soon. Better get you to the hospital and—"

"Jesus, Tommy. The stolen candlesticks and VCR were just a ruse to make it look like a burglary. Last night, somebody intentionally messed with the furnace. Somebody tried to kill me and my children."

SEVENTEEN

Every Little Breeze

THE NEXT MORNING, the furnace was in normal operation, and Lauren and I had made our peace, of sorts. She spoke about it all being "water under the bridge." That was true. But how much water could relationships withstand before the bridge washed out?

During the past week, I'd kept my parents somewhat informed of my troubles, though my accounts were glossed over so as not to alarm them into notifying the National Guard. Specifically, they knew about the two deaths and my head wound. But I'd decided to wait to tell them about the break-in, for they would want us all in protective custody.

However, there was another bit of unpleasantry I could no longer delay. Stephanie Saunders. This was a person who hated me, maybe even enough to want to kill me. A visit to her might help me learn if she was the one who'd tried to asphyxiate my children and me.

Before I could get to the phone and set up a rendezvous, the doorbell rang. Surely this wasn't Stephanie reading my thoughts and glumming my day even more than I already was, a day after I'd narrowly escaped being murdered.

At the door was a barrel-waisted middle-aged man wearing a workman's uniform. A patch on the light blue shirt pocket read, Bob's Home Repair.

He murmured, "Came to fix your window, ma'am."

I watched him work as I dialed Stephanie from the kitchen phone. Fortunately his repair job required little bending or squatting. His particular body type had inspired the invention of the belt, but he wasn't wearing one. His was not a rear end I wished to be mooned by.

Stephanie was home, blast it all. By the time I'd made arrangements to go to her house, Man of Bob had completed his job. He hiked up his pants, which stayed in place for a half second. As he headed for the door, he said over his shoulder, "Must be a high-crime district. This is the third call we've had for a repair on Little John Lane in two weeks."

"You had two other repair jobs? At which houses?"

"Actually, both were next door."

Lauren's house. The kicked-in door was one repair, but what was the second? How could I ask him that without appearing incredibly nosy? "So you repaired their door. You did a nice job. What other type of work do you do?"

He grinned and gave me a lecherous once-over. "What type of *work* were you interested in having me do for you?"

Oh, spare me! I forced a smile. "The septic tank needs an overhaul."

He left abruptly.

I was determined to put on a good appearance for Stephanie so she wouldn't have cause to goad me into another argument. I applied makeup and changed into tan cotton pants and a Windex-colored blouse, since Windex was definitely one of my colors and Stephanie was sure to notice. Now I was all gussied up for someone I intensely disliked.

I drove slower and slower as I neared her house, but my sense of direction failed to fail me.

Stephanie, who in her flowing royal blue dress and elegant gold jewelry was nothing short of stunning, took me on a tour of her home. The huge country-style kitchen was done in hand-painted tiles, with windowpaned cabinets and copper pots on the walls. The family room was awash in maroon and earth tones. Navajo rugs and tasteful Indian statues graced the cherrywood bookshelves. We climbed a spiral staircase and viewed the bedrooms furnished with antiques, poster beds, oak dressers, and braided throw rugs on the hardwood floors. The three bathrooms each had separate shower stalls and sunken ceramic-tile tubs.

She finally led me to what she called her "sitting room," which I would've called a den, but we did sit in it so no sense nitpicking. She had a coffee carafe and cups waiting for us. This room had a cathedral ceiling that accentuated the stained-glass hangings and coffee table. No matter what I thought of the woman, her eclectic taste in home decor was flawless.

"Your house is gorgeous," I admitted as we settled into the couch, a flowered patten of rich, dark hues.

"Thank you. I did it myself. Perhaps you haven't heard. I'm an interior designer. Let me get you one of my cards." She started to rise.

"Thanks, but that's all right. I can't change the interior of my parents' house, nor would I want to, and we'll be moving back to Boulder afterward."

She sat back down and cocked a perfectly tweezered eyebrow at me. "After what?"

"My husband's assignment in the Philippines will be finished in August. We're going home to Colorado as soon as he comes back."

She leaned over, patted my hand, and said, "Of course he'll come back, darling."

I shot to my feet. "Excuse me for a moment. I left something in my car." Namely my self-control. And losing my temper now would defeat any possibility of my learning whether or not she had messed with my furnace. Did she hate me so much as to want to kill me? Hard to say, but she sure was one hateful person.

To allow myself to vent in private, I marched out, locked myself in the car and indulged myself in thirty seconds of foul language aimed at Stephanie. Afterward, I locked the car again, pocketed the keys, and reclaimed my seat in the sitting room.

Stephanie took a dainty sip of coffee, pinky extended, then set it down. "While you were gone I went ahead and poured for us. Did you want cream?"

"You poured my coffee?"

"Yes. Cream?"

Uh-oh. If Stephanie indeed wanted to poison me, my brief exit had given her ample opportunity. I looked in *her* cup, black, and said, "No, thanks," reasoning that this at least eliminated my chance of cream poisoning. I took a sip of coffee, praying it wouldn't be my last. It was an almond blend and was delicious. *Wait! Isn't there some deadly poison that tasted like almonds?* I set the cup down so fast, coffee sloshed into the saucer.

"Stephanie, let's get right to why I called you. You and I are radically different people. We're never going to be bosom buddies."

Focusing on my chest, she said, "You can say *that* again."

I silently called her several nasty names, but said only, "I'd rather not." A deep calming breath or two was in order. I reminded myself of the purpose for my visit: My plan was to give her the opportunity to slip up, to reveal knowledge she shouldn't be privy to. "Somebody has been sending me death threats."

"Death threats?" For just an instant, her eyes lit up, but then her expression became one of deep concern. "You poor dear! How dreadful. I had no idea!"

"So do you have any idea now about who might be doing this to me?"

She looked thoughtful for a moment. "None. Absolutely none. What exactly did the threats say?"

"I'd rather not go into that."

"Of course. Too painful." She sighed and shook her head. "When did you...receive these threats? And how? Were they mailed to you?"

So much for my plan. She would try to badger me into giving details, not reveal any herself. I decided to take a different tack. "Why didn't you ever let on that Lauren was the one who put that poem of mine in the school newspaper?"

"You're still worried about that? Good heavens. That was a lifetime ago." She sighed and delicately sipped from her cup. "There was no point in letting Lauren take the blame. I desperately wanted out of my editor's job anyway, while Lauren wanted the position. She begged me not to tell you, so I didn't."

Stephanie being decent without an ulterior motive? No way. "You let me go on all this time thinking you did it. Why?"

"It would've destroyed your friendship with Lauren. You and I never got along anyway, so why rock the boat? I figured it was the least I could do for Lauren."

I crossed my arms. "Lauren must've had something big to use against you."

She shrugged. "That, too. In a"—she gestured into the air—"weak moment I'd told her I hadn't been faithful to Jack. She threatened to tell him about my dalliances if I told anyone she was the one who published your tour de force.''

I grimaced.

She scoffed. ''I never claimed to be Mother Teresa, for Christ sake. But I've never sent you any death threats, if that's what you're getting at.''

As I studied her face, I was unable to decide if I believed her last statement. ''Stephanie, even though we can't be friends, we don't need to be archenemies either.''

''*Enemies?*'' She made a wry smile. ''That's a term I haven't used since grade school.''

The remark stung, and I found myself wondering how she could be so gifted at needling me in my most tender places.

She met my eyes. ''You never liked me, Molly. You made that clear from day one. It's not easy to care for someone who obviously dislikes you. But I've tried my best to like you anyway. That's all I can do.''

For once, I knew her words were the truth; I never liked her, and I like most people. She'd given me plenty of reasons for my dislike. ''Well, Stephanie, what can I say? I don't *care* about whatever it was that got us off on the wrong foot years ago. I *do* care about how you treat me now, and that is, in a word, badly.'' *Shitty* would've been more like it, but badly was descriptive enough.

She looked thoughtful for several seconds, then said, ''Sorry,'' as nonchalantly as a gesundheit after a sneeze.

That's it? Sorry? I watched her take another sip of coffee. Apparently that was all she had to say about the matter. She eyed my deserted cup. ''Don't you care for the coffee?''

"It's delicious, but I'm allergic to almonds."

"I'll brew something different for you."

"Thanks, but I should be going."

She walked me to the door, then said, "I'm glad we had this little chat. Drive carefully."

Automatically I thanked her for her hospitality, but staring into her blue eyes, all I could think was, This is a person I truly don't wish to spend time with.

As I drove home, I chastised myself. I'd learned nothing about whether or not she could have murdered Steve Wilkins or Mrs. Kravett. She *claimed* not to be the one threatening me, but I remained unconvinced either way. I did know that if I were Lauren and had slept with Preston, I would be watching *my* backside. Since I couldn't understand Stephanie, I couldn't predict her behavior.

At home, I went immediately to my office and checked my fax machine. Nothing. Why had Poison Pen stopped sending threats? Possibly the rationale was that the pen is mightier than the sword, but not mightier than carbon monoxide.

I sat at my desk and doodled, drawing two mice. Eventually the doodle led to an especially inane cartoon. Two mice are walking down a road on a windy day. In the air are the words *Psst. Swiss cheese.* One mouse says to the other, "Is it my imagination, or does every little breeze seem to whisper Swiss cheese?"

How could I market this? The song I'd gotten the idea from predated my parents, so I was probably one of the few people under fifty who remembered it. Who would buy the card? A convention of old cheese salesmen? As opposed to salesmen selling old cheese, I suppose.

None the less, I decided to scan it into my computer. I nearly panicked when my keyboard didn't respond, till I realized it had been disconnected. I plugged the keyboard cord in, unplugged it, then plugged it in again, trying to figure out how this had happened. Perhaps the same person who'd tampered with the furnace had disconnected the keyboard cable. But why?

I searched my disk, and looked for any time-stamps that indicated that someone other than me had used the computer last night. Everything checked out fine, but I ran the computer through an operation that flagged altered files. Still fine. Was someone's fiddling with my computer related to Steve's death while using his? But if so, why disconnect my keyboard? Maybe the motive had been to keep me in my basement office, near the source of the carbon monoxide, while I checked out my computer. If this were yesterday morning, prior to Tommy's discovery of the furnace problem, that might have proven to be very effective.

Feeling uneasy, I scanned the card into a file.

It occurred to me how well matched Stephanie and Preston were. Perhaps they had an open marriage and were both fooling around. If so, hopefully from now on it would be with equally hedonistic people.

That reminded me. I hadn't verified the rumor that Preston and Sam's import company was no longer under investigation. I dialed the enforcement office of the US Customs Service and suffered through a brief conversation with a customs agent who interrupted my every other word to say, "What?" Then he said, "I dunno anything about that. Let me let you talk to somebody else." To my relief, he put a woman on the line who both spoke and understood English. She referred me to an enforcement agent of the Fish and Wildlife division in the department of interior. Now *there's* a catchy job title.

He was a nice, helpful man whose name, given at the start of our conversation, was lost by its conclusion. I told him what little I could about Saunders and Bakerton Imports and how I'd learned those few disputed facts. He told me that, frankly, Preston and Sam had escaped prosecution by the "skin of an elephant's tusks." The company had insisted that the shipment had been received prior to January 1, 1990, and the government had lacked sufficient evidence to prove otherwise. Lucky for Preston and Sam. The smuggling plus conspiracy charges carried a maximum penalty of $250,000 and up to five years in jail each.

After hanging up, I sat thinking, back to my original question: Who had killed Steve Wilkins and Mrs. Kravett? In my various gyrations over the past couple of days, had I eliminated any of my dinner party suspects?

If anything, Lauren looked massively guilty. I was so mistrustful of Stephanie, I wouldn't drink coffee with her. As for Preston and Sam, that report of Cherokee's had already been examined and ultimately dismissed by the authorities. But could I say with any certainty that Cherokee's report had nothing to do with why two people were murdered? It didn't take a whole lot of thought to conclude I couldn't.

To put it another way, I had reached a dead end. And all I had to do to remind myself that time was running out for me was look at my heat registers.

THAT AFTERNOON, after both children had settled down for cartoons, I went downstairs. My fax machine had a message in the tray. I read:

You're still alive. Don't worry. Next time I won't go so easy on you. But I do wonder about your children. If you think they're safe from me, you're

wrong. Killing them would be all too
easy.
  If you were any kind of a mother,
you'd protect them. You'd leave town!

"Damn you to hell!" I smacked my desk with the heel
of my hand and stared at the letter. *First you threaten
me, then my marriage, now my children. Whoever's doing this is a summa cum laude graduate of the Marquis
de Sade Torture School.* "By God! I'm going to find you
and make you pay for this!"

This time the fax had been sent from a self-service
business center. Maybe the creep's computer was down.
I needed to show this threat to Tommy, and I would drive
it to the police station myself. But I had another stop to
make first, and there was no time to lose.

I got the kids in the car, and the three of us drove to
the business center. Inside were dozens of copier machines and four fax machines along one wall. Half of the
copiers were in use; none of the fax machines. At the
back of the store, an overweight woman in her late twenties or so sat behind the glass counter, reading a paperback.

Now to find a safe diversion for the children. To one
side of the counter was a display that held hundreds of
pens in some twenty shades. I told Nathan and Karen I
would buy them each a pen in whatever color the store
had the most of. They complained a little, but then dutifully started counting.

"How long have you been here today?" I asked the
woman.

She looked up from her book, studied me, then said,
"Too long. Why?"

"Have you been here for more than two hours? I'm

trying to get a description of someone who sent me a threatening fax from one of your machines. It was at twelve forty-eight this afternoon.''

The girl snorted. "During the lunch hour? Good luck. Place is a mob scene." She set her book upside down beside her and came toward me. "Bet we've had twenty to sixty customers today. Most never even come to the counter, just put money into the machines, use 'em, and leave."

Listening in one ear to Karen and Nathan count aloud, I handed her a list of names of everyone at my dinner party and asked her to compare the list to her checks and charge receipts. There were no matches.

"Did you see any blonde women about my age and size with really skinny legs, or a brunette less than five feet tall? Or a balding man with a ponytail? Or a man with an egg-shaped head? Or a handsome, classy, white-haired man?''

She shook her head and chortled. "Wow. Least *you* ask interesting questions. Most just ask me how to operate the machines or clear a paper jam."

"I've got a yearbook here. Whoever it was would be seventeen years older now, but I've marked the pages with their pictures."

"This is a joke, right?"

"Please, just look at the places I've marked and tell me if any of them look familiar." I opened the book to the first marked spot, where youthful Stephanie eternally beamed. I rotated the book toward her and pointed.

"Nah." She flipped to the next marked page, where Denise Meekers was shown. She shrugged. She shrugged again at the photo of Tommy Newton. She started paging through toward Jack Vance's and Lauren's photos, and suddenly stopped. "Wait!" She grinned. "I can't believe this actually worked, but the girl here looks real familiar.''

I looked at where she was pointing and sighed, realizing now what a futile exercise this was. "That's me."

She widened her eyes and looked from the picture to me, and back. "Gee, lady. You were sure ugly in high school. No offense."

EIGHTEEN

Where Were You?

THE NEXT MORNING was gray and drizzling, yet Nathan was in a wonderful mood, in contrast to his sister and mother. He sniffed the air at the bus stop and said with a big smile, "I love the smell of rain."

"So do I," I told him, and walked back home after the bus arrived thinking how much joy my children brought me. My life would be so diminished were they not here to remind me to stop and smell the rain.

It was all I could do to let Karen and Nathan out of my sight, but the police were aware of the threat I'd received yesterday and Tommy promised he'd keep them and the school under protective surveillance for the next several days. I'd even asked Tommy about bodyguards, but he convinced me that would do more harm than good. Also, he agreed with me that the thrust of the threat was that the sender wanted *me* out of the picture, not to harm my children. It made me all the more determined not to leave, but to solve this mystery.

I had misplaced my drawing pad and finally found it upstairs next to my bed. Searching for my pad reminded me how annoying it is to be looking for something in the presence of someone else, who invariably asks, "Where were you when you last had it?"

I emphasized that question's uselessness in a new card design. Two men are stranded on a tiny island. One is looking around at the sand by his feet. The compass is plainly visible next to the other man, yet he says, "Lost your compass again, huh? Where were you when you last had it?"

It occurred to me that I'd missed an opportunity to drum up some repeat business from the woman who'd ordered the faxable advertisement for her office equipment store. Though self-promotion is neither something I'm good at nor enjoy, I decided to take a trip into the city and show her my wares. I grabbed my stack of recent greetings and placed them in a manila folder, which brought my absent husband to mind. Why couldn't he have been stationed in Europe? We'd all have been thrilled to spend several months there. All of us except Nathan, that is, but he would have adjusted eventually.

It was still drizzling. Knowing the sweatshirt I'd worn while walking the kids to the bus wouldn't make a good impression, I grabbed a waterproof jacket from the closet, an olive-colored Gore-Tex. Stephanie would've said it sucked the color from my flesh. No doubt by the time I reached the store in Albany, people would wonder who the vampire in the coat was.

As I started out the door, I caught sight of the ceramic bowl on my refrigerator. I could return that bowl to Denise on a single trip from the house. Such efficiency.

The drive was long, slowed by traffic overreacting to the rain. I gave myself a pep talk to boost my confidence, and by the time I finally arrived, I was fired up.

The parking lot was empty, business apparently being adversely affected by the weather. I strode into the store, found a salesman, and asked to speak to the manager. He directed me to a woman at the counter. I gave her the prerequisite self-introduction and launched into my rehearsed spiel about how she could use my faxable greetings for demos in her store, as a gimmick to help sell fax machines.

Unlike when I rehearsed my speeches in the car, halfway through I ran smack into a basic coordination problem of mine. I can't talk and breathe at the same time when I'm nervous. I caught my breath before passing out and handed her my faxable card designs.

My nervousness grew, because the otherwise-unoccupied salesmen chose to come over and check out my presentation to their manager.

The manager grinned at my cards. She laughed and said, "I love the one with the mice and the whispering breeze."

"That's my favorite, too," I lied.

A salesman tapped me on the shoulder. "You have Rice Krispies stuck to the back of your raincoat."

This roused the curiosity of all three of the other salesmen. They also peered behind me. One said, "Yep. Those're Rice Krispies, all right. How'd that happen?"

The last time I'd worn this jacket must've been the time we were running late and I'd stupidly given Nathan cereal to eat in the car. A useful parenting tip those radio-talk-show counselors never give: When you've got to feed your children on the run, don't arm them with anything that'll stick to your backside.

I eyed the salesman who'd asked the question. He was in his early twenties, a definite nonparent. "I was at a wedding earlier this morning, and we threw rice cereal instead of rice at the bride and groom."

He nodded, not sure if he should take me seriously or not. Then the store manager thanked me for coming in and said she'd consider my suggestion, and I left with as much dignity as I could muster with breakfast food stuck to my derriere.

Denise lived near Stephanie. Judging from the outside, Denise's house appeared to be one or two steps down from Stephanie's; nice, though not nearly as well appointed.

To my surprise Sam opened the door. He was wearing jeans and a flannel shirt. For once, his brown hair wasn't greased back and hung down on his forehead in boyish-looking bangs. It was quite an improvement. "Hi, Molly. I'm so glad to see you. Come on in."

His friendly attitude made me leery. Last time someone greeted me with such open arms, Stephanie'd made me PTA secretary/treasurer. "Thank you. I'm just returning your bowl and wanted to thank Denise once again for the Jello-O salad."

Denise rounded the corner, smiling broadly. Her hair was in wild curls. With her petite frame and current carefree demeanor, she looked like a teenager. "Molly! You're here. How appropriate!"

"Appropriate?"

"Sam just quit his job." She wrapped her arms around his waist, and he grinned, resting his arm on her shoulders.

"It looks as though you're both happy about that, so congratulations."

"Yes, we're very happy," Denise said. "Thank you. And it's partly your doing."

"*My* doing?"

"That's right," Sam said. "If you hadn't forced Preston to rehash that whole business of Cherokee's report, I'd have probably gone along with the status quo for Lord knows how long. Now you've got him so anxious, it reminded me how bad things were last year when the investigation started. Everyone walking on eggshells around Preston, him carping at me constantly. I nearly quit then, and should have.''

I played dumb. ''So Cherokee's report had upset Preston?''

Sam rolled his eyes. ''The guy's willing to live his life one step ahead of prosecution. I'm not. I gladly sold him my half of the business. I'm going to do something I've wanted to do all my life.'' He grinned. ''I want to work at a grocery store.''

''Really. So you're applying for managerial jobs?''

''Nah. I'm starting at the bottom, like everyone else: Bag boy.''

It felt odd to be congratulating a man older than me for achieving the position of bag boy. ''That'll be quite a switch from business owner, but if that's what you want to do, I'm happy for you.''

Denise smiled at me and said, ''And guess what else? I've joined Gamblers Anonymous.''

''That's wonderful, Denise. If there's anything I can do to help, moral support or anything, don't hesitate to call.''

She thanked me. It was wonderful to see those two so happy. This was something we needed more of in Carlton and everywhere: happily married couples.

FIVE MINUTES or so after I'd reached my home, someone was leaning on my doorbell. The noise was so obnoxious I threw the door open without first looking through the window, intending to yell, ''WHAT!''

Stephanie, looking deathly ill, lunged inside and murmured, ''Gotta use your bathroom.''

She held her hand over her mouth and barely made it to the toilet.

''Can I get you anything?'' I called after her.

"Just close the door and leave me alone," she cried between groans.

I obliged, wondering exactly what had led her to this point. Our houses weren't even a five-minute drive from each other. Perhaps she'd awakened this morning and thought, I think I'm going to be sick to my stomach. Better drive to Molly's house and throw up there.

Then I chastised myself for not being more charitable to the poor woman. I glanced out my window. Her Mercedes was parked at a haphazard angle in my driveway. She must have been suddenly overcome as she neared my neighborhood. As soon as the bathroom noises ceased I knocked and asked if she was all right.

"That's a stupid question, Molly" came the answer through the closed door. She slowly emerged from the bathroom, my dampened washcloth covering most of her face. "If there's one thing I appreciate about you it's that you rarely ask stupid questions."

"Would you like to lie down on the couch?"

She kicked her shoes off, made her way to the couch, and lay down, spreading the washcloth to cover all of her face. "What I'd *like* is someone to serve as a surrogate mother for this baby. I'm pregnant. And by the way, that bathroom of yours could use some air freshener."

"You're *pregnant?*"

"Yes, and you're the first to know. Not counting me."

"That's wonderful. Congratulations."

"Call my husband and tell him I'm too sick to drive. You can reach him on his car phone. He's got to come get me."

And say what when he asks me what's wrong? "Oh, she's perfectly fine for a pregnant woman." That hardly seemed romantic. "How 'bout I just hand you the phone?"

Stephanie sighed, but accepted the portable phone. She dialed, waited a moment, then said, "Where are you?" Pause. "Good. Turn around and pick me up at Molly's house. I'm pregnant and puking my guts out." She hung up. "That ought to get him here in a hurry."

"Can I get you a glass of water or anything? Soda cracker? Pickle?"

She dropped the cloth back on her face and moaned. Then she said, "So how long have you known about Preston's affair with Lauren?"

Fortunately her eyes were covered, so I didn't have to mask my shock. "Um, about a week ago, Lauren told me."

"At least I've known longer than you. I found out at that damned party of yours."

Perhaps she'd taken my knife intending to use it on Lauren. "Did you take my carving knife?"

"Your knife? No. And if I had, Preston would've been the dead body, not Steve. As soon as Rachel said, 'Oh, hi Preston' and Lauren blushed, and Steve acted as if he'd just been goosed by a grenade, I knew. I restrained myself till we got home, of course." She snatched the cloth off her face and eyed me. "Tell you what, Molly, I missed my calling. I was born for the stage. Maybe there's some part for a pregnant actress on Broadway."

"So what are you going to do?"

"I think I'll start small. Local productions, that sort of thing."

"I meant, what are you going to do about Preston and Lauren, and your baby."

"Oh, that. I've told him he's on probation. One more screwup, literally, and he can kiss everything he's got good-bye."

"How did you know I knew about it?"

She frowned, refolded the cloth, and draped it on her forehead. "I didn't. But now that I *do* know you knew, thank you for not lording it over me."

That was a tough one to respond to, so I simply said, "You're welcome."

Just then there was a tremendous squeal of rubber on pavement. Before I could get to the window, the door flew open and Preston burst into the room. He was wild-eyed, panting. "Molly. I'm sorry. I was going too fast and had to swerve to miss Stephanie's car. I drove into your front garden."

"Well, I hope you ran over some rabbits."

My remark was ignored. He rushed over to Stephanie, who had managed to position herself with one arm over her forehead.

"Stephie, darling. My car phone isn't as clear as it should be. Did you say you were pregnant?"

"That's right."

Preston paled, then crumbled to the floor. For a moment, I thought he was overacting.

"Damn," Stephanie said, knitting her eyebrows. "He fainted. He did the same thing in the delivery room. Am I supposed to drive *myself* home now? God, how annoying."

NINETEEN

Catch You at a Bad Time?

WHEN PRESTON'S MERCEDES had left my dirt bed, I managed just barely to get my Corolla past the other, diagonally deserted, Mercedes. I glanced at the license place. STEFFY. No telling how long STEFFY would block my driveway. I'd decided to drop into the children's classes, mostly to reassure myself that they were safe there. Maybe Nathan would even deign to accept a ride home from me.

I tried the outside door to the kindergarten rooms and was glad to find it locked. A new sign said all visitors must enter through the main lobby and get a visitor's pass from the office. I dropped in on Karen's class first, but stayed only long enough to get a hug from her. Nathan's class was involved in a coin-sorting activity when I entered. The teacher passed a magnifying glass and a penny to her students and said if they looked carefully at the tail side, they would see the statue of Lincoln inside his memorial.

Nathan seemed reasonably happy to see me, though we were both more concerned with keeping our spots in line for the magnifying glass than with greeting one another. Impatient, I took advantage of my status as a moneymaking citizen and found my own penny. Sure enough, there was our tiny dead president, marginally visible with the naked eye. All that time I'd spent during childhood folding dollar bills so that George Washington's portrait looked like a green mushroom. To think there were a hundred little Lincolns to each mushroom, and I'd never even noticed.

At the bell, I led Nathan toward the office to return my pass. Ms. Barracuda was still there. She peered down her spectacles at us and said, "Mr. Vance wishes to speak to you, but he's stepped out."

Before I could reply, Jack Vance came around the corner, smoothing his ponytailed hair as if he'd just emerged from checking his looks in the men's room mirror. He said to me, "Just the person I need to see. You know quite a bit about computers. I found something interesting in our computer logs. Come on back."

I started to follow him into the office, but Nathan stopped so suddenly his sneakers squeaked.

"What did I do wrong?" Nathan asked.

"Nothing. I just need to talk to Mr. Vance."

"Every time someone goes to the principal's office it's 'cause they're bad." His little downturned face was frozen with fear of punishment.

"That's not true, Nathan. Not this time. Neither of us did anything wrong. Did you know I used to go to school with Mr. Vance?"

Jack doubled back and knelt in front of Nathan. "Would you feel more comfortable in the nurse's office next door? There are some books and games in there you can use."

Nathan nodded, still too scared to look up from the floor. We led him into the nurse's office, which was currently empty.

"My office is right next door," Jack said. "If you want your mommy before we're through talking, just knock on this wall."

After ensuring that Nathan felt reasonably happy, I followed Jack into his office. I took a chair in front of his desk while Jack remained standing behind his desk, flipping through some papers. "Do you have any children, Jack?"

He sighed. "Five hundred and eighty-three in this building alone. That's, of course, not counting the ones in high school and junior high the other two principals are in charge of." He gave a little shrug. "But to answer your question, no, though that hasn't left a crater in my life, considering my line of work." He lifted a short stack of computer paper and waved the top sheet past my face. It appeared to be a list of names with one entry that had been highlighted in yellow.

"See this?"

Instead of actually showing me what it was I was supposed to see, he held it up so *he* could read it.

"One of the first things Steve Wilkins did was set up the computer to print out records of which users have logged on to the system each day. He said he was going to use the printout to help him analyze our needs. He had the master report set so that he could print a daily and a weekly record of all users."

"So did anyone print the master report on the day Steve was killed?"

"No, unfortunately. And since then, the data got overlaid. That was a Saturday, so if we had thought of it on Monday we could have printed it. But Steve had only just started his work here, and it took me a few days to figure out what he'd done so far and how to get the reports I wanted."

"Back when they arrested Lauren, Tommy told me about some report that showed that Steve *hadn't* been logged on to your system that day."

"Right. I didn't know about the master report of all users then. All I knew about was the monthly reports Steve had set up for each user."

"Oh," I cried, excited. "So you're saying you gave Tommy the printout of *Steve Wilkins's* log-on, and he hadn't used the system that day under his *own* user ID. So whose unexpected user ID *did* the reports show?"

Not to be rushed, Jack held the papers against his chest. As if he hadn't heard my last statement, he said, "I naturally assumed that Steve always signed on to the system using his own ID."

"Right, right, but the day he died he didn't. He used someone else's. Whose? Yours? Mrs. Kravett's?"

"You see, Molly, we didn't have a policy concerning what to do with the user reports, since Steve died prematurely. Just today, I asked my secretary to sort through them all and stick each user report in the corresponding teacher's box."

He paused. At this point, I was ready to sock him. What was he doing? Trying to drag this out to the commercial break? What in blazes did the report show?

"My secretary gave me this report a few minutes ago. She didn't know where to file it, for obvious reasons."

At last, he lowered the report and I snatched it from him. The report was for the user ID KRAVETT. It showed her logged on to the computer for two minutes. The date was a week ago Saturday, the day Steve died, almost a week after Mrs. Kravett had died.

"If only this listed her password, we'd be all set."

"Right," Jack said. "But remember, Steve wasn't going to take the system down to *find* the password in the computer base until the following day. So he must've figured out the password himself, otherwise he couldn't have logged on as KRAVETT."

"Maybe, but not necessarily," I replied. There was no way of knowing for certain that it was Steve who'd logged on as Mrs. Kravett. It could have been anyone. "Are there any other teachers who might have known her password and logged on as Mrs. Kravett?"

"Steve Wilkins asked every single person with an authorized sign-on, and not one of them knew her password."

"Or admitted to knowing it. Did everyone know the computer would be recording their computer usage?"

He nodded emphatically. "Absolutely. So they all should've been aware that this report showing that someone signed on as Mrs. Kravett would show up eventually."

"Okay." My mind raced. Steve *was* the most likely person to have signed on. Perhaps he'd signed on to the system and pulled up files of Mrs. Kravett's that were so incriminating someone stabbed him before he could divulge what was in them. "All we have to do now is figure out Mrs. Kravett's password ourselves, and we'll have our killer. Steve once told me a lot of computer users make the mistake of making a password personal so they can remember it."

Jack rotated his screen to face me, then scooted his chair beside me. I looked at him, hoping he might spout the name of Mrs. Kravett's dog or something that would magically bring up her secret files. Instead, he said, "The restrictions on our passwords are that they have to be two to eight characters long, with at least one number and one letter."

"That narrows it down," I said under my breath. We would be here forever. "It has to be something Steve could've figured out, even though he never had Mrs.

Kravett as his teacher. What room number did she have?"

"Two-oh-two."

I tried combinations of the number plus a letter: 202A. 202B. A202. B202. 202KRAV. Nothing. I could go on like this for hours and not get any place.

"Did Steve ever ask you what room number she had?" He shook his head.

"Did he ask you any personal questions about her, as if he were trying to figure out her password?"

"No, and now that you mention it, that seems odd."

"He didn't ask, so...maybe he looked it up. Have you got our old yearbook around? Steve would've had access to that through Lauren."

"It's at home."

There was a knock on the wall.

"Mine, too," I said to Jack. "Just a minute," I hollered to the wall.

A thought hit me like one of those lightbulbs-over-the-head in cartoons. Lauren had probably told Steve about my poem about Mrs. Kravett. She may have even saved a copy of the school paper. If so, there was a number-letter sequence within it that he may have thought to try. I held my breath and typed: 20YEARS.

The screen changed, signing me on as KRAVETT and giving me full access to her private files. A directory appeared. There was only one file in it. The file was named PTA.DOC.

"You did it!" Jack cried.

"Yeah." I swiveled in my chair, glad to see that Jack looked sincerely pleased and wielded no murder weapons. "But surely this *wasn't* the file someone was willing to commit murder to hide. *That* file was probably erased."

Jack shook his head. "I disagree. Steve was an experienced security consultant. He wasn't so stupid as to pull up some file right in front of a potential...hacker...stabber...whatever." He spread his hands and donned his patient-teacher voice. "Let's suppose Lauren's innocent, right?"

"That's easy. She *is* innocent."

"So the killer had to be someone *Steve* let into his house. And, if Steve knew he had a guest after he'd signed on to Mrs. Kravett's private disk, you can bet he'd sign *off* of her disk before letting 'em into his office."

I thought for a moment, then shook my head. "Steve would have simply exited the system and run a screen saver. He would never have pulled up some personal letter he wouldn't want anyone but Lauren to read."

Jack tapped the sheet of paper that listed how long KRAVETT had used the computer on Saturday. "But, Molly, Steve was only logged onto the computer for two minutes. That's no time at all."

"It's an eternity for a computer. Besides, how long do you suppose it takes to type a delete-file command?

A pounding on the wall.

"Not now, Nathan. Just a minute." I returned my attention to Jack. I was still unconvinced, but was willing to concede that his theory was within the realm of possibility. "Well, maybe you're right, Jack. Let's take a look at it." With trembling hands, I executed the commands that let me display the file.

To Whom It May Concern:

Denise Bakerton has been taking funds from the PTA to pay for her gambling debts. I'm covering those debts and intend to continue to do so. My personal funds are more than sufficient, and I can

easily afford this. I'm doing everything in my power
to help Denise, to convince her to seek professional
counseling.

Sincerely,
Phoebe Kravett

"Oh, my God," Jack muttered. "Denise?"

"That's too weird. Even *I* knew about her gambling
problem. Why would she kill to protect it?"

"Exactly. We *all* knew about her gambling."

"It's time we showed this to Tommy Newton. Excuse
me while I see what Nathan wants."

"DON'T MEAN DIDDLY," Tommy said as he read our
printout of Mrs. Kravett's file. Jack had called Tommy
only a few minutes earlier, while I was in the teachers'
lounge wrestling up some lunch for Nathan. If you considered a bag of popcorn and a can of soda *lunch*. "Might
help us pin down the time of death, is all. At that time
Saturday morning, Steve was home. If he *was* signed on
using Mrs. Kravett's ID, he had to have used his modem.
We'll compare phone message units. Even still. Call
could've been placed by the killer afterwards." He glared
at me. "Actually, it does mean one thing significant."
Tommy leveled a finger at me. "You're still buttin' into
police business."

"That's *my* fault. I asked her to," Jack said gallantly.

"Uh-huh."

"It *also* means that someone other than Lauren had a
strong motive to kill Steve Wilkins and Mrs. Kravett," I
said.

Nathan knocked on the wall. He must have finished
his popcorn.

"How you figure?" Tommy asked as I stood up.

"He'd signed on to Mrs. Kravett's system minutes before he was killed. He'd just called up the letter to Lauren to cover his actions."

"Or maybe Lauren stabbed him in the back, just as we figured all along."

I met Tommy's glare with one of my own, then turned toward the door. *Fine. Be that way.* Now I knew why Mrs. Kravett had predicted that Tommy might become an accountant. He was stodgy and ploddingly methodical. "I've got to take Nathan home."

"Thanks for your help, Molly," Jack called after me.

I drove home, utterly frustrated. There was a reason I was a greeting card writer and not a criminal investigator. I had just exhausted the very best lead I'd had so far, and it took me exactly nowhere.

Nathan played in my office while I sketched out a design that was, well, tasteless. My rationale had been this: The vast majority of cards are purchased by women. A well-known fact. Though computer usage between males and females was probably about equal, the majority of computer equipment was *purchased* by men. Therefore, to catch the eye of fax machine buyers and users, I wanted to try some male humor. My husband and son always laughed at scatological references, but I didn't want to sink that low. On the other hand, sexual jokes…It was just a design. That didn't mean I had to market it.

I drew a man clutching a sheet around himself as he opens the door for a priest. Behind the man is his bed, where two voluptuous women are sitting, wearing only hats with woolly sheep ears. The priest is saying to the man, "Did I catch you at a bad time?"

I stared at the drawing for a while. How demoralizing. I filed the thing, thinking if I decided to give up greetings, this one might sell to *Penthouse* magazine. Wouldn't *that* look nice on my résumé. Right above the line about being a mother of two. I ran back upstairs to my son.

"Nathan, let's go over to Lauren's house. If she's home, maybe we can wait there till Karen and Rachel's bus comes."

Nathan jabbered to me about something as we walked. I answered him mindlessly, hoping not to be caught agreeing to something dreadful, but unable to concentrate on his words. Lauren answered her door quickly. She winced and said apologetically, "Molly, I'm sorry. This just isn't a good time."

Not a good time? Talk about life imitating art. Was Preston's Mercedes hidden on some back street again? "That's okay. I was—"

"It's all right, Lauren" came Carolee's voice from within. "She may as well hear about this now."

"Come on in," Lauren said. "Hi, Nathan. Want to go play in Rachel's room while I talk to your mom?"

Nathan looked at me, and I put on my oh-so-happy mother's face, which roughly translated to: Let's all pretend you don't know we want you out of the room. He went along with it and climbed the stairs. My, but was I falling in debt to that little guy. He'd spent a good half hour in the nurse's office. Now he was in someone else's room, alone with her toys. Not that that was exactly Chinese water torture.

I followed Lauren into the kitchen. At the table sat Carolee, her eyes red-rimmed and puffy. On the table was a pile of small items. I recognized my sugar spoon right away. So, the klepto comes clean was my first thought. I was glad I hadn't blurted such a nasty thing.

"Hi, Molly," Carolee said. "I've asked for Lauren's help to try and figure out who owns this stuff I've nabbed over the last couple of years. Guess this is no big surprise to you, is it?''

"Uh..." There was no good answer to that question. I looked at Lauren. She was red-faced. She had introduced me to Carolee. In a letter Lauren had written some time ago, she'd first mentioned Carolee as the wonderful person who'd bought the house across from her parents. Lauren's expression told me she had never suspected this in all that time. "Could I get myself a glass of water?"

"Let me get it," Lauren said, seemingly grateful for the chance to turn her back on the situation that had developed in her kitchen.

I took a seat. Carolee and I studied one another. She said, "I was fired from the hospital today."

"Why?"

"I have these"—she gestured at the tableful of hot items—"impulses at work too, occasionally. But this is a big first step for me. Admitting my problem to my friends, I mean. I'm pretty sure the hospital will rehire me, once they can see I've reformed."

"Have you told Tommy?"

"Not yet."

"That's going to be...interesting." Talk about a couple with conflicting careers.

Lauren set the glass down in front of me and pulled up the nearest chair. She stared at the pile and removed from it a corkscrew with a chipped handle. "Always wondered where this went. I figured Steve had lost it."

There was an awkward silence.

"So, Lauren, Molly, I wonder if you two would write letters of recommendation to my bosses. Tell them that you'll vouch for me, that I've learned my lesson, that sort of thing?"

What nerve! How could *I* vouch for Carolee even if I

wanted to? What would I say? She only stole a cup and
a spoon from me—never a full place setting, so by all
means, give her her job back?

Lauren and I exchanged glances. She grimaced,
slapped the table, and said, "Why sure. That'll get you
rehired in no time. Just tell your boss I murdered my
husband, and I can tell a reformed criminal when I see
one."

Carolee blushed, and my cheeks grew warm. Without
another word, Lauren rose and left the room.

TWENTY

I Missed a Step

I LEFT WITH NATHAN promptly after Lauren's remark, with the excuse that I'd decided to wait for the bus outside, in case it came early. Minutes later, we met Karen, told her that, no, it wasn't a good time to have Rachel over, and went home.

Since tomorrow was Friday, my weekly call from Jim, I decided I might as well fax him a letter getting him at least partially caught up on our goings-on. When we'd last spoken, I hadn't told him about finding my missing knife in Steve Wilkins's back. I'd also not mentioned the faxed threats.

After some twelve years of marriage, I had a pretty good idea he was going to be, oh, a little miffed at me for not having kept him apprised of the situation. Justifiably so. I had plenty of excuses: not having his number at the temporary hotel, not wanting to burden him while he was vomiting, time flying by while scared for one's life, not wanting to alarm him when there was nothing he could do.

None of these excuses withstood scrutiny. I could have and should have sent daily faxes to Jim at his office in Manila. That no such messages were sent was a clear indication that I was punishing him for being overseas when I needed him, even though that wasn't by his choice. I'd become the stereotypical, PMS-afflicted female, prone to whining, "If you don't know what's wrong I'm certainly not going to tell you."

Yet every time I told myself to get on the horn and let Jim know what was happening to his beloved family, part of me rebelled—argued that Jim might well fly home, lead the cavalry to rescue poor helpless me. That would've made Jim feel great about himself, but what about *my* ego? By God, I didn't need or want to be rescued. Yes, Jim, you had a right to know your family was in jeopardy, but bottom line, it *was* your decision to accept your boss's request to take a year-long assignment in the Philippines at the drop of someone else's hat. You knew full well how hard that would be on me and the kids. You went along with the overseas assignment, so unwilling to make waves at work you wouldn't even dare test the water. And by the way, you leave toothpaste splatters all over the mirror. Do you have to stand that close to your reflection? Don't you know where your teeth are by now?

With the tune for *Full House* screaming from the TV set, I wrote a letter:

Dear Jim,

I know this is going to come as a big shock to you and I'm sorry to tell you this way, but I'll just give you a quick breakdown of the events of the past couple of weeks.

Two weeks ago on Monday, I got two threatening faxes accusing me of being at fault for the death of some unidentified woman. The woman was apparently Mrs. Kravett, whom you might recall was the subject of that poem in my school paper that I told you about. She had a heart attack, but the police found someone had tampered with her medication.

After the dinner party here, my knife was stolen. I got a help message I thought was from Rachel, but went over there and found Steve Wilkins stabbed to death with my knife. A couple of days later, Lauren was arrested for the murder. She got out on bail and is awaiting trial. I used to be certain she was innocent, but lately I'm starting to have doubts.

Then Monday night, someone broke into our house and stole the VCR and the brass candleholders. That was just a ruse, though, because they also jerry-rigged the furnace to pump carbon monoxide at us. The furnace has since been fixed and we're all healthy.

I'm sure you're upset with me for keeping you uninformed till now. My doing so has made me realize that deep down, I'm bitter that you chose to accept the assignment in Manila without putting up a fight. On the positive side, the time we've spent apart has also helped me realize that you and I are married because we choose to be together, not out of fear that we couldn't function separately.

When you call tomorrow, we should discuss the possibility of the kids and me renting a house for the year and returning to Boulder.

                                        Love,
                                        Molly

I didn't especially care for the idea of my letter sitting on his fax machine till he got into work, so I calculated the time in the Philippines. It was 4 p.m. in New York, which made it 5 a.m. in Manila. Jim would be at work in an hour or two.

I waited till dinnertime here, then sent it. Not fifteen minutes later, Jim called. "I'm at work now, so I can't stay on the phone for long." His voice was a couple of octaves lower than normal, which meant he was deeply hurt. "I've been in contact with my boss every day this past week. I'm still trying to get reassigned to Albany. None the less, the best thing to do under the circumstances is for you to get yourself and the children back to Boulder as soon as possible."

"That's what the person sending the threats has wanted all along." As soon as the words were out of my mouth, I knew that was the angle I should have been looking at this from all along. *Why* did someone want me out of town?

Jim said something. I asked him to repeat it.

"Some murderer wants you to leave town, you leave town," he said pointedly. "We're parents and we need to protect our children, not try to outdraw the fastest gun in the West."

This was the East, but no point in quibbling. "I agree. It'll take a few days for me to make the arrangements. I'll have to notify all my customers and run new ads that say I'm going to have a new address and fax line. Then I'll—"

"You can't do that, Molly! If you run new ads and let the world know where you'll be, you'll be telling whoever's got it in for you where to find you!"

"So what am I supposed to do? Close my business? Give up everything I've worked so hard for? Spend the rest of my life looking over my shoulder?"

He didn't answer, but I thought I heard a sigh.

"This is so unfair," I said, struggling to keep my voice steady. "All I wanted to do was raise my children to the best of my ability and still be my own person. I shouldn't have to give up my business. Should I?"

There was a long pause. "I don't know. I'll talk to you

tomorrow night. We'll figure something out." He hung up.

The children were quiet as I dished up our spaghetti: Karen, sauce on the side; Nathan, no sauce, butter, three tablespoons of parmesan cheese. We go through a lot of parmesan cheese at our house.

"Are you sad, Mommy?" Karen asked.

"'Fraid so." In truth, I was very close to losing my battle not to burst into tears. "Do either of you know any jokes to cheer me up?"

Nathan said, "How about a song?" He started singing in a loud voice, "Old MacDonald had a poop."

I burst into laughter and tears, then postponed dinner for a lengthy three-way hug, while I assured my children that no matter what happened, everything was going to be okay because we had one another.

After tucking them in their beds, I lost track of how long I just sat on the couch, staring, trying to figure out why the killer wanted me to leave so badly that he was willing to call attention to himself. If it weren't for the faxes, Mrs. Kravett's death might have remained the perfect murder.

Though I ran everything around in my head countless times, I couldn't answer that one. Finally, I took my frustrations out by composing a cartoon. A man on a bridge is reading a document entitled "Bungee Cord Assembly Instructions." In his hand is the unfastened end of the cord, and in the background are feet in the air belonging to someone who has just jumped off the edge. The man with the instructions is saying, "Oh, wait a sec. I may have missed a step."

LATE IN THE MORNING the next day, I trotted over to Lauren's house. She looked exhausted, and sorely in need of good news. I didn't have any. I told her about Jack and my figuring out Mrs. Kravett's password yesterday, and the disappointing outcome of finding only the one letter about Denise's gambling.

I said, "There's only one reason I can think of that someone would risk sending me threats and letting on that Mrs. Kravett's death wasn't a simple heart attack. Greed. Someone did this who might have inherited the money and hoped to get me out of the picture to stop the scholarship fund."

"At one point, before Denise developed a gambling problem, *she* would've been the logical person for Mrs. Kravett to choose to control the fund. The two of them were very close. Maybe Denise was hoping to get rid of all the evidence about the gambling, and drive you away so she could take your place. Maybe her husband was in on it, too."

"That could be. I wish we had some proof, though."

Lauren sank farther into her chair in the living room. "What was the password?"

"'Twenty years,' like in my poem."

She winced. "So Steve was trying to guess what Mrs. Kravett's password was when he died. Maybe that explains why the police found my box of memorabilia from school in his office."

"They did? Nobody told me that."

She chewed on her lip for a moment, then said, "Your poem had been clipped out of my old newspaper."

"Then *that's* where someone got the copy of it to send to Mrs. Kravett. Why didn't you tell me that right away?"

"When you first told me about it, I didn't even stop to think it might have been from my old paper. I had my hands full with my marriage breaking up. Then, when the police showed me the clipped-out page after I'd been arrested, I figured you might think *I* did it.''

I paced, combing my fingers through my hair. "You were set up. First the killer makes it look like I'm a maniac sending threats to my teacher. Then he makes it look like you're behind it." I headed toward Steve's office. "Can we go through Steve's office together?"

"Why?"

"I've got a strong feeling we've all overlooked something that might point to who really killed him."

Lauren followed me into the office. His desk chair was gone, probably removed by the police as evidence. In the far corner was a storage box. *Carlton Central* was written on the side in Lauren's handwriting. I pulled another chair up to his computer and tried not to think about the fact that this was Steve's position when he died.

"I don't know what you could possibly find," Lauren said. "The police took everything they thought was important."

I turned on Steve's main computer and fax machine. "I don't know how much you know about fax machines, Lauren, but they keep a running log of their most recent communications. The log shows when and where documents were sent to or received from. Except, of course, in *my* case with the death threats. Since the sender suppressed his phone number and user ID, all my machine recorded for those was the time and number of pages I received. Has anyone printed the log from this fax machine?"

"Yeah. The police printed it. They showed me three transmissions to your house and asked me to identify them."

"What were they?"

"The first was that fax Rachel sent to Karen, and the

second was your response. When you asked her to have me call you. The third turned out to be that bogus help message supposedly from Rachel. The police took the log with them, along with the original help message.''

"I'll print another log."

Moments later, Lauren and I were looking at the report, and just as she'd said, there were only the three transmissions to or from my fax line.

I punched my thigh. "Damn. Another dead end." I looked around the room making a quick appraisal of how many fax machines Steve owned. "He's got a second fax machine and a couple of notebook computers. They may have built-in data/fax modems. We'll have to check their logs."

"Why? What are you looking for?"

"Even though my fax machine couldn't record the number of the sender, the machine that sent the fax to me has to log *my* number as the receiver."

"What makes you think it's one of Steve's fax machines?"

"Because *everyone* knows phones can be traced. So the person who sent those faxes to me wouldn't have wanted to risk using their own home phone or business phone."

"So? If I were doing this, I'd use a portable computer, go to a phone someplace where I wouldn't be seen, call you, and send my threatening fax from there. I wouldn't use someone else's phone and fax machine."

"Exactly. But if you wanted to make someone *else* look guilty, you'd use *their* machine and *their* phone, right?"

"Oh! I see what you're getting at," Lauren said. "But wouldn't the police have already done this?"

"Probably. And that's just what the person setting you up wanted."

Lauren said, "The thing is, though, with our house alarm, nobody could... Preston! Oh my God. What if he really *was* trying to break in through the office window?"

We printed out Steve's second fax machine's log.

The last three entries were for one-page documents sent to my fax line. Two transmissions were made on the Monday afternoon before school started. The third was made a few hours after my party—a couple of minutes after midnight. I pounded the desk with both hands. "I knew it. These are the first two threats. The third was when I got an anonymous fax accusing me of not being a good wife."

Lauren grabbed both of my shoulders and shook me. "I'm cleared! This proves I didn't do it!" She put a hand to her chest. "I was at the grocery store both of these times on Labor Day, and at the hotel fighting with..." She stopped suddenly, then winced and cried, "Oh, shit! I just thought of something. This may not have anything to do with Steve's murder. Steve might have sent you those threats himself."

"What?" I cried, utterly shocked.

"He could've had his fax machine with him on Monday when he was at some client's office. And that Friday, it was all so crazy. Steve followed us to the hotel and grabbed Rachel. I sneaked back home a couple hours later, snatched her out of bed, and checked into a different hotel. He might've sent the third threat when I wasn't around."

Still stunned, I stared at her. "Why would Steve have sent me threats?"

"I don't know. He went a little crazy when he first

found out about my affair. He put his fist through a wall, and I had to hire someone to come fix it."

"Man of Bob," I murmured as I studied the guilty fax machine. That would have been the unexplained repair call to our street. "But Lauren, this fax machine is programmable. You can read a fax into its memory and specify the time it will be sent. You don't need to physically be here operating it."

Lauren's spirits deflated so abruptly it was like watching the air go out of a balloon.

"Besides, it couldn't have been Steve. I got a fourth threatening fax just a couple days ago. I never told anyone but the police about it. *That* one was sent from the self-service center."

Lauren chewed on her lip. At length she said, "It doesn't look good for me. This is just one more piece of evidence pointing at me. Tommy won't believe I didn't know how to program the fax." She searched my eyes. "*You* believe me, don't you?"

"Yes." I averted my eyes. I did believe her. But no matter what I tried, I couldn't prove it. I combed back my hair in frustration.

"Wait." I whirled around in my chair to look at the box in the corner. "When did your storage box get moved down here?"

"I have no idea. I keep all that stuff in the attic, and I rarely go up there or into Steve's office. Why?"

"That poem was sent to Mrs. Kravett *before* her death. So when Steve brought this stuff down to his office, he saw that the poem had been cut out. Didn't he ask you about it?"

She shook her head and said, "We were barely communicating by then. The *last* thing he cared about then was—" She broke off abruptly and her eyes widened. "I just remembered. You told both of us about Mrs. Kravett's getting that poem when you picked your kids up after the PTA meeting. Afterward, Steve didn't say anything about it. But then just before your party, he asked me if I remembered what the poem said, and I recited what I remembered and told him he could find it in the attic if he was so curious. Then he made some remark like 'You can't be truthful about anything.' I never found out what he meant.''

"He might've meant that he'd already learned the poem was missing."

Lauren nodded, her face pale. She wrapped her arms around her waist and leaned down as if ready to faint. "I have a terrible feeling. Putting together some of the things Steve said to me the last time I..." She paused, and after a moment of reflection, she said, "He thought *I* was sending you those threats. I'll bet he checked the log on his second fax machine, then he saw the poem was missing. He thought *I* was responsible."

Lauren looked so wounded by this realization, it wasn't my place to point out to her that only minutes before, she'd accused Steve of the very same crime.

It hit me then how truly evil this murderer was. It wasn't enough to kill someone, or even two people. All the survivors wound up mistrusting one another. My friendship with Lauren was perhaps irreparably damaged. Lauren's memories of her husband were destroyed.

Here at last was the motive I could never find for Stephanie Saunders. She's pregnant. She learns her husband is having an affair. She wants revenge against his mistress. Perhaps she knows Lauren has a habit of going through people's medicine cabinets. She kills Mrs. Kravett merely to make Lauren look guilty and points a finger at me as well, to keep Lauren's best friend from rallying to her defense. Then she kills Lauren's husband, as the ultimate way to get even.

"That's it!"

"*What's* it?" Lauren asked.

I grabbed the logs from the two fax machines. "Listen, I'm going to run home and check these against the log for my machine. Can you meet Nathan's bus?"

"Sure. But what did you just figure out?"

"I think I know who the killer was. But I still don't have any proof, so I don't want to say just yet. Bring Nathan to my house. Maybe by then I'll have this figured out, all right?"

My head was in a whirl as I went home. All I could think about was what Tommy would say as I tried to explain my reasons for suspecting Stephanie. He would tell me again about needing evidence, not woman's intuition.

My theory had one craterlike flaw: the Wilkinses' alarm system. Even if Stephanie had managed during a social call at the Wilkinses' to sneak unseen into their office and program all three faxes in advance, she couldn't know that Steve wouldn't be in his office at those times. Possibly she'd been with Steve the Monday afternoon when the first two were sent. But after my party, Steve had been arguing with Lauren in a hotel lobby during the transmission. Maybe she was watching the Wilkinses' house then, but she *should* have been home with Preston. Eating cheesecake. Therefore, she'd have to have defeated the alarm, given Preston an excuse for being gone, and then spied on the Wilkinses' house till they left, not knowing in advance that they *would* leave.

I could imagine Tommy's face as I tried to sell him on *that* story. Something still wasn't adding up.

I printed my fax log. I had gotten too many faxes over the past two and a half weeks. My communications last Monday had been overlaid.

I flung open my file cabinet to search for an older log sheet. I grabbed a handful of my last twenty or so faxable designs and started to flip through them, searching for the listing.

Could I really trust my instincts and let Nathan be alone, even briefly, with Lauren? By God, I'd been manipulated enough. My loyalty for thirty years of friendship was not to be second-guessed. I owed her—and myself—at least that much.

"Oh my God!" I froze and stared at one of my designs. I had indeed missed a step. My subconscious had not. The answer was right there in one of my greeting cards.

My heart pounding, I called Tommy Newton and got his recording. I left a message saying to get over to my house the instant he got the message, that I knew who the killer was. As a precaution, I dashed a note on the edge of the greeting card and faxed it to his office.

I had to get Nathan home safe behind locked doors.

I looked out the window and saw my son walking toward our house, hand in hand with the murderer.

TWENTY-ONE

We've Got Each Udder

I RUSHED OUT of the house toward them, willing myself to stay calm. If I could just hang on and pretend not to be upset, maybe she'd go home.

After all, there had to be a simple explanation for her being here. Surely she hadn't just shot Lauren dead at the bus stop. If that were the case, Nathan would've looked upset. Instead, he smiled and waved at me.

"Hi," I said. "Uh, what happened to Lauren? She was going to wait at the bus stop till I could get there."

"She got a phone call from her lawyer, who said it couldn't wait."

I stood directly in her path, but she walked around me as if she was supposed to lead the way into my house.

"I told Carolee I'd show her my truck collection," Nathan explained.

"This isn't a good time. The house is a mess, and—"

"I promised Nathan I'd see his trucks," Carolee said firmly. "And there's something important you and I need to talk about."

This is still going to be okay, I thought. In a few minutes, Tommy would get my message. As long as Carolee and Nathan weren't left alone, everything would be fine. Besides, I knew Carolee was guilty, but was still extremely short on proof. Maybe I could trick her into saying something incriminating.

I let Nathan lead us into the house, watching Carolee.

Maybe I should send Nathan to Lauren's house. No, that
would mean that unless I could keep Carolee with me
until she was arrested, I would eventually be letting both
Nathan and Carolee out of my sight. Best scenario was
Nathan and I getting rid of Carolee till the police arrived.
Second best was me keeping Carolee far away from Nathan till help arrived. I left the front door wide open,
shutting only the screen door, in anticipation of the
troops' arriving.

Nathan showed Carolee the trucks in the cabinets in
the family room. She did an admirable job of feigning
interest; a better acting job than my current nothing's-
wrong routine, complete with a sweaty upper lip.

"There's some more upstairs in my room," Nathan
said, rising to lead the way.

"That's all right, sweetie. Why don't you watch some
TV while I talk to Carolee in my office."

"But there's nothing on."

"Put a tape in."

"I don't want to."

"Then go to your room! Now!"

Nathan took a look at my face, which was no doubt
showing my panic. He started crying and went up the
stairs. Good. Soon there would be two whole flights between him and Carolee.

She narrowed her eyes at me but said nothing.

"I was a bit harsh on him. It's hard to be a parent, let
me tell you. Come on downstairs and we can talk."

She dutifully followed me down the stairs, though
turning my back on her even momentarily was scary in
and of itself. I kept expecting to feel a knife between the
shoulder blades at any minute. We reached the office.

"So, you said we had something important to talk
about. What's up?" I pulled my chair way back so that
I'd be nearest the door and able to watch her, but she

grabbed it from me and sat down, which meant I had to take the director's chair in the corner.

She didn't answer. She reached over and grabbed my stack of greetings. "I've never actually seen your cards before. Mind if I flip through these?"

"Not at all." The incriminating one was in the original document tray in the back of the fax machine. She would never think to look for it there. I hoped. While she read through the ones in her hand, I looked at the fax machine, unable to keep my eyes off it, trying to calculate how visible the one I'd sent to Tommy was. It wasn't in sight. I was fine. I breathed a sigh of relief.

The fax machine began to whir with an incoming fax. I cringed.

"So this is how your machine works? Automatically?"

I nodded, knowing she knew at least as well as I how to operate a fax. My throat felt dry. My lips were sticking to my teeth as I tried to smile at her.

"Have you gotten any more of those threats lately?"

"Threats? You heard about those?"

"From Lauren." She reached over and snatched up the faxed message. *Please don't let this be a response from Tommy!*

She glanced at it, then held it out toward me. "Here. It's from someone named Mrs. Wesley Styler. You do Christmas letters for customers?"

"Uh, I, yes."

She studied my face for a long moment. I felt frozen to the chair, unable to move. "You're acting awfully strange, Molly. As if you're hiding something." She reached back and grabbed the original document out of the tray on my fax machine. "Is there something you don't want me to look at?"

"That's nothing."

She glanced at it and narrowed her eyes. After a mo
mentary pause, she said evenly, "Cindy the Locked-Nes
Monster. It's not all that good a likeness of me. The leg
are right, but the hair is all wrong."

She rotated it to read my note to Tommy. I had writter
that Carolee was the only person who could have seer
when the Wilkinses weren't home and gotten into thei
house without tripping the alarm. That *someone* had t
have let himself into the house Saturday morning, for i
Steve had known anyone else was in the house, he
wouldn't have been in his office chair with an embar
rassing letter about leaving Lauren on his compute
screen. As the "Locked Nest" had reminded me, Carolee
had a key.

She looked at me. "You're right. I was the only person
other than the Wilkinses who had a key to their house
and knew their security code. But so what?"

"You used their fax machine to send those threats t
me. Every time I got one, nobody was home. Your fron
windows face their driveway. You could easily see wher
they were home and when they weren't."

"So fry my butt in a chair. What does that prove
Molly? That I *might* have sent you some threats? You've
got diddly-squat on me."

"We'll see."

"Right." She stood up, and before I could fully come
to my feet, she had me in that old school-yard wrestling
grip, twisting my right arm behind my back. Almost in
stantly I was in agony, and as I struggled to pull free
she twisted harder and slammed me face first into the
wall.

"What evidence do you have?"

*A smashed face and a wrenched arm, for one thing
Please God! Make Tommy hurry!* She tugged again or
my arm. I had to tell her something. Anything. "A note

written by Mrs. Kravett claiming you'd swapped her medications and were trying to kill her. She stored it on the school's computer." I was lying through my teeth, of course, but she loosened her grip.

"You're lying. You didn't have the password. That's why I... Steve wasn't going to be able to get the password till Sunday."

"He did, though. Just before you sneaked into his house and stabbed him. And then I figured out the code too."

"When?"

"A few minutes ago."

"Damn you to hell! That money was mine! I earned it! I sucked up to that old bitty and her goat of a husband for four years! They said I was the daughter they never had. When her husband finally kicked the bucket, it was *my* shoulder she cried on. Then the word spreads that Molly's coming back to town. Everything changes. Suddenly, she starts talking about how this was the answer to her prayers. That *you* would have the energy and determination to head up a scholarship program in Bob's name. 'All our savings don't need to go to waste now.' Like *I* was a waste? Jesus. She cut me out entirely! I couldn't meet my mortgage on my salary, let alone have a life!"

"But why..." I paused, answering my own question before it was asked. Rather than risk yet another murder, she'd hoped to scare me into leaving and giving my control of the money to Tommy. And someone—either Lauren or Mrs. Kravett, had told Carolee about my poem, so that was the Achilles heel she attempted to use against me. Then, intending to become the next Mrs. Newton, she could swindle that money into her own pocket. "So how have you managed till now? Stealing?"

"Penny-ante stuff. A few dollars here and there when

someone at the hospital was too careless with his walle
The Kravetts were my ticket. I'd waited for someone lik
them, nurtured them, played them perfectly. When M
Kravett died, I became Mrs. Kravett's dearest compan
ion—ran errands for her, went shopping for her, took he
to movies and out to dinner. She promised me she wa
leaving me her money. She would have, too, until yo
came along. The day Mrs. Kravett died, I went to visi
her. She said she was on to me, that she finally realize
I'd swapped her prescriptions and was going to her doc
tor. I denied it, of course, but she knew. I told her I ha
one last pill I wanted her to swallow, one which woul
kill her instantly.'' Carolee chuckled. ''I didn't, really
Just grabbed an ibuprofen tablet from my purse and mad
like I wanted to jam it down her throat. Scared the ol
bitty so bad, she went into cardiac arrest. She told me
as she was dying, that she'd already written about wha
I'd done. She said that her note would be read in the
event of her death. I searched her house, but... Whe
Steve said she had a secret password for the school'
computer, I knew that must be where she stored it. I ha
no choice.''

Jesus. Steve died for nothing. There was nothing in
criminating on the disk.

She let go of my arm. ''You've got a modem. Sign on
to the school computer using Mrs. Kravett's ID and cal
up that file. Now! If I delete it, it's just your word agains
mine, and *I* have the sergeant in my pocket.''

A staggering realization suddenly came too clear to
me. Under imminent fear for our lives, Mrs. Kravett and
I had pulled the exact same bluff about an incriminating
letter that never existed. Mrs. Kravett had been dead for
almost three weeks. If she'd actually written such a letter
it would've surfaced by now.

How would Carolee react if I pointed that out to her?

"Think about this, Carolee. It won't do you any good
to—"

She picked up my heavy desk chair as if it were doll
furniture and flung it at the door. The crash shook the
entire house. "Do it! Now! Or I'll kill you!"

So much for rational conversation. "Okay." I desperately needed to stall. There was nothing on the disk that
I could pull up to appease her. "We'll have to call the
school to get the phone number for their computer. Plus,
you've made this harder. I'll have to type standing up
now." *Shit! Where was Tommy Newton?*

"Mommy?"

I gasped and whirled in the direction of Nathan's
voice. He had heard the noise coming from my office.
He stood in the doorway, his little Wiffle bat in his hands.

"Go back upstairs!" I screamed.

Carolee swooped him into her arms and wrenched the
plastic bat away from him. He kicked and screamed with
all his might, but she lifted the razor-sharp arm on my
paper trimmer. "Better get signed on to the computer
quick, Moll. 'Less you want to watch your son bleed."

In one fluent motion born of desperation, I disconnected my keyboard and swung it at her head with all
my strength. The impact of the blow reverberated through
my upper body. She released Nathan and slumped to the
floor. Blood oozed from a deep gash on her head, but I
ignored it. I grabbed the phone, looped the wall cord once
around her neck, and knelt with one knee on her back,
gripping the phone cord.

"Go upstairs, Nathan. Lock yourself into my bedroom
and don't unlock it for anyone except me or the police.
And call nine-one-one. Just leave the phone off the hook
if you're scared to talk."

He just stood there, staring at Carolee.

"Go on, sweetie. It's okay. Carolee is a very bad woman and I had to hit her to get her to let go of you."

"Is she dead?"

"No."

"She needs to go on time-out, doesn't she?"

His childish innocence brought tears to my eyes. "That's right. Now go on upstairs."

Carolee soon regained consciousness. She groaned.

"Move one muscle, and I'll strangle you." I'm sure the pain in her head let her know I meant it.

Within minutes, the police arrived. They banged on the door and I yelled as loud as I could, "Come in. We're downstairs."

Only when three uniformed officers were in the room did I loosen my grip on the cord and let her rise.

"Jesus," Carolee said as she got to her feet. "I'd never have believed you were that strong."

"You made a stupid mistake when you grabbed Nathan. You don't mess with my children. Nobody hurts them. Not now. Not ever."

If it weren't for the fact that an armed policeman was staring at my face, I would have told her honestly how lucky she was that I hadn't killed her.

WE PICKED UP KAREN from school. Tommy drove us from the station after I'd given my statement. I asked him if he could try to find out from Carolee where my parents' VCR and brass candlesticks were, and he assured me he'd do his best to get them back. He took us all out to lunch at McDonald's. When we arrived back home, Karen took Nathan's hand, and he finally left my side as we opened the door.

Tommy declined my offer to come inside. He kicked at a dead leaf on my porch. Sensing he had something he wanted to say to me in private, I lingered on the front porch with him and closed the door.

"Molly, I feel so bad about what happened. Your son getting threatened like that. Is there anything I can do?"

"It was my fault. I should've just given you the information and let you take it from there. Can you recommend a child psychologist? Someone who can help Nathan and Karen talk about what they experienced?"

"I know the perfect person," he said, taking a pen and pad from his pocket. "She was wonderful with my boys when my wife died. They were older, you know, but she's great with younger ones, too."

"I'm sorry about Carolee."

"Me too." He reddened. "She just wanted to get at Mrs. Kravett's money through me. Guess I shoulda realized that right away."

"Tommy, any woman would be lucky to have a man like you. I'll bet Carolee realized that, too, despite all her problems."

He sighed. "Least I'd rather have it be her than Lauren. For Lauren's little girl's sake."

I nodded, swallowing the lump in my throat.

"What does your husband really do?"

"He's an electrical engineer."

He nodded. "Sometimes...you remind me of my late wife. Your husband is a lucky man."

I took a halting breath, feeling such a rush of gratitude and sorrow for Tommy that I nearly cried. "Thanks. Your sons are lucky to have you as a father."

He shrugged. "Take care of yourself."

"You too, Tommy." He handed me the note with the psychologist's name.

"Sometimes I wish..." He stopped and smiled sheepishly. "I won't forget to return your letter from Mrs.

Kravett, after the trial.'' He touched the brim of his hat, then left.

I went inside and read a pair of picture books to Karen and Nathan, my mind only half focused on the words. There were so many things I didn't understand about people, about the choices each of us makes. I knew now that part of the reason I'd been so intent on coming back to Carlton was to achieve some level of peace with my past. Only time would tell if that goal had been accomplished.

With Carolee under arrest, I didn't have to fear notifying my customers about a change of address. It was possible to think about going home, back to Boulder. If we left soon, the children would have missed only the first couple of weeks of school. I'd give Jim a call, and we'd decide together what was best for everyone.

Promising I'd be right back, I slipped downstairs intending to call Jim, then realized it was four-thirty on Saturday morning there. With little else to do on weekends, Jim told me he always went to the office on Saturdays, but he'd probably be asleep for at least three more hours. My machine had a message. It was from the woman I'd spoken to at the office-equipment store. She wasn't the manager of just that particular store, but of the entire national chain. She wanted permission to use my ''breeze whispering Swiss cheese'' to coincide with their introduction of a high-end fax machine. She suggested I call her on Monday to discuss the matter further.

I jotted Jim a note that ''Carolee Richards, the nurse who lives across the street from Lauren, was Steve's and Mrs. Kravett's murderer.''

My friends always find it a little odd that I rarely send cards myself. That was probably due to some easily explained neurosis. This time, though, to accompany my note I made an absurd little drawing of a man and a woman, who looked roughly like Jim and me, being dragged by a cow. The woman says to the man, "Well, at least we've got each udder." I faxed it to Jim's office, knowing he'd see it at some point that day.

Then I went upstairs where my children were currently riveted to the couch, staring at the TV screen. I turned off the set and announced, over their groans, that I was going to read aloud to them. Karen and Nathan uttered another token complaint or two, then helped me build a fire, and we tossed some pillows in front of the hearth. I located my childhood copy of A.A. Milne's *Now We Are Six* and read in the flickering yellow firelight, Karen resting against one of my shoulders, Nathan against the other.

An hour or so later, I asked the children to excuse me for just a moment, then dashed downstairs to check my fax, hoping Jim had sent a response. There was a letter in the tray. I literally leapt and wept with joy as I read:

```
Molly,
  The greatest news! My boss finally
came through with a replacement for me
here. He's reassigned me to Albany for
the year after all. Have to get packed.
Flight's leaving in two hours. See you
soon! I love you.
                                      Jim

P.S. Your drawing of a cow needs a lit-
tle work. It looks like an ugly horse.
```

RANSOM FOR OUR Sins

First Time in Paperback

A Jeremy Ransom/Emily Charters Mystery

The body of a young man has been found nude, the marks on his palms and feet revealing a grim fate: he has been crucified. The body is identified as a member of the cultlike Community of the Lord church.

Chicago police detective Jeremy Ransom—along with insightful help from his surrogate grandmother, Emily Charters— investigates, convinced that a killer lurks in the church community, especially when another victim meets the same torturous death. The truth did *anything but* set these victims free....

FRED W. HUNTER

"Ransom and Charters make a formidable and enjoyable detecting team..." —*Publishers Weekly*

Available in September 1997 at your favorite retail outlet.

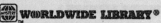

THE COFFIN TREE

First Time in Paperback

A Commander John Coffin Mystery

"An intelligent, challenging mystery." —*Booklist*

When two of his officers fall victim to suspicious "accidents" while investigating a money-laundering ring, Commander John Coffin is forced to recruit replacements for the dead officers. One of his recruits is Phoebe Astley, Coffin's former lover. But when a bizarre fire yields the body of the wife of one of the dead officers, Coffin is certain that a killer is behind all the "accidents."

GWENDOLINE BUTLER

Available in September 1997 at your favorite retail outlet.

NOT FOR SALE IN CANADA.

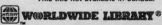